Always Saw the Real You

M.C. DANIELSEN

COZY ENDINGS IN RIVERBEND BOOK 3

To those who don't feel seen.

You matter simply because you're here.

You're important without being seen, because you're part of this world.

If it's a need of your soul, may someone with a good heart see you.

Contents

1

Geese Flying South in a V

Nate

I stopped paying attention to soccer.

There was no pattern, no order in kids tripping around a field. No connection to the kids randomly running in a field.

Soccer had rules. I'd memorized most of them. No one was following the rules. Not when all the players ran at the ball. Not when all the players tried to kick it the ball. Especially not when what got kicked was another kid who ended up crying.

Without pattern, order, rules, the game was just dumb. I'd lost interest and wandered to the edge of the soccer field. I heard the geese before I looked up and saw them flying in a V. The geese were a team working together. The lines of the V might wobble. I thought maybe it was windy up where the geese were making their V.

I squinted, trying to imagine any other letter they could use to fly. Nothing seemed as good as V. It was simple—only two lines—and pointy which made it *sharp*, maybe? Made the V like a knife to cut through air?

Air was there even though you saw through it. Air could push and blow and change. I hadn't figured out how something invisible could be so much. The geese, though, in their sky-V? The geese had air stuff figured out. Whenever a line of the V wobbled they fixed it.

The geese leader, the point of the V, moved to the side and a different one took over. The V had a new point and kept moving. That was cool to watch. Way better than the dumb soccer team Mom signed me up for.

The geese curved over the trees and seemed to be flying lower. I followed the tree line. They went over the creek. I did too—where the flat rocks made a path across. The geese kept going. So did I.

I wasn't lost. I could get back to the field. The geese were interesting and I was right, they were flying lower. And lower. I wanted to see if they'd land. And they did. They landed in a field of tall and short grass and weeds. I counted twenty-three geese.

When they landed they didn't pile on each other like soccer kids would. They landed like they flew, spaced out, bringing the V down to the ground. So cool! I sat down at the edge of the field to watch more.

The grass was wet. My pants would be muddy, but the geese were right there. I could stay still, quiet enough to not scare them. They'd stay and I could watch. All the interesting geese things happening in front of me filled my mind and blocked out everything else.

The geese honked to each other. Maybe noise or maybe goose talk. A goose honked three times, short. Another goose honked back twice, longer. It felt like a goose secret being shared.

I don't know how long I sat there. I was there long enough for the geese to settle into feathery piles across the field. Long enough that the sun moved lower and the air got colder.

I realized I was cold and uncomfortable. My pants had gotten soaked through from wet ground. I realized I'd been there too long. People would be mad, shake their heads at me. No one would understand how wonderful the geese were. No one would want to hear about them.

I hear my name being shouted. I stood up, scaring the geese. They flew up in a blast of flapping and honking. People came through the trees edging the field. My mom came through, running. Behind her came Dad and then police?

"NATE!" Mom dropped to her knees. She grabbed me, holding so tight I heard myself creak. "Oh my God, Nate. Oh my God."

"Mom?" I said. My voice was muffled against her shoulder.

"Are you okay? What happened? Where have you been been? What were you doing? We couldn't find you—" She was crying now, hard.

"I was watching the geese. They were flying in a V. The front bird—"

"You can't just leave!" She pulled back to look at me, hands on my shoulders. "You can't just walk away without telling anyone!"

"I told the coach I was going to watch the geese."

"He didn't hear you, Nate. Nobody knew where you were."

That didn't make sense. I'd said it. I'd said it too quietly maybe? Had I just thought about saying, but really didn't say it out loud?

Dad was there too kneeling beside Mom. He looked at me for a long time without saying anything. His face was wrong—like something had broken and the pieces wouldn't go back together.

"You're okay," he said finally. Not a question. Like he was telling himself.

"I'm okay," I agreed.

The people in uniforms asked me questions. Where did I go? Why did I leave? Was I scared?

I wasn't scared. I was watching geese. I told them about the V being the best letter shape, that it could cut the air. The geese flew using a pattern. They landed with order. I could've watched longer. As I tried to explain, I knew-nobody else cared about the geese.

2

What I was Supposed to Be

Jenna

The stadium lights made the cheerleaders glow, a bright, white-blueish glow. Magical. I sat between Mom and Dad in the bleacher. My feet didn't touch, so I scooted forward and let my legs dangle.

Down on the field cheerleaders were lined up. Uniforms lit up, purple and gray. Silver added sparkles. Ponytails bounced and danced. Big smiles caught the light.

Hailey cheered in the first line. Amber cheered behind her. They were 16 and 13 and no one else was as pretty as my sisters. No one else looked as perfect in their cheer uniform. Their ponytails were higher and bouncier, tie around with a silver ribbon. Both wore a big shiny smile.

"There's your sisters!" Mom said.

I nodded. I'd been watching the whole time.

Music started—loud and fast. The cheerleaders moved together. Arms up, arms down, turn, clap. It looked easy, like a dance and game mixed together.

Hailey flipped backwards in the middle. Everyone cheered. Mom grabbed Dad's arm. Dad did his high, loud whistle to let her know we were watching.

Amber hopped onto someone's shoulders next, arms up in a V. More cheering. Everyone in the stands watching with smiles as big as the cheerleaders. Hailey and Amber were so important to the school. When they finished, everyone in the stands stood up and clapped really loud.

"Aren't they wonderful?" Mom asked me.

"Yeah," I said. "They're so pretty."

Mom laughed. "They work so hard. Lots of practice."

I thought about that. Lots of practice to look like that. I could do that.

"Can I be a cheerleader?" I asked.

Mom's face got so happy. "Oh, sweetie! Yes! When you're old enough, we'll sign you up."

"Will I look like them?"

"You'll be perfect," Mom said, hugging me. "Just like your sisters."

Just like your sisters.

That sounded good. Sounded like what I wanted to be.

3

Pretend Sarah and Other Imaginary Kids

Nate

After the geese, Mom and Dad watched me. Like they worried I might fly away, on purpose—not because I followed something interesting. They put me in more things—not soccer, that was done forever. Other things. Art class, swimming, T-ball. Usually one of them stayed and watched.

The worst thing they put me in was a group for eye contact, feelings, and taking turns. Stuff called social skills. We sat in a circle and talked about the feelings of pretend kids that weren't there.

"How do you think Sarah felt when you took her toy?" and we were supposed to give a good answer.

I didn't take other kids' toys. That was mean and I wasn't a bully. I didn't know who Sarah was. If I was a bully who took toys would I even want hers? Not if it was a stupid Barbie doll.

I tried to tell Mom and Dad why it was stupid, but Mom got tears and Dad's face started breaking. So I kept going. I kept on making guesses about pretend kids' feelings about mean things. Stuff I'd never do to real life kids. After each class Mom looked happier and said it was important. Dad's face smoothed and he said I'd make friends.

I wasn't the same as the other kids. I knew that. I suppose other kids knew. I didn't know if they cared. Grown-ups definitely thought I was different. When I did things differently they got worried faces. When I wanted to watch the ants instead of play freeze tag a grownup would ask if I was sure. I was sure. Sure that ants were doing something more interesting than freeze tag.

Other kids didn't need groups to practice talking about pretend problems. Just me. Because geese were more interesting than soccer and ants better than freeze tag.

The social skills room had posters on the walls. Mrs. Morris, the teacher, said they were *Feelings Faces* and each one had a *feelings* word. Mad, happy, sad, angry, scared, surprised. The faces were round, yellow, and simple. Pretend faces, because nobody's real face was bright yellow- except minions. And real faces weren't simple. Real faces had eyebrows and foreheads and eyelids.

Mrs. Morris had a soft voice and always wore a sweater with pockets. She kept tissues in one pocket and stickers in the other.

There were five other kids in my group. I didn't know their names at first because Mrs. Morris just called us "friends."

"Let's sit in our circle, friends," she'd say. We'd sit on carpet squares—mine was blue, always the same one because I picked it first every week.

Tommy was bigger than the rest of us and chewed on his sleeve. Emma picked at carpet fuzz and didn't look at anyone. Jacob rocked a little when he sat. Lily answered every question fast and loud. And there was a girl whose name I never knew because she only came twice.

I watched them while Mrs. Morris talked. They were all different from each other, but none of them acted like the kids at soccer had. Nobody here ran into each other or kicked another kid by accident. We all stayed on our carpet squares.

"Today we're going to talk about sharing," Mrs. Morris said. She picked up a big picture from the floor. "This is Sarah. Sarah is playing with her doll. Her friend wants to play with the doll too. But Sarah won't share. How do you think her friend feels?"

Lily's hand shot up. "Sad!"

"Good, Lily. Yes, sad. Can anyone think of another feeling?"

I thought about it. If I wanted something and couldn't have it, I might feel frustrated. Or annoyed. But the friend in the story wasn't real, so did it matter what the friend felt?

"Mad," Tommy said, still chewing his sleeve.

"Yes, that's right. Mad is another word for angry. Now—" Mrs. Morris picked up another picture. "Here's the friend taking Sarah's doll away. How does Sarah feel?"

I knew the answer they wanted. "Sad," I said.

"Very good, Nate!" Mrs. Morris smiled big. She pulled a sticker from her pocket—a star. "You're thinking about other people's feelings. That's wonderful."

I stuck the star on my shirt. Mom would be happy about the star. But I still didn't understand why we needed to guess about pretend Sarah's feelings. Feelings about pretend toys weren't real.

If I really wanted to know how someone felt, I could ask them. If I wasn't busy watching ants or geese and the real kid was interesting. If they were pretend, then I couldn't ask them anything.

After too much talking about pretend Sarah and her toy—somehow I knew it was a stupid Barbie doll—I got tired. I got tired of Sarah. Tired of her pretend feelings. I had real feelings about saying wanted to pull the stupid Barbie's head off, even if it was pretend. I knew that I couldn't say that out loud, for real.

The kind of tired I got wasn't a need-sleep-tired. It was head-tired. Tiredness from finding room in my brain to store all the stuff I-couldn't-say-out-loud. From remembering the teacher wanted to hear us say feelings words and that Mom was happier when I came out after this class.

That's when I needed quiet. Quiet like looking at the patterns in the ceiling or staring at the frost on the window to find a brand-new swirl.

I'd go to my room. The quiet felt good. Like stuff I didn't need in my brain was falling out; my mind wasn't so stuffed full.

The quiet felt it like it made useless pretend kids smaller so they took up less space.

Mom would knock on the door. She'd use a quiet voice. Quiet but still somehow like the voice she had in the geese field.

"Nate? You okay, honey?"

"I'm fine."

"Do you want to come downstairs? We could watch a movie. Play a game."

"I'm okay here."

Long pause. I could feel her standing outside the door, deciding if I needed to be given something to do.

"Okay. But if you need anything..."

I didn't need anything. I just needed quiet. Time for my brain to make room for important things. Mom and Dad were worried about my quiet times. It sounded like they thought I might get lost in my room or even lost in my own brain. I could hear them talking when they thought I wasn't listening.

"He's withdrawing again."

"Should we call Dr. Patterson?"

"Maybe he needs more social interaction. More structure."

I didn't need that stuff. I needed quiet. Time to let ideas rearrange in my brain. I didn't try to say otherwise though because I didn't want Dad's face to break and Mom's voice was always a few seconds away from the geese field voice.

In art class made patterns of shapes and lines. Other kids painted houses or families or bunnies or minions. The teacher said my patterns were "interesting" but never looked real close at what the patterns were doing.Mom stayed for the whole class, sitting in the back with the other parents. Most parents dropped their kids off and left. Mom stayed.

At swimming, I liked the way the pool echoed. Everything sounded bigger and farther away. It was loud and quiet at the same time. I could float and look at the ceiling. Listen to the sounds change.

The instructor told Mom I was "doing great with the basics" but didn't engage with the other swimmers. I didn't know what that meant. Was I supposed to figure out what the other kids learning to swim were feeling?

At T-ball, I stood in right field. Nobody ever hit the ball to right field. It was the perfect spot to watch clouds and dragonflies. I didn't follow anything though, I stayed there in right field even when my body itched to walk away.

Then Coach moved me to first base where I had to pay attention all the time and people yelled instructions that didn't make sense. Mom said it was good for me to try different activities. Dad said I'd find something I liked.

I liked clouds and pool echoes and painting patterns. Geese and ants and dragonflies. But all that didn't seem to be what they wanted.

Every Wednesday was social skills group. Every Wednesday, new pretend kids with pretend problems.

Sometimes pretend Sarah wanted to play with pretend Tommy but he wouldn't let her. Sometimes pretend Alex took pretend Jordan's snack. Sometimes pretend everybody had feelings I was supposed to guess.

I got good at guessing. I learned the patterns. When someone took something: sad or mad. When someone wouldn't share: frustrated or upset. When someone did something nice: happy or good.

Mrs. Morris gave me more stickers. My collection of stickers grew. Mom stuck them on a paper hanging on the fridge. Mom told Dad I was "making progress." Dad said I was "learning important skills." I learned the skill to say the right feelings words at the right time, to say or guess what they wanted to hear. Was that what I was supposed to be learning?

One day Mrs. Morris, stopped me at the end of group.

"Nate, you've been doing so well," she said. "You really think about how other kids might be feeling."

I nodded. I had gotten good at it.

"How do you feel about coming here each week?"

I shrugged. How did I feel?

"Okay."

"Just okay?"

What was I supposed to say? That pretend kids with pretend problems were dumb? That pretend Sarah was whiny sometimes and I didn't like her? That I'd rather lay on my back and look at things overhead?

"It's fine," I said.

She smiled. Not the fake smile grown-ups used they didn't understand you. Mrs. Morris was never pretend nice. Sarah wasn't real, but Mrs. Morris' niceness was.

"You know, Nate, everyone learns differently. And that's okay."

I didn't know what to say. It sounded like a good thing, so I nodded my head.

She pulled a sticker from her pocket. Not a star. A rocket ship.

"Keep doing your best."

I stuck the rocket ship in my pocket. Mom could stick it next to the stars on the fridge.

Mom asked what Mrs. Morris had said.

"She said I'm doing good."

Mom's face changed. The worry-crease between her eyebrows got smaller.

"Oh, honey. I'm so glad. You're working so hard."

I was working hard. I don't think she knew what I was really working at-making her face look less worried. At keeping Dad's face from breaking apart. At collecting stickers and giving right answers about pretend problems. I was working hard at being what they needed me to be.

Even if I still didn't understand why pretend Sarah's feelings mattered more than watching the geese.

4

A Smile is Part of the Uniform

Jenna

My sisters Hailey and Amber were both cheerleaders. Both captains. Both got scholarships to college for it.

I was five when I decided I'd be a cheerleader too. Just like them.

Mom signed me up for Little Tumblers when I turned seven. Not because I asked—I'd already decided, so asking wasn't necessary. She just knew.

"You're going to love it," Hailey said, braiding my hair before my first class. "Coach Denise is amazing. She taught me and Amber everything."

Amber leaned against the door frame, home from college for the weekend. "Just remember to smile. Always smile, even when you're tired. Especially when you're tired."

"Why?"

"Because that's what cheerleaders do." She said it like it was obvious. Like smiling when you didn't feel like it was just part of the uniform.

I nodded. I could do that.

The gym had the sharp smell of cleaner and sweetness like a fruity lip gloss. Mats covered the floor in bright blue squares. A long mirror took up one whole wall.

Coach Denise had blonde hair in a high ponytail and wore workout clothes—purple with white stripes. She smiled the whole time she talked.

"Welcome to Little Tumblers!" She clapped her hands together. "We're going to have so much fun learning cheers and jumps and tumbling. But first—biggest rule. Can anyone guess what it is?"

A girl next to me raised her hand. "Listen to the coach?"

"Good guess! But no. The biggest rule is..." Coach Denise pointed to her own smile. "Always smile! Even if you fall. Even if you're tired. Even if your toe hurts. Cheerleaders smile!"

We all smiled. Some kids looked confused. I understood though. Amber had already told me.

There were twelve girls in the class. Most I didn't know. A few went to my school.

Coach Denise had us sit in rows on the mat—six in front, six in back. I picked the front row without thinking. That's where Hailey and Amber would've sat.

"Let's start with jumps," Coach Denise said. She demonstrated a toe-touch—arms in a T, legs straight out to the sides mid-air, toes pointed. She landed perfectly and held her arms in a V. "Ta-DA!"

We clapped.

"Now you try! Remember—point those toes, smile big, and stick that landing!"

I stood up with the others. I'd seen my sisters do this a thousand times. I knew what it was supposed to look like.

I jumped. Got my legs out. Kind of. My toes weren't very pointed and my landing was wobbly.

"Good try, Jenna! Next time, tighter core and bigger smile!"

I smiled bigger. Jumped again. Better.

"There we go! Much better!"

The praise felt warm. Like I'd done something right just by trying harder and smiling more.

We practiced jumps for twenty minutes. Toe-touches, herkies, pikes. My legs got tired. My cheeks hurt from smiling so big.

A girl in the back—Marissa, I'd learn later—stopped smiling during her third herkie. Just concentrated on getting her legs right.

"Marissa!" Coach Denise called. "Where's that sparkle? Smile, honey!"

Marissa smiled immediately. But her jump got worse because she was thinking about her face instead of her legs.

I noticed that. If you thought too hard about smiling, you messed up the jump. But if you messed up the jump while smiling, Coach Denise still said "Good job!"

If you did the jump perfectly but forgot to smile, she corrected you.

The smile mattered more than the jump.

I tucked that information away.

After jumps, we learned a basic cheer.

"Go! Fight! Win!" Coach Denise demonstrated the arm motions—sharp, clean, ending in a high V. "Nice and sharp, girls! Cheerleading isn't ballet. It's power! Snap those motions!"

We copied her. My arms felt loose and sloppy compared to hers.

"Tighter, Jenna! Like you mean it!"

I tried again. Sharper. Stronger.

"Yes! That's it!"

Another warm feeling. Another thing I'd done right.

We ran through the cheer six times. By the end, I had it memorized. The motions felt more natural. My arms knew where to go.

"Beautiful!" Coach Denise clapped. "You girls are going to be amazing! Next week we'll add tumbling. For now, let's do our cool-down stretches."

We sat in a circle and stretched. My legs were tired. My arms were tired. My face was tired from smiling.

But I'd done it right. Coach Denise said so.

Mom picked me up after class. "How was it? Did you love it?"

"It was good," I said.

"Just good?" She looked worried. Like I should've had bigger feelings.

"I mean—it was really fun!" I smiled bigger. "Coach Denise is nice. We learned jumps and a cheer."

Mom's whole face relaxed. "Oh, good! I'm so glad. Hailey and Amber are going to want to hear all about it."

In the back seat, I looked out the window. My reflection looked back at me—hair messy from jumping, cheeks still pink.

I'd done it right. Said the right thing. Mom was happy.

That felt important.

At home, Hailey and Amber were waiting at the kitchen table.

"So?" Hailey asked. "How was your first class?"

"Good. We learned jumps and a cheer."

"Did you do a toe-touch?" Amber asked.

"Yeah. Mine wasn't very good yet."

"You'll get better. It takes practice." She smiled. "Did you remember to smile the whole time?"

"Yes."

"Good girl. That's the most important part."

Hailey nodded. "Seriously. You can mess up every stunt and every jump, but if you smile through it, people think you're amazing."

I thought about Marissa getting corrected for not smiling. "Coach Denise said that too."

"See? It's the secret." Amber leaned back in her chair. "Smile, and people think you're confident. Even when you're not."

"What if you are confident?"

"Then you smile anyway. That's just what we do."

I nodded. I could do that. I was already doing that.

"Are you excited to go back next week?" Mom asked from the kitchen.

The honest answer was: I didn't know yet. It was fun, but also hard. My legs were still tired. And I wasn't sure I liked being told to smile when I was concentrating.

But the honest answer wasn't the right answer.

"Yeah! I can't wait."

Mom smiled. Hailey and Amber smiled. Everyone was happy.

I'd said the right thing again.

Every week I went to Little Tumblers. Every week I learned new jumps, new cheers, new ways to move my body sharply and confidently.

I got better at toe-touches. Better at back handsprings. Better at remembering to smile even when I was counting in my head or trying not to fall.

Coach Denise praised me a lot. "Jenna, you're a natural! Just like your sisters!"

I wasn't sure I was a natural. I *was* good at watching and copying. Good at doing what I was told. Good at smiling, when what I really wanted was to just concentrate on getting the motion right.

Other girls in the class struggled more. Marissa couldn't get her back handspring. Emma kept forgetting the words to cheers. Sophia's jumps were always a little sloppy.

I helped them sometimes. Showed them how I did it. Smiled encouragingly.

Coach Denise noticed. "Jenna, you're such a good leader! You'll be captain someday, just like your sisters."

Captain. Like Hailey. Like Amber.

That sounded good. Sounded like what I wanted to happen.

One Saturday, Amber came home from college. She watched me practice my back walkover in the backyard.

"Nice," she said when I stuck the landing. "You're getting really good."

"Thanks."

"You like it, right? Cheer?"

I thought about it. Did I like it? I liked getting things right. I liked when Coach Denise praised me. I liked that Mom and Dad were proud.

Did I like the actual cheer leading? The jumping and flipping and smiling?

I wasn't sure I'd ever asked myself that question.

"Yeah," I said. "I like it."

Amber smiled. "Good. Because you're really good at it. You could get a scholarship too, if you keep working hard."

A scholarship. Like Hailey. Like Amber. All I had to do was keep going. Keep smiling. Keep doing it right.

"I'll work hard," I said.

"I know you will." She hugged me. "You're going to be amazing."

I smiled. The smile that said I believed her. The smile that made everyone happy. A smile I could put in place and wear even when I didn't know what I felt underneath it. By the end of that first year, I'd learned a lot.

How to do a back handspring without spotting.

How to land a toe-touch with my toes pointed.

How to remember all the words and motions to six different cheers.

How to smile even when I was tired or nervous or wasn't sure I wanted to be there.

How to be exactly what everyone expected.

Coach Denise said I was one of her best students. Mom and Dad framed my Little Tumblers certificate and hung it in the hallway, right next to Hailey and Amber's old ones.

Those three certificates in a row. Past, present, future. They looked good, looked like what I was supposed to want.

5

Peas in Cookies

Jenna

Mrs. Robertson assigned partners for the North Dakota project by pulling names from a basket.

"Groups of three this time," she announced. "Jenna, Ivy, and Emilia."

I looked across the room. Ivy sat near the window, already pulling out a notebook. Emilia was two rows over, wearing overalls and a t-shirt with a sunflower on it.

I smiled and waved at both of them. Ivy gave a small wave back. Emilia grinned and shot me a thumbs up. I didn't know them well, but I knew they were nice girls, and they were cousins.

After class, we met by the lockers.

"Okay, so North Dakota agriculture." Ivy was already making notes. "There's like, a ton of options. Wheat, cattle, sugar beets—"

"Sunflowers," Emilia said immediately. "We should definitely do sunflowers. And honey. North Dakota's been number one for honey production for like nineteen years."

"Wait, how do you know that?" I asked.

She shrugged. "My family farms. We grow sunflowers."

"That's perfect!" I said. "You already know stuff!"

"She knows everything about farming," Ivy told me. "She reads farm magazines for funsies."

"You listen to classical music for funsies," Emilia added, elbowing her.

I didn't add anything. What did I do for fun now? I wasn't sure.

Ivy pulled out her notebook. "We should work on this weekend. Someone's house?"

"You guys should just come to the farm," Emilia said immediately. "I can show you the sunflower fields. We've got like a million farming books at home."

"That sounds perfect," I said.

"Saturday afternoon work?" Ivy asked.

"Yeah!"

Saturday, Mom drove me to the Preston farm. It was my first time there—long gravel driveway, big red barn, fields stretching in every direction.

Emilia met me at the door. "Come in! Ivy's already here."

Inside, Ivy sat at the kitchen table surrounded by library books and printed articles. Mrs. Preston was making lemonade.

"You must be Jenna," she said warmly. "Emilia's been excited about this project all week."

"Really?" I looked at Emilia.

"Agriculture is actually really cool," Emilia said, completely serious. "Like, people don't get how much science goes into it. Did you know North Dakota's starting to grow all this new stuff now? Chickpeas, fava beans, industrial hemp—"

"Fava beans?" I made a face. "Those sound gross."

"They're actually great for rotation," Emilia said. "Puts nitrogen back in the soil. Plus they're super good for you."

Ivy nudged Emilia. "What she means is they're good for the soil, right? You're going all Farmer's Almanac zombie again, Em."

Maybe she did get carried away, but I liked the way she talked about farming. It was the same way Hailey talked about cheer routines—like she actually cared about it. Emilia was a farmer. This wasn't just an assignment for her.

Ivy was already making lists. "So we have wheat, sunflowers, honey as the main crops. And we can mention the new ones—chickpeas, fava beans, hemp, hops."

"My dad just started growing hops too," Emilia added. "You guys want to see the fields before we start working?"

"Yes!" I said.

The sunflower fields were incredible. Rows and rows of tall stalks with huge yellow flowers, all facing the same direction.

"They follow the sun," Emilia said. "East in the morning, west by afternoon. There's this whole word for it—heliotropism."

"That's so cool," Ivy said, taking notes.

I just stared. I'd seen sunflowers before, obviously. But never this many. Never explained by someone who actually knew why they did what they did.

"Can we use some for the project?" I asked.

"Yeah, definitely. We can bring fresh ones in a vase. And I've got some dried ones that show the seed patterns really well."

We walked back to the house, arms full of sunflowers. My fingers were sticky with pollen and I didn't even care.

Back at the kitchen table, we spread out our research.

"So we'll do the poster with all the facts," Ivy said. "Maybe handouts?"

Hmmm, that was the safe option. The boring option. We needed more, but I didn't want to hurt Ivy's feelings.

"What if we did something more?" I said. "Like...made something with this stuff?"

Emilia's eyes lit up. "Like what?"

"Cookies? Using honey, maybe..."

"Chickpeas," Emilia interrupted. "My mom uses them in cookies and muffins all the time. You can't even taste them—they just make everything soft."

"Wait, chickpeas?" Ivy wrinkled her nose. "Like from hummus?"

"Ivy, it's like you don't have any farmer in you at all."

"My mom can help us bake," I offered.

"Mine too," Ivy said.

"And my dad can get us fresh honey from the beekeeper he knows," Emilia added.

We looked at each other and grinned. This project was going to be awesome.

First attempt: Complete disaster.

We met at my house the next Saturday. Emilia brought honey and a bag of hemp seeds. Ivy brought a recipe she'd found online. I had a can of chickpeas.

I measured out what I thought was sugar. Dumped it in the bowl. Ivy mixed the wet ingredients while Emilia measured the hemp seeds. We combined everything, rolled the dough, baked the cookies.

They came out looking perfect—golden brown, slightly crispy at the edges. I bit into one.

"Oh no." I spit it into a napkin. "That's horrible."

Ivy tried one too. Her face scrunched up. "What happened?"

Emilia took a tiny bite and immediately reached for water. "Did something go wrong with the chickpeas?"

Mom came over and tasted a piece. "Jenna... did you use salt instead of sugar?"

I looked at the container I'd measured from. Salt. Big block letters: SALT.

"Oh no."

"Oh no," Ivy echoed.

Emilia started laughing. "We just made the world's most nutritious salty bricks."

"Those poor bees made this honey for nothing," I moaned.

"It's okay," Ivy said practically. "That's why we're testing. Let's try again."

She wasn't mad. Neither was Emilia. They just... wanted to solve the problem.

I took a breath. "Yeah. Okay. Round two."

Second attempt: Also a disaster, but different.

This time I triple-checked the sugar. We mixed everything carefully. Except the chickpea puree. I got excited and dumped in way too much. The dough turned into sticky sludge. It glued itself to the bowl, the spoon, our hands, the counter.

"Um," Ivy said, trying to scrape dough off her fingers. "This isn't working."

"It's like edible glue," I pulled at a strand that stretched between my hands. "Maybe we can market it. Super Cookie glue."

Emilia examined the goop scientifically. "The chickpea puree is too wet. We need way less of it."

"Let's go on Shark Tank with this. Organic glue from North Dakota," Ivy said, trying to pull her fingers apart. "Make millions."

"Retire before middle school," I added.

"Live on a farm growing chickpeas," Emilia finished. "Oh wait, I already do that."

We dissolved into giggles while Mom helped us scrape dough off every surface.

Third attempt: Forgot to roast the hemp seeds first.

The cookies looked great. Smelled great. Tasted... bitter.

"Ugh." Ivy made a face. "What is that?"

Emilia checked the seeds. "These aren't roasted. Raw hemp seeds are super bitter. We need to toast them first—it makes them taste nutty."

"We brought out the dirt flavor instead," I said.

"Extremely nutritious dirt," Ivy added.

Mom suggested we take a break. We ate actual good cookies from the pantry and regrouped.

"Let's be scientific about this," Emilia said, pulling out her notebook. "Follow the recipe exactly. Roast the seeds first. Measure everything carefully. Less chickpea puree."

"And check all the labels," I added firmly.

"Definitely check all the labels," Ivy agreed.

Fourth attempt: Success.

Emilia roasted the hemp seeds perfectly—until they smelled nutty and delicious. Ivy measured everything precisely. I double-checked that sugar was actually sugar. We added just enough chickpea puree and the perfect amount of honey.

The cookies came out beautiful. Golden brown. Crispy edges. Soft centers. They tasted like honey and toasted seeds with just a hint of something interesting underneath.

"We did it!" I held up my hand for a high-five.

Emilia and Ivy high-fived me back.

"These are actually amazing," Emilia said, eating her second one. "My dad would love these."

"Really good," Mom confirmed, reaching for her third. "You girls should write down this recipe."

I felt proud in a way that was different from getting praise at cheer. This wasn't someone telling me I did a good job. This was me knowing I did a good job. We'd solved the problem together. Made something that worked.

"Should we add something else?" Ivy asked. "For the presentation?"

"Sunflower butter!" Emilia said. "We can make it from our sunflower seeds. With carrots and celery for dipping."

"Perfect!"

We spent another hour making sunflower butter—roasting seeds, grinding them, adding a little honey. Then we forgot about the seeds in the oven and burned them. Smoke filled the kitchen. Mom opened windows while we waved dish towels at the smoke detector.

"You know what?" I said, coughing. "We're never opening a bakery together."

"Never," Ivy agreed.

"Maybe a farm stand," Emilia suggested. "Where we sell vegetables and someone else bakes."

But we were all smiling.

Presentation day, I wore my favorite shirt—blue with sparkles. Hailey said presentation was half the grade. Look confident, smile big, and people would believe you knew what you were talking about.

Emilia wore her overalls with the sunflower shirt. Ivy carried the poster with neat labels and charts. I carried a vase of sunflowers from Emilia's farm, and Emilia brought two dried sunflower heads showing the seed patterns.

When it was our turn, we stood at the front of the room. The sunflowers made our presentation area look bright and professional.

Ivy held up the poster while I talked. Emilia added facts and details I didn't know.

"North Dakota leads the nation in spring wheat production," I said, pointing to the poster.

"And we grow more sunflowers than any other state," Emilia continued, holding up one of the dried sunflower heads. "My family's farm produces about two hundred acres of sunflowers every year. See how the seeds arrange in a spiral pattern? That's the Fibonacci sequence."

"We've also been number one in honey production for nineteen years in a row," Ivy added.

Then I brought out the cookies.

"We made these using all North Dakota ingredients!" I said, channeling every bit of cheer enthusiasm I had. "Honey for sweetness, hemp seeds for crunch, and chickpeas for nutrition!"

Tyler's hand shot up. "Wait. CHICKPEAS?"

"Yep!"

"Like from hummus? In cookies?" He made an exaggerated gagging sound. The class laughed.

Mrs. Robertson gave him a look. "Tyler."

"Sorry. But peas in cookies? That's just wrong."

"They're actually really good," Emilia said, glaring at Tyler. "Chickpeas have tons of protein. And they make the cookies really soft."

Tyler leaned back and smiled big at Emilia.

"Everyone should try them!" I added, still smiling.

We passed around the cookies, carrots, and celery with sunflower butter. Most kids tried everything. A few wrinkled their noses at the chickpea revelation, but nobody spit them out.

"These are actually pretty good," Aiden admitted.

Nate took a cookie, studied it for a second, then ate the whole thing. "This recipe got all the ratios right."

Tyler stared at him. "Dude. Just say they taste good."

"See?" I said. "North Dakota agriculture is delicious!"

Mrs. Robertson smiled. "Excellent presentation, girls. Very creative approach. "

After class, the three of us walked to lunch together.

"You did great with the talking part," Ivy said to me. "I would've been so nervous."

"You made it easy with all your research," I said. "And Emilia knew everything about actual farming."

"That's because I live it," Emilia said. "But you made it interesting, Jenna. And you figured out the recipe."

"We all figured it out," I corrected.

"Yeah," Ivy agreed. "Together."

Something warm spread through my chest. Not the automatic warmth of being praised for doing what was expected. Something different. Something real.

"Want eat lunch with us?" Emilia asked me.

"Definitely," I said.

We found a table near the windows. Emilia pulled out a lunch packed with actual farm vegetables. Ivy had a sandwich cut into precise triangles. I had the cafeteria pizza.

"We usually sit by Aiden and Tyler, but I wouldn't want Ty to barf because of these cookies," Ivy said, then put a lidded container with extra cookies on the table.

"And I'm not cleaning up Captain Annoying's barf, fake or not," Emilia said.

"Next project," she added, "we should do something with soil science."

"Only if there's no baking involved," Ivy said. "Or worms."

"Agreed," I laughed.

That night at dinner, I told my family about the presentation.

"And Tyler pretended to throw up when we said the cookies had chickpeas in them," I finished.

Hailey laughed. "Did everyone else like them?"

"Most people. And Mrs. Robertson gave us an A+."

"That's wonderful, honey," Mom said. "I'm proud of you for trying something creative."

"The baking was fun," I said. "Even though we messed up a lot. Emilia knew so much about farming, and Ivy organized everything perfectly."

"Sounds like you made good friends," Dad said.

"Yeah. I did."

Amber looked up from her phone. "You should stick to cheer though. That's where your real talent is."

I nodded automatically. "Yeah, I know."

But later, lying in bed, I thought about the cookies. About figuring out what went wrong and fixing it. About Emilia explaining the Fibonacci sequence in sunflower seeds and Ivy making lists and all of us laughing when things went wrong.

Cheer didn't work like that. You either did the jump right or you didn't. Either remembered the routine or forgot it. There was a right way, and you learned it.

The project felt different. Like there was room to experiment. To fail and try again. To make something uniquely ours.

I wondered if I'd have time for both. Cheer and... whatever else I might want to try. Probably not. Hailey and Amber never had time for anything except cheer. That's what it took to be captain. To get the scholarship. To follow the path.

I closed my eyes and pictured middle school. Tryouts. Making the squad. Eventually becoming captain. Just like my sisters. The path was clear.

Even if a tiny part of me wondered what it would be like to spend more time with Emilia and Ivy. To work on projects that let us mess up and laugh about it. To choose something because we wanted it, not because it was expected.

But that was silly. I did want cheer. I'd always wanted cheer. I wanted to be a cheerleader.

Right?

6

Patterns of Basketball

Nate

Dad installed a basketball hoop in our driveway the summer after I turned seven. He didn't make a big deal about it. Just came home one Saturday with the hoop in his truck, spent the afternoon setting it up in concrete.

"Thought you might want to shoot around sometime," he said when he finished. "No pressure."

I nodded. Another activity. Another thing to try. At least this one was in our driveway. No classes. No groups. No other kids.

I ignored the hoop for two days.

Then I got curious about the net. The way it was woven in a pattern—diamond shapes, each connected to the others. Mathematical. Precise.

I grabbed the basketball from the garage. Stood under the hoop looking up at the net pattern. Threw the ball up. It rattled around the rim and fell through. The net swished.

Satisfying.

I did it again. And again. Seeing how the ball moved through the net, how the pattern compressed and expanded with each shot.

"Having fun?" Dad asked, coming outside with a glass of water.

"The net makes a pattern when the ball goes through."

"Yeah, it does." He took a drink. "Want me to show you how to shoot from farther away?"

I shrugged. "Okay."

Dad showed me how to hold the ball. Fingers spread, shooting hand under the ball, guide hand on the side. Elbow in. Follow through.

"It's all about form and repetition. The more you practice, the more automatic it becomes."

I tried. Missed. Tried again. Missed.

"You're getting closer," Dad said. "See how that last one hit the rim? You're figuring out the arc."

Arc. Angle.

Those were things I could figure out. Things I could measure and adjust. I kept shooting. Dad went back inside after a while, but I stayed.

The ball had to travel in a specific arc to go through the hoop. Too flat and it hit the front rim. Too high and it bounced off the back. The angle had to be just right.

I made one basket out of twenty-three attempts.

But now I had data. I could adjust. I practiced every day after that. Not because anyone told me to. Because I wanted to figure out the pattern. How hard to throw. What angle worked best. Where to aim—front of the rim, back of the rim, directly center.

I started making baskets. One out of twenty. Then one out of fifteen. Then one out of ten.

Dad came out sometimes to shoot with me. He'd show me a move—a layup, a jump shot, how to dribble between my legs.

"You're getting good at this," he said one evening. "Better than I expected."

"I like the patterns."

"The patterns?"

"How the ball has to move in a specific way. How the angles work. It's predictable."

Dad smiled. Not his worried smile. A real one. "Yeah. I never thought about it like that, but you're right."

One Saturday, Dad turned on the TV in the living room.

"Timberwolves game," he said. "Want to watch with me?"

Usually I stayed in my room during games, even on TV it was too loud. I'd been thinking about basketball a lot. Wondering if there were patterns in actual games like there were patterns in shooting.

"Okay."

I sat on the couch. Dad settled into his recliner with a beer. The game started. Right away, I saw it. The players were moving in patterns. Not random running like soccer field kids. Actual patterns. Set plays.

One player cut left. Another moved to the corner. The ball handler waited—one second, two seconds—then passed exactly when the defender committed. It wasn't chaos. It was geometry.

"Dad?"

"Yeah, bud?"

"Why did that player wait to pass?"

"He was reading the defense. Waiting for the right moment."

"How did he know it was the right moment?"

"Experience. You learn to see when a play's going to work."

Learn to see. Like there were invisible patterns you could recognize if you knew what to look for. I stopped thinking about anything else and watched.

The Timberwolves ran another play. Similar to the first one but different. The initial setup looked the same, but then they moved differently. Like a variation on a theme.

"They're using the same pattern," I said. "But it changed."

Dad looked at me, then back at the TV. "Yeah. That's a pick-and-roll variation. Same basic play, different execution."

I nodded. That made sense. Patterns with variations. Like how geese always flew in a V but sometimes the V was bigger or smaller depending on how many geese there were.

After that, I watched games with Dad regularly. He started explaining plays to me. Not just what happened, but why.

"See number 21? Watch him. He's reading the defense, deciding where to pass."

"Like figuring out the best move?"

"Exactly. He's thinking three moves ahead."

Three moves ahead. I could do that. I did that all the time.

"It's like math," I said during a timeout. "The plays are equations. If X player does this, and Y player does that, then Z outcome is more likely."

Dad smiled big. "That's exactly what it is. Probability and execution."

He looked proud. Not worried-proud like when I got stickers from Mrs. Morris. Just proud.

I started practicing the plays I saw on TV. In the driveway, I'd pretend there were other players. Imagine cutting to the basket. Setting screens. Running pick-and-rolls by myself. Dad watched from the porch sometimes.

"You've got good court vision," Dad said one day while we were watching a game. "You see things before they happen."

I'd started to think out loud about what the plays might be.

"I'm figuring out what's most likely to happen."

"That's what the best players do. They just call it court sense instead of figuring it out."

Same thing. Different words. The announcers talked about statistics during breaks. Points per game. Field goal percentage. Assists. Rebounds. Numbers that measured performance. Predicted outcomes.

I started keeping a notebook. Tracking stats for players. Finding their averages. Comparing them to other players.

"What are you working on?" Dad asked, seeing my notebook.

"Tracking how good players are."

He laughed. "Of course you are."

But he looked happy. Really happy.

"You know, there are people who do this for a living. Sports analysts. They use numbers and patterns to help teams make decisions."

"Really?"

"Yeah. It's a whole field."

A field where people figured out basketball patterns for a job. That sounded perfect.

One night after a game, Dad asked, "Would you want to play on a team? Youth basketball league starts in the fall."

My stomach tightened.

A team meant other kids. Chaos. Noise. People yelling.

But basketball wasn't like soccer. Or maybe, the kids would be older so the structure, the rules, the positions. All that would mean something to them.

I knew basketball plays already and I could learn more. I'd know what to do. Where to be. And Dad wanted me to play. I could tell by his voice. It sounded hopeful, not pushing.

"Can I keep practicing first? Learn more?"

"Absolutely. We'll practice all summer."

We practiced every day. Dad taught me to dribble, to pass, to move without the ball.

"Keep your head up when you dribble. You need to see the whole floor."

I tried. It was hard. Dribbling and watching and figuring out everything all at once. But I got better. The dribbling became automatic. That freed up my brain to see the patterns.

By the time fall came, I'd made 1,847 baskets in the driveway. I knew six different plays from watching the Timberwolves. I could dribble without looking at the ball.

I was ready. I could see where the open spaces were. Where a pass would work. Where to move to help my teammate.

"You're a natural point guard," Dad said. "You see the game like a coach."

I didn't know what that meant exactly. But it sounded good.

"Do you want me to sign you up for basketball?"

"Yep, I'm ready."

At my first practice, I recognized two kids right away.

Tyler and Aiden.

Tyler spotted me first. "Nate! No way! Dude, you're playing basketball?"

"Yeah."

"Awesome!" He ran over. "Aiden, bro, look! Nate's on our team!"

Aiden jogged over, smiling. "Cool. Now we can play pickup games together." He held out his knuckles and I bumped them.

I felt something relax in my chest. I knew Tyler and Aiden. They were my friends from school. This wouldn't be all strangers.

Having Tyler and Aiden on the team made everything easier. During drills, Tyler would joke around and make practice less serious.

"You're really good at passing," Tyler said after I'd assisted on three of his baskets. "Like you know where I'm going before I get there."

"I figure out the angles. And you always cut to the basket the same way."

"That's awesome," Tyler said. "You see everything before it happens."

Aiden nodded. "Your passes are always right where I need them."

Coach noticed too. Started putting the three of us on the court together. "You three have good chemistry," he said. "Natural connection."

Natural connection. Because we were already friends. Already knew each other's patterns. We started practicing in each other's driveways—sometimes just playing, sometimes running plays I'd learned from watching the Timberwolves.

"How do you remember all these plays?" Aiden asked once.

"I watch the games and write them down. Then I can practice them."

"You write down basketball plays?"

"Yeah."

Tyler grinned. "See, Aiden? I told you Nate's brain is like a basketball computer."

I wondered for a moment how much brains and computers had in common.

"Is that bad?" I asked.

"Are you kidding?" Tyler said. "It's the coolest thing ever. You make us all better players because you see everything."

"Tyler's right," Aiden added quietly. "You help us understand the game better."

By the end of the season, basketball had become our thing. Not just mine. Ours. We'd talk about games at lunch. Practice at recess. Shoot hoops after school.

Mom and Dad noticed.

"It's nice that you and your friends have something you all enjoy together," Mom said.

Dad was even happier. He'd coach all three of us in the driveway sometimes, showing us moves and plays.

"You three are gonna dominate in middle school," he said. "Just wait."

Middle school felt far away. But I liked the idea of Tyler and Aiden being there too. Basketball made sense. My friends made sense.

7

Accumulation of Data

Nate

People confused me, so I taught myself chaos theory.

Math came easy. Theorems behaved. Logic solved proofs.

People skewed the graph. They flipped the equation mid-solution. They erased needed variables simply to erase something.

Chaos theory helped. It pointed to hidden patterns in unpredictable systems. It showed how small events became big outcomes. It named the invisible centers of chaos: attractors.

That's how I started sorting the data I gathered when I watched people.

By age seven, I'd begun to find my people. Tyler, then the others who clicked into place. Mom stopped worrying I'd fly away. I learned **that** I observed not to withdraw, but to order—it was my way of understanding. The kids who were really friends took me the way I came and made understanding them easier.

Jenna was part of the group that clicked, but as we got older I kept myself further from her than I did others. Observing her didn't feel neutral. What I saw pulled at me. Understanding her felt urgent in a way I couldn't explain. I stayed a safe distance away because none of the feelings words I'd ever learned in social skills groups helped me explain her. What I understood? Jenna was a person like no other. And that thesis seemed to have been formed in my heart instead of my mind.

Data Point: Birthday Party (Age 9)

Pink balloons. Pink cupcakes. Pink everything.

But Jenna's smiles were wrong. Her real smiles started in her eyes—data I'd cataloged without meaning to. Today: zero authentic smiles. Performance mode at her own birthday party.

She slipped away to the porch. I calculated: 87% probability no one else would notice. I grabbed the Creme Soda from the cooler—two cans, both hers. Nobody else drank it.

Found her on the porch swing, glitter on her face and in her hair from decorating cupcakes. Still performing sadness like she was performing happiness earlier.

I gave her the soda. Sat. Didn't make her go back inside.

"You have a lot of glitter on your face."

She touched her hair. We talked about Glitter Warriors. Her real smile—the one that started in her eyes—appeared for three minutes and forty-two seconds.

Not long enough. But data worth noting.

First conscious observation: The difference between Jenna performing and Jenna being real was measurable. And I wanted more of the real version.

Data Point: Science Fair (Age 10)

It was Kyle Mendoza's turn—tall, nervous, red in the ears. His project was evaporation: neat charts on a trifold board and a glass of water for his demo.

He tripped on the way to his table. The glass tipped, and water spread in a fast puddle across the surface.

Someone whispered, "Fail."

Kyle froze. We all knew he wanted to disappear.

"Hey, Kyle? Wouldn't it evaporate faster now—since it's spread out thinner?"

That was Jenna. Calm. Aiming to help.

Kyle blinked. "Uh... yeah. Exactly. More surface area."

His shoulders lowered half an inch. The giggling stopped. The rest of Kyle's presentation wasn't perfect, but he made it through.

No one else noticed why. I did.

One question. A small event that shifted the outcome of Kyle's day. A butterfly flapped its wings. Nobody else saw the ripple.

Data Point: Music Class Chorus (Age 12)

Ellie Kim was fine through warm-ups—every note, quiet and steady. As we moved closer to her solo—the fourth piece—she went pale.

By song two she held her music in tight fingers, head tipped toward the floor, body going rigid minute by minute.

Jenna hopped down, whispered something, and patted her arm. Ellie nodded. Maybe Jenna whispered magic words that turned her back into flesh and blood.

Later, everyone complimented Ellie on her voice.

No one mentioned the magic.

But I filed it away.

Data Point: Sophomore Year, First Day (Age 15)

The halls were chaos.

Ninth graders in packs clutching schedules.

Upperclassmen sliding through the mass like sharks.

"You're in my locker."

Data: Taylor Nichols, junior. Hair perfect, clothes perfect, mean-girl persona razor-sharp.

She loomed over a freshman holding a crumpled paper.

"I think this says 218?" the girl whispered.

Taylor crossed her arms. "This has been my locker for two years."

Three lockers down, Jenna spun her combination once, turned with a bright smile, and slid between the scared freshman and the Taylor-shark.

"Hey, Taylor! Didn't you and Casey get the cool lockers next to the lunchroom?"

Taylor blinked. She remembered it wasn't hers anymore, then huffed like the freshman was at fault. She walked away, every step precise and rehearsed.

Jenna turned. "Hi, Macie!" She smiled and lowered her voice. "It's all downhill after Taylor. You've got this."

The girl laughed nervously and opened her locker. "Thanks, Jenna."

Noise filled the hallway again.

No one else noticed Jenna pull the freshman out of the eye of Taylor's hurricane.

Data Point: Now (Age 16)

It's harder to track to organize what I see from her now. Her edges aren't as crisp, she's fraying. Harder to measure. But she's still there, a quiet center wherever she is.

Last week before a quiz, half the row didn't have pencils. Jenna unzipped her backpack and passed them out. At the pep rally, a younger cheerleader forgot her bow. Before anyone panicked, Jenna had a spare in her bag—crisis solved before it started. The candy bag is still on her locker shelf—everyone's favorites.

She still makes chaos softer for everyone else.

Something's shifted. Her smile is always there—cheerleader-perfect, the one she's had at the ready for as long as I can remember. The smile doesn't reach her eyes often now. She laughs at the right moments, says the right things, performs enthusiasm like it's choreographed.

Which maybe it is.

At lunch, when someone mentions pep rallies or games her face lights up on cue. She all in but her fingers fidget with her phone case or a pen. She nods and agrees with plans but goes quiet after.

Someone asks what she's doing this weekend. "Practice, obviously."

Someone asks if she's okay. "Yeah, totally. Just tired."

She delivers it all with a smile, but it's one the shuts the door, instead of opening to pull the other person in.

She still makes things better for everyone else. As she does, something about her grows smaller. Less certain. And worst of all—less happy. She's keeping it all disguised behind the performance she's been perfecting since she was swallowed up into cheerleading.

Even the simplest of people can seem confusing. Knowing them longer clears the confusion. Not with Jenna. She's become harder to read. I don't think she's changed at the core. I think she's questioning, but doesn't see answer.

Her smile falters when she thinks no one's watching. There's a new pause before she answers people. She deflects real questions with cheerful certainty rehearsed so it feels spontaneous.

I haven't stopped trying to understand her. Understanding her feels more urgent now. Not to fix her. To see her. To understand why someone who makes chaos softer for everyone doesn't have anyone doing the same for her.

8

Things I Could've Posted

Jenna

People work for likes and shares and reactions—online and in real life.

Nate Berglund, though? He's about actions done quietly. Living without flash or the volume cranked up. His quietness is the infrastructure we take for granted—solid and trustworthy.

Wherever he is, whoever's around, Nate doesn't push to the front. I just know he's there.

Because he isn't chasing notice or approval, he catches what the rest of us miss.

My sisters Hailey and Amber were both cheerleaders. Both were captains. Both went to college with scholarships. I watched them from the bleachers when I was five, decided that's what I wanted to be too.

Just like them.

I've been following their script ever since. Learning to smile the right way, say the right things, be the girl everyone expects. The performance became automatic.

But Nate? He's never cared about the performance.

He sees what's underneath. Always has.

Age 9 —

My ninth birthday party.

Everything looked perfect. Pink cupcakes, pink balloons, pink everything Mom thought I'd love. A tower of Jell-O I hated but pretended was cool. Guests who were really my parents' friends' kids.

My sisters left before cake. Cassidy Miller said even they didn't want to stay at my boring party.

I smiled bigger. Joked louder. Performed harder.

Then I snuck to the porch swing.

Nate found me. Brought me Creme Soda from the cooler—the only kind I actually liked. The kind Mom bought two of because no one else wanted it.

He noticed.

We sat there, not talking much. He said I had glitter in my hair from decorating cupcakes. Said it looked like I'd survived the Glitter Games.

"I'm a Glitter Warrior," I said.

His eyes crinkled. Real smile, not performance.

Mom came to get me. Time to say goodbye to guests, be the birthday girl again.

Nate didn't make me go back to performing. He just... let me be.

First time I remember someone seeing past the smile and not needing me to explain.

I tucked that feeling away. Kept it safe.

And if I had been able to post I'd have said this:

Post Zero: The Glitter Warrior

Caption: "Some people don't make you go back and fake it." Vibe: being seen, quiet refuge, authentic moment Hashtags: #GlitterWarrior #CremeSoda #SomeoneNoticed

Age 14 — Post One: End-of-Summer Bonfire

Caption: "Steady fire, steady hands." Vibe: quiet action, unnoticed stability, background presence Hashtags: #BonfireNights #QuietStrength #Noticing

The fire started to burn low. Everyone else was mid-conversation or half-listening to a playlist.

Nate got up, shifted a log until it settled, coaxed the coals, and sat back down.

Not blazing. Not dramatic. Steady.

No one said anything. No one looked up.

I noticed and tucked it away.

Age 14 — Post Two: Group Project Panic

Caption: "Biology but make it March Madness." Vibe: group chaos redirected, low-key teamwork, quiet leadership Hashtags: #GroupProject #Noticing #HeHadItHandled

Freshman-year Biology.

We got assigned groups for the big "kingdoms of life" project.

My group: me, Tyler, Aiden, Nate—four completely different strategies.

Tyler cracked jokes while drawing a classification chart that looked like a March Madness bracket.

Aiden focused but kept second-guessing, erasing until the paper tore.

I kept worrying about the presentation—trying to make us sound like we had it together.

I stressed and nudged, mostly failing to pull focus back.

A few minutes in, Nate flipped through the packet, tapped his pencil, and finally looked up.

"Archaea switched conferences a while ago. Might want to update your bracket before Selection Sunday."

A joke with purpose—Ty understood instantly.

Result: Tyler re-worked the chart like it was an actual seeding diagram.

Aiden stopped erasing and joined in.

I made notes for presenting.

Class ended and the project looked organized.

As we packed up, Nate slid me his packet.

"I saw you making notes for the presentation—you'll do better than me. Those two will pretend they're on SportsCenter."

It was a compliment—but better than that. It was him seeing me. Seeing my work.

Seeing me unfiltered and uncaptioned.

I felt seen and tucked the feeling away.

Age 15 — Post Three: Sprinkles Help Maddie Smile

Caption: "The quiet way of making sure the birthday girl felt special." Vibe: unnoticed preparation, shared credit, quiet kindness Hashtags: #BirthdayRescue #QuietSpecial #Noticing

Maddie never made a big deal about her birthday. She'd barely mentioned it that year. She shrugged and said her parents were busy—code for they forgot again. She said it like it didn't matter.

But it did.

All morning I kept thinking about how to make her day better.

My plan: sit with her at lunch and cheer her up.

Right before lunch, Nate stopped me in the hall.

He handed over grocery bags full of ice cream, sprinkles, and toppings. Paper bowls and Happy Birthday napkins. Candles—he'd already checked we could light them.

He'd even borrowed an ice-cream scoop from the lunch ladies.

He wanted me to be the one who started it. I smiled and took everything.

Most of us ate only ice cream that lunch, while Maddie smiled bigger than she had in days.

She thanked me, and when I tried to correct her, Nate nudged me—ears pink.

I got the credit. It didn't matter. What mattered was that Maddie felt better.

I smiled and stored the memory somewhere safe: Nate's pink-tipped ears, Maddie's real smile.

Holding himself back is still his way. Nate never pushes forward or tries to be in the center of everything. When he has something to say, people get quiet without him asking. They know—it'll matter.

When did I start seeing him clearly? It must've been slow, a quiet understanding. I pay closer attention now. I don't giggle thinking about Nate, don't feel butterflies or plan hallway run-ins.

What I feel is better. When I smile so hard my face hurts, I think he'd understand if I sat near him to rest. Maybe even leaned my head on his shoulder. He'd understand because he sees.

He sees me behind the always-there smile in a way that's terrifying and comforting. With Nate, I could stop smiling all the time and just rest. So no giggling. I notice things about him that matter more than other things I see. I thought he noticed me too, but then he surprised us all and started dating Jenny Coleman.

It was strangely painful when the person I thought saw the real me put all his focus on someone else. I'd been depending on him to anchor the real part of me since we were nine years old. Since glitter and Creme Soda on a porch swing.

And if he stopped seeing me, where did the real part of me go? It's terrifying to think that maybe the always-smile version became who I really am. Or who I was supposed to be.

If no one sees even a sliver of the real me, I'm not sure I can find my way back.

How I'd Like to Post About Him

Draft: "Some people shout to be heard. Others don't need to."

Caption: "Noticed him noticing, but if he stopped."

Hashtag: #QuietMatters #DoesHeStillNotice?

End of Summer before 11th Grade

The golden ratio is
approximately equal to 1.6181.
It is considered aesthetically pleasing
and is found in nature, art, and architecture.

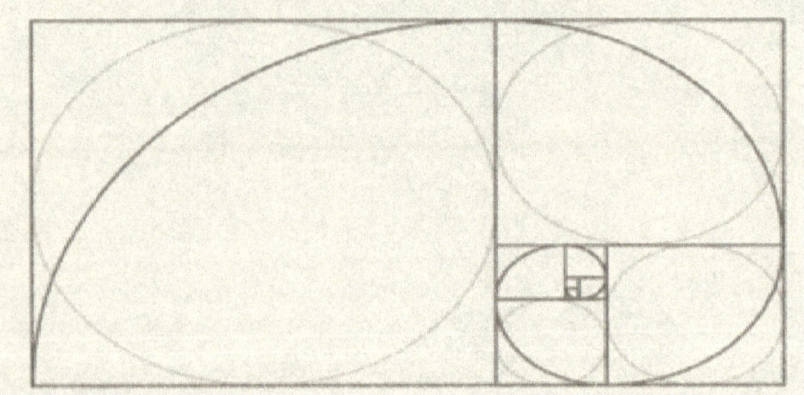

9

Life Lessons and a Pick-up Game

Nate

In the driveway, Tyler's portable hoop creaked every time the rim rattled. We'd been playing pickup at each other's houses since we were kids, and by now the games had evolved into quiet competitions—side bets on who could drain threes while trash-talking.

The ball in my hands felt different—as if the usual equation—grip, spin, release—wasn't solving right anymore.

"Berglund!" Tyler called, jogging backward to set for the rebound. "You planning to join the game or just do math in your head all afternoon?"

"Still getting a feel for the ball."

I held it still, dribbled twice, then pulled up from the corner—driveway version of a corner three. Clean shot. Perfect arc. All net.

Tyler rolled his eyes. "What were the variables this time? Earth's core temperature? Methane from North Dakota cows? Ratio of heat we can blame on Aiden's hot air?"

He tossed the ball to Aiden, who paused for a fraction of a second before shooting. Aiden's shot was smoother than mine—less calculated, more instinctive. His DNA worked the equations for him.

Tyler snagged the rebound, spun once, and chucked it one-handed, backward, off the garage. It rattled in. He threw his hands up. "See? No variables. The ball was overwhelmed by my charisma and wanted me to look good."

Aiden snorted and I just shook my head at him.

We cycled through a few more plays. I tracked angles, spacing, reaction times. Running through variables made my moves sure, almost automatic. When we stopped, we grabbed water bottles and dropped under a tree for shade. Grass and sweat—itchy.

"So," Tyler said, stretching out on the grass. "Jenny's gone, huh?"

"Yeah, moved end of July."

"And you're...?"

"Not doing long-distance."

"Wow. That's ice cold, Berglund."

I took a drink. "It wasn't like that."

"Wait—" Aiden sat up. "You dumped her when she moved?"

"We both just... agreed to end it."

Tyler snorted. "That's the most Nate breakup ever."

"We weren't some big romantic drama," I said, picking at the grass. "Our moms worked together. Kept putting us together. One day someone asked if we were dating and we both just said yes."

"So why say yes?"

"I don't know. It was just... easy? Like, she was there, it was comfortable, our moms were happy about it—"

"Dude," Tyler said. "That's not a relationship. That's carpooling."

Aiden frowned. "Sounds like choosing where to get gas."

"Good thing they weren't expecting marriage and grandkids," Tyler added.

"He might've just said yes," Aiden agreed.

I sat up and shoved at his shoulder. "She moved. We said we'd stay in touch. We probably won't."

Tyler studied me. "You don't seem that broken up about it."

"I'm not." That felt important to say out loud.

"Jenny's great, nice, smart. We were easy. I never had to think about anything."

"Dude, sounds like you were dating the girl version of you," Tyler said, grinning. "Basically you chose a relationship that was like counting by twos," Aiden said.

"Easy is boring, but that was okay, because—" Tyler leaned forward. "We all know Nate likes to solve difficult math equations but wants people stuff easy."

I didn't answer, but dropped my head back and groaned.

"I'm pretty sure hard is better than easy and boring," Aiden said.

"You manufactured a lot the of hard between you and Ivy, bro," Tyler added.

Aiden shoved Tyler. "I'm aware of that. I just meant that for it to be good, there's gonna be work."

"Berglund's got an idea of the work he wants to do," Tyler said. "Just doesn't know if he wants to stick to the easy path yet. Right?"

"I don't—"

"Dude," Aiden said. "Everyone knows you like Jenna, don't start."

"Yeah, he's been observing her like a science project for years," Tyler added.

I didn't deny it.

Pickup basketball was starting to feel like *Social Skills Group: Survivor Edition.*

"So what's the difference?" Tyler pressed. "Between Jenny and Jenna?"

I thought about it. About the way Jenny was easy to be around because I never wondered what she was thinking. About Jenna, who I'd been observing for years without understanding why it felt different.

"With Jenny, I never wondered what she was thinking. Didn't need to. With Jenna..." I stopped. "I want to know, figure things out, understand..."

"You've left science behind, just admit that you're up in your feelings about her," Aiden said.

"That you're pathetically gone for her," Tyler added.

"Shut up."

"See? Not denying it."

Tyler clapped me on the shoulder.

"Well, this is gonna be fun to watch. You both coming to Em's on Saturday?"

"Yeah." I stood up, brushing off grass. "I'll be there."

Aiden was gulping down more water. He gave Tyler a thumbs up.

I headed out a few minutes later. On the way home, I passed the school. At the stop sign, movement caught my eye near the gym's side door. Summer cheer camp was letting out.

Jenna stepped outside, a little behind the rest of her squad. She didn't see me idling half a block back, waiting for cross-traffic.

Her posture straightened the second she hit the pavement. Smile locked into place like a stage light flipped on. Deliberate. Calibrated. Not real.

10

Banner Operation

Jenna

I'd spent forty-five minutes perfecting a purple-glitter outline on the letter R before I realized I'd messed up.

GO RIVERBENDUSTANGS.

I stared at the banner stretched across the gym floor—a riot of blue and gold on white poster paper—and felt a hysterical laugh rise in my throat.

"Please tell me you just noticed," Maddie said, dropping beside me with another pack of markers. "I've been waiting for you to see it."

"Why didn't you say something?" I groaned, falling backward onto the floor and covering my face.

"Because it's hilarious. And fixable." She nudged my shoulder.

"I'm losing it," I muttered through my hands. "Completely losing it."

"Not completely," she said cheerfully. "You're still color-coordinating the glitter."

I peeked between my fingers. She was grinning, head tilted, braid slipping over one shoulder—so normal, so Maddie—that it pulled me back from the edge.

"You're enjoying this way too much," I said.

"Jenna Lundquist making a mistake? It's like witnessing a solar eclipse." She handed me a gold marker. "Here. Operation Banner Cover-Up begins now."

The gym was empty except for us and we'd been chatting as we worked on a banner for the upcoming spirit week.

"It's been fun getting to know Dayne. Bet you love having his family here now."

"Yeah," Maddie said, as she cut out a paper Mustang to cover my typo, "I really love his family. Dayne and I have always gotten along. I always wished they lived closer."

"He's got a little brother and sister right?" I focused on redesigning the layout.

"Oliver and Sophia. They're a pair, so much fun and so much trouble. Dayne's a good big brother to them." She set down her scissors. "You know, Dayne wasn't dating anyone before they moved here."

"And you're telling me this because?"

"Because you're you. You're fun and sweet and pretty and not dating anyone. And he might have asked me about you."

"What?"

"You heard me. Why are you always so surprised when any guy is interested in you? You're amazing."

I waved her off. "I doubt whatever he asked meant anything."

"You're going to spend junior year pining after Nate again then, huh?"

I froze. "Seriously, Maddie? When did matchmaking become your default mode?"

"Seriously Jenna, how can you believe that none of your friends have noticed the mutual pining situation taking place right in front of us."

"There's no mutual anything," I scoffed reaching for the glitter pen. "Our families have been friends for years. There's no pining happening."

Maddie gave me her full attention. "Okay, I'm invoking the Sixth-Grade Sleepover Pact."

I groaned. The sacred rule: one honest answer when directly asked.

"We're juniors, too old for a sixth-grade pact."

"No, no, no you don't. It's sacred and you know we'll never outgrow it," she said, crossing her arms. "One honest answer, Lundquist."

I stared at the crooked word on our banner, then looked up at her. "Okay, Thompson, I'm not hearing a question, and the window for forcing an answer through the sacred pact is fifteen seconds. Time is running out—10, 9, 8, 7..."

"Do you still have a big, old, possibly unrequited crush on Nate Berglund? Truth. Now—go."

"So mean, so mean," I whined. "Fine. I don't know what I've got, Maddie. Let's just call it a crush. A definitely unrequited crush."

Maddie's eyes narrowed. "I don't think it's as unrequited as you think. Problem is, neither of you does anything about it."

"Okay, Sixth-Grade Sleepover Pact sacred window is closing and the subject is officially closed," I replied. "Anyway, whatever you think you see is just Nate being Nate. He's nice to everyone. And he's dating Jenny Coleman, so there's nothing to do."

"I might have heard something about Nate and Jenny..."

The gym door creaked open causing us both to jump. Tyler burst in, followed by Maddie's cousin Dayne, both with wet hair—clearly fresh from the locker room.

"Ladies! Just the artistic geniuses I need," Tyler announced.

"Speak for yourself," Dayne said, grinning at Maddie. "I came for Cousin Time. Hey, Maddie-Monster."

"Hey, Dayne-Dum-Dum. You're interrupting important banner work."

"I can see that." He pointed. "Dustangs. Nice touch."

"We're busy," Maddie said, gesturing at the chaos.

"This is important." Tyler crossed the gym in three strides. "Coach Wilkins wants the record board updated. We need fancy lettering. You're the experts."

"There are no experts here," I said. "Just two girls with glitter and questionable spelling."

"Wait," Maddie said, narrowing her eyes. "Did you just assume we'd be good at fancy lettering because we're girls?"

Tyler held up his hands. "No! I just meant—"

"—that girls automatically have better handwriting?" I added.

"Or that we spend our free time doodling exquisite hearts with Timothée Chalamet's initials?"

Dayne laughed. "Dude, you walked right into that."

Tyler glanced at our banner. "Okay, fair point. But... Dustangs?"

"It's a work in progress," Maddie said, holding up the Mustang cutout. "What's the emergency?"

"Coach wants the display cases cleaned before the alumni flood in for homecoming. So—can you help? Today?"

"It's almost six," I said. "And the banner's not done."

"I'll help," Tyler said. "Nate's already working on the record board, but there's a reason he's our stats guy, not our sign guy."

My heart did a weird double-beat at the mention of Nate. Tyler gestured toward the hallway.

"He's just around the corner by the trophy cases."

I caught the knowing gleam in Maddie's eyes.

"I don't know…" I gestured at the banner. "We've got a lot left."

"Go," Maddie said, shoving me lightly. "Tyler and Dayne can help me."

"I'm helping?" Dayne asked.

"You are," she said. "You owe me for giving you a friend group when you moved here."

"Fair point."

I gave Maddie a betrayed look. Her eyes gleamed. Trapped. Perfect.

"Fine," I said, gathering my markers. "But only because I care deeply about proper lettering."

"Your dedication to penmanship is inspiring," Tyler said solemnly.

"Not another word out of you, Alred." I punched his arm on my way out. "By the way, aren't you wondering what initials Emilia doodles in her notebook?"

He froze. "What? Of course she doodles mine."

I laughed and headed to the gym doors. Behind me, I heard Tyler call, "Wait—she does, right?"

The trophy hallway glowed with late-day light filtering through high windows, illuminating decades of Mustang trophies and photos. Nate knelt by the basketball records display, brow furrowed, focused on a list in his hands. A few markers lay scattered beside him.

I hesitated. Yes, Maddie. I did have a big, old crush on Nate. I'd been crushing for years. Now here he was. Before I could retreat, he looked up.

"Hey," he said, surprised.

"Hey," I replied. "Tyler said you needed help with lettering?"

He looked at the paper, then back at me.

"Tyler says a lot of things. Most of them are conspiracy theories." He held up the sheet. "My handwriting's decent, but help layout would be great."

I knelt beside him, close enough to notice his clean, soapy scent. Close enough that focusing on the board took effort. Because I did have a crush on Nate, a years-old crush. If I was brave enough to do anything about my crush, I couldn't. He'd been dating Jenny Coleman since the middle of sophomore year.

"So these names get added?"

He nodded. "And a few records updated."

"Easy enough." I picked up a blue marker. "I'll do the names; you handle the numbers?"

"Deal."

We worked in silence for several minutes—only the squeak of markers and the faint echo of voices somewhere down the hall. It wasn't uncomfortable—just charged.

"How's the banner?" Nate asked eventually.

"Oh, you know. The Dustangs are going to crush it this weekend."

He frowned.

"I misspelled it," I explained. "Attention to detail was not present."

A small smile. "Everyone makes mistakes."

I shrugged. "I guess so. Hey, how's Jenny doing? I haven't seen her yet."

"Her family moved in August. Her dad got a job transfer to Minneapolis."

"Oh, I'm sorry to hear that. You must miss her."

His expression was placid. Then he shrugged. "She was upset about moving, starting at a new school will be hard. We're not doing the long-distance dating thing."

She was upset. What about you, Nate? Nate was never easy to read. This moment? I had no clue what he felt about his girlfriend moving away.

We fell into silence, into rhythm. I lettered names, he updated numbers. Left, right, in sync. We finished the record board in steady, companionable quiet. I'd always been comfortable with Nate. I rarely understood him.

"Looks good," he said, capping his marker. "Much better than mine would've been."

Footsteps approached—Tyler and Maddie's voices drifting closer.

"Guess we're done," I said, gathering markers and handing them to Nate.

He stood. "Thanks for the help. Jenna, I...."

Maddie rounded the corner, Tyler close behind.

"Banner's fixed. No more Dustangs!"

My phone buzzed at the same time and I pulled it from my back pocket.

> EMILIA: Something tells me you know why Tyler's texting me about doodling initials and demanding screenshots of my notebook margins.

I laughed.

"I'll help you cleanup," I called to Maddie and looked at Nate. Had he been about to say something?

"Hey, Jenna," Tyler called. "You were joking about the doodling, right?"

Nate shook his head. He was used to Tyler's drama and didn't need to have the whole story to be amused.

"Thanks, Jenna." His eyes held mine for a beat longer than necessary. "See you around."

As I followed Maddie back to the gym, I replayed that moment—*Jenna, I...* What had he been about to say?

Early
September
11th Grade

The golden ratio is
approximately equal to 1.6181.
It is considered aesthetically pleasing
and is found in nature, art, and architecture.

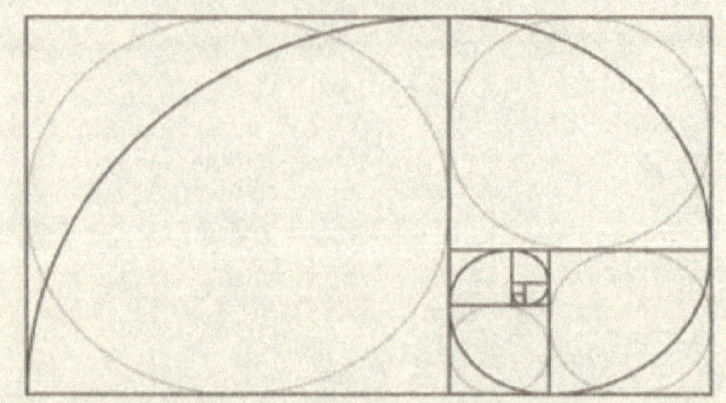

11

Variables Do Tik-Tok Dances

Nate

The gym still smelled like fresh wax and summer sweat.

It was early enough in the preseason that our plays were sloppy and nobody had remembered to refill the water cooler. We weren't even scrimmaging yet—just running drills and resetting muscle memory.

I was packing up when Coach Greene called my name. "Berglund. Hang back a sec."

My heart did that stupid half-skip it always did when an adult used that tone. I jogged over. He kept flipping through papers on his clipboard, not looking up.

"You've been nominated for team captain."

I froze. "Wait—what?"

Coach raised an eyebrow. "You heard me."

I must've blinked too long because he added, "This isn't a prank."

"Who nominated me?"

"Doesn't matter. A few names brought you up. And I think it's worth considering."

I rubbed the back of my neck. "I haven't even— I mean, I'm not—"

Coach cut me off. "You show up. You don't talk to hear yourself talk. You're steady. You lead by example. That matters more than hype."

I didn't say anything. I didn't know what to say.

He handed me a folded paper from his clipboard. "Here's what it involves. You don't have to decide now."

I nodded.

"I'll need an answer two or three weeks before the first game at the latest," he added. "Take your time. Think about it."

Then he turned and walked off like he'd just asked me to bring snacks to practice.

I stood there staring at the paper in my hand. Would it turn into trig homework if I stood here long enough?

Captain.

I didn't feel like a guy who got nominated. This didn't feel like it added up.

I grabbed a basketball from the rack and moved to the free-throw line.

The variables wouldn't cooperate.

Usually, I told the variables to jump. They asked "How high?" and then jumped.

But today, the regression coefficients kept scrolling social media to find trending TikTok dances to learn. Instead of solving equations, they were too busy posting their own dance versions and checking for likes.

The high school gym had emptied except for me. The last stragglers were long gone. The overhead lights buzzed faintly, casting everything in harsh fluorescence that made the polished hardwood gleam. The scent of floor cleaner mingled with sweat and the faint metallic tang of the drinking fountain by the door. Familiar constants in my otherwise unsettled equation.

The problem wasn't the team captain question. That was just another variable in a system that had recently become... unstable.

The problem was yesterday—the trophy hallway with Jenna. Working on the record board with her. The tug and pull I'd always felt around her. The fact that I no longer had a reason to step back, though stepping back had always felt safer.

The problem of feelings from being around Jenna that were unlike what I felt with anyone else and still didn't understand. I didn't usually act on impulse. I made sure my steps were calculated. Lately, around her, calculation felt insufficient.

The gym door opened again.

"Figured you'd still be here." Tyler walked in, dropping his bag on the bleachers. "Thought I'd check to see if your brooding levels were in the safe range."

I bounced the ball once.

"This about the nomination for captain?" Tyler asked. "Or about a certain cheerleader?"

I shot him a look. Of course he already knew about the nomination.

"Both, probably." Tyler grabbed a ball from the rack. "Though I'm still processing the fact that you accidentally dated someone for a year and a half."

"Can we not—"

"Accidentally. Like you tripped and fell into a relationship." He bounced the ball. "That's impressively passive, even for you."

"Our moms worked together. It just... happened."

"Yeah, that's the problem. Nothing with Jenna is just gonna 'happen.' You're gonna have to actually try."

I didn't respond. He was right.

"Thought so." Tyler took a shot. "You like her."

"It's more complicated than that."

"Yeah, you've got that look—like your brain's chewing through emotional data without a safety net."

"I don't chew through data. I savor it."

"Right. Slowly. Intensely. Like it's a five-course meal of existential dread."

Tyler huffed. "You turn a crush into a math thesis. That's your brand."

Maybe he was right. Maybe I was overcomplicating a simple equation. Boy notices girl. Girl lets guard down slightly. Boy wants to understand why that matters so much.

Except Jenna Lundquist had never been a simple equation.

She was a complex system of variables, each one carefully calibrated to present exactly what she thought people wanted to see. And somehow, I'd been cataloging those variables for years without ever fully understanding the pattern they formed.

"She's different," I said finally.

"Different how?"

I hesitated, unused to articulating the observations that filled my mental notebooks. "She's calculated but not like me. I calculate to understand. She calculates to perform."

Tyler blinked. "In English, please?"

"She's always adjusting. Smile angle. Voice pitch. Word choice. Response time. It's like watching someone solve equations in real time, but the goal isn't accuracy—it's acceptance."

"And this fascinates you because...?"

Because I recognized it. Because I did my own version of the same thing. Because beneath all her sparkle algorithms was someone nobody actually saw.

Except maybe me.

"I notice things," I said simply.

Tyler shook his head. "You notice everything about everyone. You've been doing that since elementary school. But you've been noticing Jenna Lundquist with extra intensity since approximately forever."

"Since we were kids," I said. "But I remember seventh grade science fair specifically. Her volcano erupted prematurely. Everyone laughed. She smiled anyway—smile variation #4, amused at herself even though she wasn't. I thought it was interesting that she'd rather pretend to laugh than let anyone see she was upset."

Tyler stared. "That's... both incredibly insightful and mildly concerning."

I shrugged. Observation was what I did. Jenna was just the subject I'd observed most carefully.

Tyler paused, then added, "You know who else notices? You know Maddie's cousin whose family moved here? Dayne? He's been here for summer breaks, we've all met him. He's been collecting his own data on Jenna for a few years except his is—funny, pretty, smart, I think I might like to ask her out."

My hand tightened on the basketball. The variable I hadn't accounted for.

"So what are you gonna do?" Tyler pressed. "Calculate the odds for another six months while someone else actually asks her out?"

"No." The word came out harder than I meant.

"Good." Tyler nodded. "Keep talking to her. Build on yesterday."

"Probability of meaningful interaction: 17.8%."

"I have no idea if that's good or bad."

"It's an improvement from last week's 12.4%."

Tyler laughed. "Progress! Next you'll be telling me the statistical likelihood of asking her to homecoming."

I didn't tell him I'd already calculated those odds. Multiple scenarios. Variable outcomes. The numbers weren't promising.

"One step at a time," I said instead.

Tyler nudged my shoulder. "Captain? That's big."

"It's unexpected."

"It's deserved. You see the game differently than the rest of us."

I bounced the ball again, the sound echoing in the empty gym. "Seeing isn't the same as leading."

"Sometimes it is." Tyler stood and grabbed his bag. "Just like noticing someone isn't the same as helping them. But yesterday? Working on that board together? That was something."

He headed for the door, then paused. "Maybe it's time to recalculate some of those variables, Captain."

I stayed after Tyler left, running drills automatically while my mind processed new data. The rhythmic bounce of the ball against hardwood created a steady background for irregular thoughts.

Dribble. Calculate. Shoot.

Jenna's face in the trophy hallway. The way the performance had dropped when it was just us. The realness underneath.

Dribble. Calculate. Shoot.

The team captain decision. Probability of success: high. Probability of comfort in the role: moderate at best.

Dribble. Calculate. Shoot.

Dayne. The new variable. Someone else collecting data. Someone else who might act first.

Dribble. Calculate. Shoot.

I lined up for one last shot—three-point line, left corner. Basketball was geometry in motion. Life was messier, less predictable. But the principles remained: assess the variables, calculate the odds, take the shot.

The ball arced through the air. Rotation perfect. Trajectory optimal.

Swish.

I'd been recording data on Jenna Lundquist for 5.7 years. Cataloging smile variations, tracking voice modulations, noting the subtle tells that signaled the difference between her performance and her reality. I'd built an entire database without ever really asking myself why I needed the data.

Yesterday in the trophy hallway, I'd started to understand.

As I locked the gym door behind me, my phone buzzed.

> **TYLER:** Officially appointing myself your coach for Operation S.T.A.T.S.

> **TYLER:** Stop Thinking and Take a Shot

> **TYLER:** first assignment: find an excuse to see her this weekend

> **TYLER:** second assignment: don't calculate the odds first

I typed back:

ME: That's not how I operate.

TYLER: exactly the problem berglund

TYLER: new system. you'll thank me later

I sighed tucking the phone away.

Tyler wasn't wrong. I'd spent years observing, calculating, analyzing. Maybe it was time to recalculate the entire approach.

As I walked to my truck, the evening air heavy with an autumn chill, I reached a conclusion that wasn't about probabilities or statistics.

12

Operation STATS Commences

Nate

Sunday, 8:23 PM

> TYLER: officially appointing myself ur coach for Operation S.T.A.T.S.

> TYLER: Stop Thinking and Take a Shot

> TYLER: new system

> TYLER: u'll thank me later

Sunday, 9:47 PM

> TYLER: been thinking

> TYLER: about ur training program

> ME: I don't have a training program.

TYLER: u do now

TYLER: starting w fundamentals

ME: Basketball fundamentals?

TYLER: HUMAN fundamentals

ME: I'm adequately human.

TYLER: debatable

TYLER: preseason tomorrow

TYLER: report 0600

TYLER: mental conditioning

ME: I'm not reporting anywhere at 6 AM.

TYLER: fine

TYLER: 7:30

TYLER: but u WILL do the exercises

ME: What exercises?

TYLER: u'll see

TYLER: mental training

ME: Absolutely not.

TYLER: too late

TYLER: already designing ur program

Monday, 7:31 AM

TYLER: rise and shine athlete

ME: It's 7:31.

TYLER: ur late

ME: You said 7:30.

TYLER: punctuality = success

ME: You texted at 7:31.

TYLER: don't dis coach

ME: Dis is not a real word.

TYLER: Ok u just showed why w r here

TYLER: Human fundamentals

TYLER: 1st up - affirmations

ME: No.

TYLER: look in mirror & say "I am capable of human conversation"

ME: I'm not doing that.

TYLER: science says it will help

ME: Talking to reflective surfaces doesn't alter outcomes.

TYLER: it alters UR outcome

TYLER: UR CONFIDENCE

ME: My confidence is appropriately calibrated to my actual abilities.

TYLER: avoiding jenna in hallways

ME: I don't avoid her. I navigate efficiently.

TYLER: u calculate her route and take the long way ME: That's just optimal navigation.

TYLER: it's AVOIDANCE

TYLER: say the affirmation

ME: I'm going to school.

TYLER: BERGLUND

Monday, 3:52 PM

TYLER: did u do the morning affirmation

ME: No.

TYLER: why not

ME: Because I don't require verbal self-assurance to function.

TYLER: u require SOMETHING

TYLER: bc ur current strategy is failing

ME: I don't have a strategy.

TYLER: EXACTLY THE PROBLEM

TYLER: new affirmation

TYLER: "Jenna Lundquist would benefit from knowing me better"

ME: That's presumptuous.

TYLER: it's TRUE

ME: It's an unverifiable hypothesis.

TYLER: oh my god

TYLER: u can't even COMPLIMENT urself hypothetically

ME: Self-assessment should be evidence-based.

TYLER: fine

TYLER: what's the evidence that she WOULDN'T benefit from knowing u better

ME: ...

TYLER: see?

TYLER: no data

TYLER: which means the hypothesis stands

ME: That's not how burden of proof works.

TYLER: it is in STAT coaching

Monday, 9:15 PM

TYLER: evening check-in

ME: Still not doing affirmations.

TYLER: u don't even know what I was gonna say

ME: I extrapolated based on previous patterns.

TYLER: use that big brain for ROMANCE not AVOIDANCE

ME: Pattern recognition is useful across domains.

TYLER: including the domain of "noticing jenna lundquist has smiled at u three times this semester and u've responded with the nate nod"

ME: The nod is efficient.

TYLER: the nod is escape

ME: It's non-verbal communication.

TYLER: it's HIDING

TYLER: tomorrow morning

TYLER: mirror

TYLER: 5 minutes

ME: Five minutes doing what?

TYLER: affirmations

TYLER: I'm texting u a list

ME: Don't.

TYLER: too late

Monday, 9:17 PM

TYLER: OFFICIAL STAT PRESEASON AFFIRMATION LIST

TYLER: 1. I am capable of normal human conversation

TYLER: 2. Jenna Lundquist is a person, not a statistical anomaly

TYLER: 3. Eye contact will not cause physical harm

TYLER: 4. Using actual words is better than nodding

TYLER: 5. I will not calculate probability before saying hello

ME: I'm not reading these to a mirror.

TYLER: u don't have to READ them

TYLER: just SAY them

ME: Same objection.

TYLER: do u want to be 50 and alone with ur spreadsheets?

ME: At 50 I'll have significantly more sophisticated data models than spreadsheets.

TYLER: SO SAD

Tuesday, 6:47 AM

TYLER: morning report

TYLER: did u do the affirmations

ME: No.

TYLER: BERGLUND

ME: I brushed my teeth. That's sufficient mirror time.

TYLER: ur impossible

ME: Consistent.

TYLER: those are not the same thing

ME: In my case they overlap significantly.

TYLER: I'm adding a sixth affirmation

ME: Please don't.

TYLER: "I will stop hiding behind vocabulary and actually express human emotion"

ME: I express emotion appropriately.

TYLER: u express CALCULATION

TYLER: that's different

ME: Calculation is how I process the world.

TYLER: and how's that working out with jenna

ME: ...

TYLER: EXACTLY

TYLER: mirror

TYLER: tonight

TYLER: all six affirmations

TYLER: I'm checking in at 9pm

ME: You can check in. I won't have results.

TYLER: we'll see

Tuesday, 9:03 PM

TYLER: report

ME: I attempted the affirmations.

TYLER: U DID???

ME: Attempted. Past tense. Did not complete.

TYLER: why not

ME: Because saying "Jenna Lundquist is a person, not a statistical anomaly" to my reflection felt absurd.

TYLER: that's the POINT

TYLER: you've been treating her like DATA

ME: I observe patterns. That's different from dehumanization.

TYLER: is it though

ME: Yes. Observing someone's behavioral patterns doesn't negate their personhood.

TYLER: but ur not ENGAGING with her personhood

TYLER: ur CATALOGING it

ME: ...

TYLER: yeah

TYLER: think about that

TYLER: tomorrow

TYLER: all six

TYLER: five minutes minimum

ME: This is an inefficient use of time.

TYLER: this is an ESSENTIAL use of time

TYLER: u've spent YEARS watching her

TYLER: maybe try TALKING to her

ME: I talk to her.

TYLER: "here's ur pencil back" doesn't count

Wednesday, 7:02 AM

TYLER: I'm adding a 7th affirmation

ME: Of course you are.

TYLER: "I deserve to be known as more than the quiet guy who does math"

ME: I'm fine being known as the quiet guy who does math.

TYLER: but are u fine being UNKNOWN to jenna

ME: She knows who I am.

TYLER: does she though?

TYLER: like ACTUALLY know u?

ME: We've known each other since elementary school.

TYLER: u've been in the same BUILDING since elementary school

TYLER: that's different

TYLER: she knows u return lost items and nod in hallways

TYLER: she doesn't know u stay up until 2am reading about chaos theory for fun

TYLER: or that u notice when someone's faking a smile

TYLER: or that u've been quietly cataloging her smile variations for YEARS bc u think she's fascinating

ME: I don't think I should share the smile catalog.

TYLER: DEFINITELY NOT

TYLER: but maybe share SOMETHING

TYLER: something REAL

ME: This is getting complicated.

TYLER: relationships ARE complicated berglund

TYLER: that's why u need a coach

Wednesday, 9:34 PM

TYLER: evening report

ME: I said three of the seven affirmations.

TYLER: PROGRESS

ME: It felt ridiculous.

TYLER: but u DID IT

ME: Barely.

TYLER: still counts

TYLER: which 3

ME: One, three, and four.

TYLER: so u admitted u can have normal conversation

TYLER: that eye contact won't kill u

TYLER: and that words are better than nodding

ME: Correct.

TYLER: that's actually huge

ME: It's three sentences to a mirror.

TYLER: it's 3 sentences u NEEDED to say

TYLER: tomorrow: all 7

ME: We'll see.

TYLER: "we'll see" is nate-speak for "probably yes but I'm too stubborn to admit it"

ME: Accurate.

Thursday, 6:52 AM

TYLER: final day of preseason

TYLER: today u do all seven affirmations

TYLER: PLUS an eighth I'm adding

ME: What's the eighth?

TYLER: "I will take one small risk today"

ME: Define small.

TYLER: u'll know it when u see it

ME: That's not a definition.

TYLER: trust the process

ME: Your process is chaos.

TYLER: YOUR process is paralysis

TYLER: pick ur poison

Thursday, 9:17 PM

TYLER: report

ME: All eight affirmations completed.

TYLER: WHAT

TYLER: seriously???

ME: Yes.

TYLER: I'm actually shocked

ME: Your confidence in this program is underwhelming.

TYLER: no I just didn't think u'd actually DO it

TYLER: what changed

ME: I calculated the probability that you'd stop texting me if I didn't comply.

TYLER: and?

ME: 3.7%. Not worth the continued interruptions.

TYLER: ur the WORST

TYLER: but also I'm proud of u

ME: Don't be emotional about it.

TYLER: too late

TYLER: I'm VERY emotional

TYLER: preseason complete

TYLER: real training starts Monday

ME: I'm not ready for real training.

TYLER: nobody ever is berglund

TYLER: that's why u have a coach

13

OPERATION S.T.A.T.S. - WEEK 1

Monday, 7:18 AM

> TYLER: week one official training begins now

> TYLER: assignment 1: say hi to jenna

> TYLER: actual words

> TYLER: use her name

ME: I say hi to people regularly.

> TYLER: the nod doesn't count

ME: The nod is efficient communication.

> TYLER: the nod is AVOIDANCE

> TYLER: words

TYLER: today

TYLER: report back

I saw her between second and third period, near the east stairwell. She was reorganizing her backpack, books stacked on the floor around her in a careful arrangement.

Probability of successful interaction: 34.2%.

I kept walking.

Monday, 3:47 PM

TYLER: report

ME: Working on it.

TYLER: that's nate-speak for "I didn't do it"

ME: Timing wasn't optimal.

TYLER: there's NEVER optimal timing

TYLER: that's the whole point

TYLER: tomorrow

TYLER: no excuses

Tuesday, 12:17 PM

My phone buzzed under the lunch table.

TYLER: dude for real 8 feet away from u

I glanced up. Tyler sat across from me, phone hidden under the table, eyebrows raised in challenge. Emilia was next to him, mid-conversation with Ivy about some chemistry lab. Aiden sat beside Ivy, quietly eating while she gestured enthusiastically.

Jenna sat at the far end of the table with Maddie, Dayne, and Aria, laughing about something I couldn't hear over the cafeteria noise.

Eight feet. Might as well be eight miles.

ME: I'm aware of proximity.

TYLER: then use it

TYLER: lean forward

TYLER: make eye contact

TYLER: say LITERALLY ANYTHING

ME: We're at a group lunch table. That's already interaction.

TYLER: ur at OPPOSITE ENDS

TYLER: u literally picked the seat farthest from her

ME: I sat in my usual spot.

TYLER: ur usual spot that HAPPENS to maximize distance?

ME: Correlation isn't causation.

TYLER: it is when u do it EVERY DAY

Emilia leaned over Tyler's shoulder to read his phone, then looked directly at me and shook her head. Tyler grinned.

TYLER: em agrees with me

ME: Emilia doesn't know what we're discussing.

TYLER: she knows ur being stubborn

TYLER: just say hi when we leave

TYLER: that's it

TYLER: I'm not asking for a marriage proposal

ME: Noted

TYLER: that means no

ME: That means noted.

We didn't leave at the same time. Jenna and Maddie headed out first. I stayed until Tyler finished his third helping of fries. Optimal timing: 0%.

Wednesday, 6:45 PM

TYLER: next assignment

TYLER: cheer practice Friday, bball out early, no xcuses

TYLER: north field

TYLER: ur walking by

TYLER: casually

TYLER: like ur headed somewhere

ME: Where would I be headed?

TYLER: literally anywhere

TYLER: the parking lot

TYLER: truck

TYLER: ANYWHERE

TYLER: the point is u WALK BY and u WAVE

ME: A wave.

TYLER: a manly wave

TYLER: acknowledgment of her existence

ME: This is getting absurd.

TYLER: this is getting u OUT OF UR HEAD

TYLER: Friday

TYLER: 3:30pm

TYLER: be there

Friday Afternoon

I'd calculated seventeen reasons not to go. Then I went anyway.

Tyler's coaching had gotten under my skin—not the affirmations or the awkward lunch table surveillance, but the underlying question: When did observation become a substitute for action? The north field was visible from the parking lot. I could walk to my truck, happen to pass by, execute Tyler's "manly wave," and leave. Total exposure time: 90 seconds maximum.

Probability of catastrophic failure: 23.6%. Acceptable risk.

I grabbed my gym bag from my locker and headed out. The practice was already running when I approached. Music pulsed from a portable speaker. The squad ran through a formation—pyramid build, I thought, though I wasn't well-versed in cheer terminology. Jenna was at the base. Left-front position. Her stance looked solid, hands positioned to support.

The formation shifted. The timing was off. Someone's grip adjusted too early, throwing everything out of sync. The flyer—Jessie, I recognized her from the hallways—compensated, but her weight redistributed wrong. The structure didn't collapse, but it tilted. Jenna caught most of the imbalance, her right ankle rolling slightly as she braced. They held. Barely.

"Let's reset," someone called.

No correction. No analysis of what went wrong. I'd stopped walking. Stood there at the fence line like an idiot, gym bag in hand, watching. Another run. Same formation. This time the base positions weren't aligned properly from the start. Jenna overcompensated before the lift even began. Her ankle took the strain again.

Coach Marquez was nowhere in sight.

Pattern recognition kicked in.

Formation timing: inconsistent across multiple attempts

Structural issues: base positioning misaligned

Jenna's positioning: consistent overcompensation for group errors

Coach Marquez: absent

Squad response: no one correcting fundamental problems

I should have left. Should have executed Tyler's wave plan and walked away. Instead, I pulled out my phone and opened a note.

Observation Log:

Formation-Pyramid

3-Tier

Multiple instances -timing discrepancies

No correction

Coach: Not present

Jenna's ankle – visible strain

Squad fatigue visible

Late afternoon practice

Duration of Observation-14 min

I added one more line:

Pattern – unsafe conditions.

Saturday, 3:23 PM

TYLER: REPORT

ME: I went.

TYLER: AND???

ME: Walked by. Observed practice.

TYLER: did u WAVE

ME: No.

TYLER: BERGLUND

ME: I was gathering data.

TYLER: this wasn't a RESEARCH PROJECT

TYLER: this was operation STATS remember?

TYLER: the S stands for STOP THINKING

ME: Something's off.

TYLER: what do u mean off

ME: At practice. The timing's inconsistent. Formations aren't being corrected. Jenna's compensating for structural problems. Coach Marquez isn't supervising.

TYLER: …u went there to wave and ended up doing SAFETY ASSESSMENT?

ME: I went there and observed unsafe patterns.

TYLER: of course u did

TYLER: okay but did jenna SEE u at least

ME: Probably not. I was at the fence line.

TYLER: so u WATCHED her practice from a distance and didn't even say hi

ME: I observed safety concerns.

TYLER: from BEHIND A FENCE

ME: It's a chain-link fence. Visibility is optimal.

TYLER: ur impossible ME: I'm going to keep watching.

TYLER: watching JENNA or watching PRACTICE

ME: Both.

TYLER: …I don't know if this is progress or a setback

ME: Progress. I'm acting based on observed data.

TYLER: that's not the action I meant

ME: It's the action that matters right now.

I couldn't stop thinking about it.

The pyramid formation. The inconsistent timing. The way Jenna's ankle had rolled—just slightly, not enough for injury, but enough to notice if you were paying attention.

And I was always paying attention.

By Sunday afternoon, I'd created a spreadsheet.

Cheer Safety Analysis

Formation types observed: 1

Timing discrepancies: 4

Structural compensations by Jenna: 6

Coach presence: 0/1 practices observed

Squad fatigue level: high

Probability of injury under current conditions: 67.8%

The number bothered me. Too high to ignore. Too low to act on without more data.

Sunday, 8:14 PM

TYLER: week one debrief

TYLER: u said hi zero times

TYLER: u waved zero times

TYLER: u did however conduct SURVEILLANCE

TYLER: which was not on the assignment list

ME: I identified a potential safety issue.

TYLER: u identified an excuse to avoid actually talking to her

ME: This isn't avoidance. This is observation.

TYLER: it's BOTH berglund

TYLER: week two: ur going back

TYLER: but this time ur actually engaging

ME: I'll go back. But not for the wave.

TYLER: why are u going back

ME: Because someone needs to pay attention to what's happening at that practice.

TYLER: and that someone is u?

ME: Apparently.

TYLER: ...this is either really noble or really weird

ME: Probably both.

TYLER: yeah that tracks

I opened the spreadsheet again before bed. Added another column:

Intervention threshold

Left it blank. Because I didn't know yet what would be enough to act. Didn't know what "enough" even looked like. But I knew I'd keep watching. Not for Tyler's Operation S.T.A.T.S.

For Jenna.

For the data that said something was wrong. And for the certainty—growing stronger with every observation—that no one else was paying attention.

14

OPERATION S.T.A.T.S. - WEEK 2

Nate

Monday, 7:03 AM

TYLER: week two

TYLER: escalation phase

ME: That sounds ominous.

TYLER: it's STRATEGIC

TYLER: today's assignment: actual conversation

TYLER: more than three words

ME: Define conversation.

TYLER: back and forth exchange

TYLER: questions

TYLER: answers

TYLER: HUMAN INTERACTION

ME: I interact with humans regularly.

TYLER: grunting at aiden about basketball plays doesn't count

ME: We communicate effectively.

TYLER: jenna needs WORDS berglund

TYLER: SENTENCES

ME: Noted.

TYLER: ur doing it again

Monday, 12:22 PM

Tyler kicked my foot under the lunch table.

I looked up. He jerked his head toward the far end where Jenna sat with Maddie and Aria, discussing something about homecoming decorations.

My phone buzzed.

TYLER: she just mentioned the record board u worked on

TYLER: PERFECT OPENING ME: I'm eating. TYLER: u finished ur sandwich 4 minutes ago

TYLER: ur just sitting there doing NOTHING

ME: I'm observing.

TYLER: ur HIDING

Tuesday, 3:47 PM

TYLER: practice tomorrow

TYLER: 3:30

TYLER: ur going

ME: I went last week.

TYLER: and u OBSERVED

TYLER: this week ur ENGAGING

ME: How?

TYLER: walk by

TYLER: say hi

TYLER: ask how practice is going

TYLER: LITERALLY ANYTHING

ME: What if practice is running?

TYLER: then u WAIT until they break

TYLER: or u wave

TYLER: or u do SOMETHING other than lurking behind a fence taking notes

ME: I wasn't lurking. I was assessing safety protocols.

TYLER: u were AVODIING

ME: I identified four separate timing discrepancies and—

TYLER: I DON'T CARE ABOUT UR DATA

TYLER: I care about u talking to an actual human girl

ME: She's aware I exist.

TYLER: is she though?

TYLER: bc from where I'm sitting u've been a GHOST

Wednesday, 3:30 PM

I went to practice.

Not for Tyler's wave. For the data.

The spreadsheet from last week had seventeen entries now. I'd added projections, calculated risk factors, cross-referenced injury statistics from USA Cheer safety reports. Probability of significant injury if patterns continue: 78.4%. Too high to ignore.

The practice was already midway through when I arrived. Same formation as last week—pyramid, three tiers. Jenna at base left. I positioned myself at the fence line. Close enough to observe. Far enough to avoid detection.

First run: clean. No discrepancies.

Second run: the timing slipped. Half a second delay in the count. Jenna adjusted mid-lift, ankle rolling slightly as she compensated for the misalignment.

"Hold steady on the base," someone called. Generic correction. No specific guidance on what went wrong.

I pulled out my phone, added another entry to the log.

Practice observation #2

Same formation, different timing issues

Timing discrepancy: 1.3 seconds delay on lift

Jenna's compensation: visible ankle strain, right side (again)

Coach presence: absent

Squad response: no corrective instruction given

Fatigue factor: increasing

Pattern: confirmed unsafe conditions.

Third run started. The bases weren't synchronized. One moved before the count, another after. Jenna tried to hold the structure together, bracing at an awkward angle.

The formation held. Barely. When they broke for water, I should have left. Instead, I stayed. Jenna limped slightly as she walked toward her bag. Nothing dramatic. Just a barely perceptible favor of her left foot. I opened a new note.

Intervention threshold: next observed unsafe practice.

Because 78.4% was too high.

Because someone needed to pay attention. Because if I didn't, who would?

Wednesday, 5:12 PM

TYLER: report

ME: Observed practice. Confirmed previous patterns.

TYLER: did u TALK to her

ME: No.

TYLER: BERGLUND

ME: I was documenting safety violations.

TYLER: u were AVOIDING under the guise of RESEARCH

ME: The formations are unsafe. Timing's inconsistent. No one's correcting the problems. Coach Marquez isn't supervising. Jenna's ankle is showing repeated strain.

TYLER: ...okay that's actually concerning

ME: Yes.

TYLER: but u still didn't talk to her

ME: Correct.

TYLER: why not

ME: Because I don't know what to say.

TYLER: "hey jenna, are u okay"

TYLER: that's a good start

ME: What if she says she's fine?

TYLER: then u know she's lying

TYLER: and u press

ME: Or she thinks I'm overstepping.

TYLER: or she thinks someone finally NOTICED

I stared at that text for three minutes before responding.

ME: What if I make it worse?

TYLER: what if u make it BETTER

TYLER: what if someone actually paying attention is exactly what she needs

ME: ...

TYLER: friday

TYLER: practice

TYLER: ur going back

TYLER: and this time ur talking to her

ME: I'll think about it.

TYLER: ur going

ME: Probability of successful interaction—

Friday, 3:15 PM

I stood at the fence line for the third time in two weeks.

This time, I had a plan. Not Tyler's plan. Not the wave or the casual greeting or the "hey, how's practice going" small talk. My plan: wait until practice ends. Approach when she's alone. Ask if she's okay. Show her the data if necessary. Probability of success: 31.7%. Probability of her thinking I'm weird: 68.3%. Acceptable risk.

The practice ran long. Forty-seven minutes of formations, counts, corrections. The timing slipped multiple times. Jenna compensated repeatedly. Her ankle rolled once—visibly, enough that Megan glanced at her with concern.

Coach Marquez appeared for the last ten minutes, observed from the sidelines, left without comment. When practice ended, the squad scattered quickly. Jenna stayed behind, adjusting equipment, moving slower than the others.

This was it.

I walked toward the field entrance, gym bag in hand like I had a reason to be here. She looked up as I approached. Surprise flickered across her face.

"Nate. Hey."

"Hey." My carefully planned opening disappeared. "How's... practice?"

Smooth. Really smooth.

"Good." Filtered Smile. Automatic. "Just wrapping up."

"Your ankle okay?"

She blinked. "What?"

"I noticed you favoring it. After the pyramid."

Her smile faltered. Just for a second. "Oh. Yeah, it's fine. Just tired."

"Jenna—"

"I need to head out." She grabbed her bag, started walking.

I should have let her go. Instead, I followed.

"I've been watching practices."

She stopped. Turned. "What?"

"Not in a weird way. I mean—" I ran a hand through my hair. "I noticed some safety issues. The timing's inconsistent.

Formations aren't being corrected properly. Your ankle's taking repeated strain from compensating for—"

"You've been watching my practices?"

Her voice was quiet. I couldn't read the tone.

"I was concerned."

"About my practices. Specifically."

"About the safety patterns. The timing keeps slipping. No one's correcting it. Coach Marquez isn't supervising properly. The probability of injury if this continues is—"

"Stop."

I stopped.

She stared at me. "You've been calculating the probability of me getting hurt?"

"Yes."

"That's..." She shook her head. "That's really weird, Nate."

"I know."

"But also..." She bit her lip. "No one else has noticed."

"I noticed."

"Yeah." She adjusted her bag strap. "You notice things."

We stood there in uncomfortable silence.

"I should go," she said finally.

"Jenna—"

"Thanks. For... noticing. But I'm fine."

She walked away. I stood there like an idiot, gym bag in hand, knowing I'd just blown whatever chance Tyler's coaching had been building toward.

As I walked back to my truck, passing the bleachers near the practice field, I saw it—a spiral notebook. Yellow paper, worn edges. I picked it up. Jenna's name on the inside cover. She must have left it when practice ended. Or dropped it when she walked away from our conversation.

I flipped it open, meaning to just confirm it was hers. A loose page fell out.

TO DO BEFORE FALL SEMESTER

- Order banner supplies (check sale at Michaels?)

- Pick up pep rally plans from Coach M

- Shopping with Maddie – Friday @ 10 a.m.?

- Coordinate locker decorations (call Casey?)

- Finish summer reading (still need 2 books)

- Check cheer uniform alterations

The list went on. So many tasks. So many expectations.
When did she rest? When was she allowed to just... exist?
I refolded the page, tucked it back, closed the notebook.

Friday, 5:47 PM

TYLER: REPORT

ME: I talked to her.

TYLER: FINALLY

TYLER: how'd it go

ME: She called me weird.

TYLER: ...context?

ME: I told her I've been watching her practices and calculating injury probabilities.

TYLER: OH MY GOD

TYLER: BERGLUND

TYLER: that's not what I meant by ENGAGING

ME: I was being honest.

TYLER: u were being CREEPY

ME: I was expressing legitimate concern about safety violations

TYLER: by admitting u've been SURVEILLING her???

ME: Observing. Not surveilling.

TYLER: those are the same thing when u say them out loud to the person ur observing

ME: She said no one else has noticed.

TYLER: wait what

ME: She said no one else has noticed. Then she said I notice things.

TYLER: ...that's actually not terrible

ME: Then she left.

TYLER: okay that's terrible

TYLER: but she ACKNOWLEDGED that u noticed

TYLER: that's progress

ME: She thinks I'm weird.

TYLER: everyone thinks ur weird berglund

TYLER: the question is does she think ur INTERESTING weird or RESTRAINING ORDER weird

ME: I don't know.

TYLER: monday

TYLER: we regroup

TYLER: new strategy

ME: I think I'm done with strategies.

TYLER: ur not done

TYLER: ur just getting started

TYLER: u finally TALKED to her

TYLER: that's huge

TYLER: even if u did it in the most nate way possible

I sat on my bed that night, spreadsheet open on my laptop.

Added one final entry:

Direct interaction

Jenna's response: defensive, then acknowledging

Ankle status: confirmed strain, self-reported as "fine"

Pattern: she's aware something's wrong but minimizing

Intervention: attempted, poorly executed

Probability of her letting me help: 22.1%

15

Risk Assessment: Critical

Nate

Twenty-seven seconds. That's how long a standard competition dismount should take from initiation to landing, according to USA Cheer Safety Guidelines. I'd been reading about cheer safety protocols for over an hour, cross-referencing what I'd observed across three separate practices.

Two Saturdays. One Wednesday. One Friday where I'd broken my own observation protocol and actually talked to her.

You've been calculating the probability of me getting hurt?

She'd called me weird. But she'd also said no one else had noticed. The data said someone needed to keep noticing. I closed the browser window and opened my statistics notebook instead. Basketball season wouldn't officially start for months, but I'd been tracking preseason conditioning data: free throw percentages, sprint times, vertical leap measurements. Numbers that made sense. Patterns I could analyze.

Without really thinking about it, I'd started a new page:

Gym Observations:

Pyramid: 3rd attempt—timing off by 1.2 seconds

Casey adjusting grip during critical transition (4x)

Base positioning shifted during countdown

Sophie showing signs of hesitation

Jenna compensating for structure instability

Landing impact—20% greater than standard

I stared at my notes, not entirely sure why I'd written them. I wasn't on the cheer squad. Wasn't a safety spotter. Just someone who happened to be watching and couldn't stop cataloging what he saw.

Someone who noticed things.

My phone buzzed.

> TYLER: u coming to Emilia's calc thing tonight?

I glanced at my watch. The study group had started fifteen minutes ago.

ME: Lost track of time. Might skip.

TYLER: No pressure

TYLER: but there's a test Friday

TYLER: and the group needs u more than u need the group

TYLER: Maddie's still stuck on derivatives

TYLER: even Em's worried

TYLER: As Miggy would say: Don't Like it When Meela's Worried

I looked at my notebook, then back at my phone.

ME: Just thinking about something.

TYLER: Brown-haired something?

TYLER: About this tall, does impressive flips?

ME: About Friday. What I said to her.

TYLER: yeah that was… a choice

TYLER: but she didn't run screaming so there's that

TYLER: also ur COMING to study group

TYLER: em's texting u in 3… 2…

My phone buzzed again.

EMILIA: Nate. Get over here. Maddie's about to cry over derivatives and I need backup.

I closed my notebook and grabbed my keys.

The Preston kitchen table was covered in textbooks, notebooks, and scattered index cards. Maddie sat hunched over a calc problem, pencil tapping anxiously against the page. Emilia stood at the whiteboard Tyler had hung on the wall last year, working through an equation. Tyler leaned back in his chair, spinning a pencil.

Miggy was at the far end of the table with construction paper and crayons, tongue sticking out as he drew what looked like a spaceship-dinosaur hybrid. Sofía sat in her booster seat systematically destroying a graham cracker into crumbs while humming to herself.

"Finally," Emilia said when I walked in. "Voice of calc reason has arrived."

"More like voice of excessive calculation," Tyler muttered.

Sofía's head popped up. "Nay-nay!"

She made immediate grabby hands toward me, graham cracker debris raining from her fingers.

"Hey, Sofía," I said, staying a safe distance from the crumb zone.

"Up! Up, Nay-nay!"

"After I help Maddie," I told her, which she accepted with a resigned sigh and went back to demolishing her snack.

I dropped my bag and looked at Maddie's paper. "What are you stuck on?"

"All of it." She gestured helplessly at her work. "I get the concept, but then I try to solve it and my brain just... stops."

I pulled up a chair. "Show me where you're getting stuck."

She walked me through her process. The setup was correct. The approach was logical. But she kept second-guessing herself halfway through, erasing and restarting.

"You're overthinking," I said. "Trust your initial instinct. You had it right the first time."

"How do you know?"

"Because I've watched you solve these before. You get to the critical step and then panic. But your work is sound."

Emilia wrote another problem on the board. "Okay, Maddie. Try this one. Nate will sit here and NOT let you erase."

"I think I've got this," Maddie said, not looking up from her work.

I looked over the problem.

"Yep, looks great. Stop doubting yourself you've got this."

Tyler cleared his throat and hmmmed.

"Maybe the calc coach needs to follow his own advice and stop doubting himself."

"What are you talking about Ty?" Emilia asked.

"It's nothing," I said quickly.

"Nate's love life," Tyler said at the same time.

Emilia turned from the whiteboard. "Wait. Nate? What's going on in your love life?"

"I'm coaching him about Jenna," Tyler interjected." I'm helping him stop pining and actually DO something about it."

"I'm not pining."

"It's Operation S.T.A.T.S. Operation Stop Talking And Take a Shot. I came up with that myself," Tyler continued as if I hadn't spoken. "And you are pining."

Miggy's crayon stopped mid-stroke. He looked up. "Wait. What's pining? Is it climbing trees? The prickly, needly ones? Do you and Jenna climb prickly trees together?"

"Pining means wanting to spend time with a person," Emilia told Miggy.

"Ohh. Nate wants to spend time with Jenna?"

He'd abandoned his drawing and was staring at me with narrowed eyes.

"Do you like Jenna the way basketball head likes Ivy?"

"Basketball head?"

"Yeah, Aiden."

"Miggy—" Emilia started.

"Like Farm Guy likes Meela?" Miggy continued, warming to his theme.

Tyler grinned. "Yes. Exactly like that."

Miggy's face transformed into pure horror. "Nooo! That means you're gonna kiss too!"

He made elaborate gagging sounds and flopped dramatically across his drawing. "That's SO GROSS."

"We're not—" I started.

"SO GROSS," Miggy repeated louder. "Kissing is the worst thing that people do."

Sofía, not understanding but sensing the energy, clapped her hands. "Goss! Goss!"

"See? Even Sofía agrees," Miggy said with great authority.

Tyler was laughing so hard he nearly fell off his chair. Maddie had given up on derivatives entirely.

"Can we not—" I tried again.

"I can't believe my Nate is gonna be a kisser," Miggy said mournfully. "I thought you were different."

"Your Nate?" Tyler managed between laughs.

Sofía yelled enthusiastically. "My Nay-nay!"

"We share him," Miggy explained patiently. "But I was first."

"Actually, Sofía claimed him first," Emilia said, clearly enjoying this.

"Only because she can't say enough words yet," Miggy argued. "When I'm in charge of words, I'm first."

I rubbed my face. "Can we go back to derivatives?"

"No," Tyler said. "This is way better."

Maddie looked up from her problem. "Nate, it's no secret that you like Jenna. And Jenna probably likes you."

Emilia said, "It's Aiden and Ivy lite. Just more analysis. We can all see what's there."

"Or Tyler and Emilia," Maddie added. "Except Nate, you're way less obnoxious than Tyler."

Tyler pressed his hand to his chest. "Obnoxious? I think you meant charismatic."

Emilia set down her marker, then grinned and patted his arm. "She said what she said."

Then she focused on me. "I need more information. About this coaching situation."

"I'm working as his social translator," Tyler answered. "So he'll stop noticing all the different ways she smiles and talk to her."

"Noticing all her smiles? Hmm, that's kind of sweet, actually," Maddie said.

Emilia added, "We all know you have your own way of thinking. What's the big deal?"

I hesitated.

Tyler didn't. "He's been watching her cheer practices and noticed some safety issues. Then he TOLD her he's been watching her practices and calculating injury probabilities."

"Ooo-kay, again different," Maddie said. "But super tuned into her well-being. Strange with a big hit of sweet."

Miggy's eyes got bigger. "You've been watching Jenna? Like a spy?"

"Not like a spy," I said. "Like someone concerned about safety protocols."

"That's what spies say," Miggy said sagely. "I saw it on a show."

"In my defense," I said, "something is wrong at those practices. Casey's timing is consistently off in ways that put Jenna at risk. Coach Marquez isn't supervising properly. I've documented four separate—"

"Nate." Emilia's voice was gentle. "What did Jenna say when you told her this?"

"She called me weird."

"Well, kind of accurate," Maddie laughed.

Miggy nodded vigorously. "Spies are weird. But good-weird. Like superheroes."

Sofía had lost interest in the conversation and was now trying to stack cracker crumbs. It wasn't going well.

"But then she said no one else had noticed," I continued. "And she's been favoring her right ankle for two weeks. The data suggests—"

"The data," Tyler interrupted, "suggests you care about her and you're worried she's going to get hurt."

I didn't respond to that.

"Up! Nay-nay, UP!" Sofía had apparently decided now was the time for shoulder rides. She stretched her arms toward me with maximum determination.

I walked over to Sofía's chair. She lunged at me with the confidence of someone who'd never been dropped, and I caught her under the arms, settling her on my shoulders. She immediately grabbed fistfuls of my hair for stability.

"So high!" she announced to the room. "Bigger dan Fahm Guy."

"Yeah, that's right, Sofía. Way bigger, way smarter, way more logical," I muttered. "No wonder you prefer me."

"Prefers you for what?" Tyler asked innocently.

"Prefers me for shoulder rides."

Tyler pressed a hand to his chest. "I've felt the sting of betrayal and dealt with it. Continue on being tall for Sofía."

Sofía patted the top of my head like I was a very good horse. "Nay-nay nice up."

"See?" Miggy said. "Even Sofía knows you're a good spy. You should tell Jenna you're being a superhero for her. Girls like that."

"I'm not a superhero."

"You noticed she was getting hurt when nobody else did," Miggy said with the kind of simple logic that made arguments impossible. "That's what superheroes do."

Emilia leaned against the counter, fighting a smile. "He's not wrong."

"I'm five," Miggy added. "I know things."

"Almost five," Emilia corrected.

"Mamá said I've got an old soul, so I'm at least five now. And wise."

Tyler was grinning. "This is the best study group we've ever had."

I stood there with Sofía on my shoulders, her hands still tangled in my hair, while an almost-five-year-old explained superhero ethics and my friends watched with entirely too much amusement.

"Can we please go back to calculus?" I asked.

"No," everyone said in unison.

Sofía bounced slightly. "No! No! No!"

Emilia looked at the homework. "Okay, actually, we do need to finish this problem set. Maddie, how's that one coming?"

Maddie held up her paper. "Done. And I didn't panic."

"Because Nate didn't let you," Emilia said. "See? Superhero."

"Emilia..."

"Superhero Nate," Miggy tested. "No, that's not right. Spy Nate? Nah. Just Nate is better."

Miggy inhaled deeply and his eyes went wide with wonder. "Nate the Great," he said reverently.

"That's a book series, Miggy," Emilia said.

"Books can share names." Miggy turned and squinted at me. "But you're still gonna kiss Jenna and that's still gross."

Tyler laughed so hard he fell off his chair.

We worked through the rest of the problem set with Sofía periodically patting my head and announcing "Nay-nay nice" to no one in particular. Miggy added helpful commentary like "High school math is angry couting."

By the time Maddie finished her last problem, Sofía had fallen asleep on my shoulders, her grip still firm in my hair. Emilia carefully extracted Sofía and carried her to the couch, covering her with a blanket.

Miggy had gone back to his drawing, now adding what appeared to be a cape to his spaceship-dinosaur. "This is you being a superhero for Jenna," he explained, holding it up. "See? You have muscles and everything."

"I don't have muscles like that."

"You do in my picture. Artists have a license to draw the way they want," he said, clearly repeating something he'd heard. "And I'm an artist."

"Artistic license?" Maddie asked.

"Yeah and it tells I'm an artist."

He went back to coloring, then added without looking up, "You should tell Jenna you like her. Before the kissing part. That's the rule."

"What rule?"

"The rule I just made up. But it's a good one."

Tyler leaned over to whisper, "Miggy's got a point."

"I've got an old soul," Miggy said.

I pulled Jenna's notebook from my bag and set it on the table. "Found this at the practice field. Can one of you get it to her?"

Emilia and Maddie exchanged a look.

"Or," Emilia said, "you could return it yourself."

"I already talked to her today. It didn't go well."

"Which is exactly why you should be the one to return it," Maddie said. "Show her you're not just the weird guy who calculates injury probabilities. You're also the guy who notices when she drops her notebook."

"That's still noticing," Tyler pointed out.

"But it's not statistical noting," Emilia countered. "There's a difference."

I looked at the notebook. "She thinks I'm weird."

"She thinks you're weird AND she said no one else noticed," Maddie said. "That's not rejection. That's... complicated."

"Everything with Jenna is complicated," I muttered.

"Then uncomplicate it," Emilia said. "Return her notebook. Have a normal conversation. Don't mention injury statistics."

"Or surveillance," Tyler added.

"Or data collection," Maddie said.

"Just be a human person returning a notebook to another human person," Emilia finished.

I picked up the notebook. Felt its weight.

"Fine. I'll return it."

"Tomorrow," Tyler said. It wasn't a question.

"Tomorrow," I agreed.

I left the farm an hour later with Maddie's confidence restored, Tyler's commentary still ringing in my ears, and

Miggy's drawing folded carefully in my bag ("So you remember to be a superhero").

By the time I got home, it was past ten. I pulled out my laptop and opened the cheer safety research again.

The statistical probability of serious injury in cheerleading: 4.2 per 1,000 participants annually.

But those were general statistics. They didn't account for lack of correct training. For coaches who weren't supervising. For athletes compensating for structural problems that weren't their fault.

What I didn't know: how to stop it.

My phone buzzed.

TYLER: hey

TYLER: for what it's worth?

TYLER: u did the right thing

TYLER: noticing. saying something

TYLER: even if it was weird

TYLER: someone needed to pay attention

TYLER: glad it's u

I set the phone down and looked back at the screen. Something about the pattern bothered me. Coach Marquez's absence wasn't random—it was consistent.

The timing errors weren't being corrected because no one in charge seemed to care enough to fix them. And Jenna kept compensating, kept taking the strain, because someone had to hold the structure together.

I didn't have enough data to prove negligence. But I had enough to know this: if nothing changed, someone was going to get seriously hurt. And in this equation, the person most at risk wasn't just a number.

It was Jenna.

16

Spiral Bound Operations Manual

Nate

The yellow spiral notebook sat on my passenger seat, its weight somehow more significant than its actual 8.3 ounces. I'd rehearsed the approach. Simple. Direct. No mention of probabilities just, "Found your notebook. Thought you might need it."

Fourteen words. Impossible to misinterpret.

I parked in front of 14 Willow Street—big white house with blue shutters, precisely trimmed hedges, the kind of North Riverbend upper-middle-class residence that looked like it belonged in a home magazine. Everything perfectly symmetrical. Not a leaf out of place.

The walk to the front door took approximately forty-seven seconds. I spent thirty-two of them questioning this decision.

Emilia's voice in my head, *Just be a human person returning a notebook to another human person.*

I rang the doorbell.

Thirty-three seconds later, the door opened.

Jenna stood there in joggers and an oversized hoodie, hair pulled back in a messy ponytail. No makeup. No performance smile. Just... Jenna.

Different from school Jenna. More unfiltered.

"Hey," she said, surprise flickering across her face.

"Hey." I held up the notebook. "Found this at the practice field yesterday. Thought you might need it."

Fourteen words. Delivered successfully.

She stared at the notebook, then at me, something unreadable in her expression. "You didn't have to drive all the way over here."

"It's 2.3 miles. Not that far." *Maybe she didn't need to know the exact distance.*

A small smile tugged at her lips. Silence stretched between us. Not uncomfortable but loaded.

"Do you want to come in?" she asked, stepping back. The offer felt genuine, not just a reflex.

"Sure," I said.

I followed her inside, past a living room that looked like a furniture showroom—pristine couch, decorative pillows arranged at perfect angles, coffee table books aligned with geometric precision. The entire house had that same calculated perfection as the exterior.

The kitchen was bright and immaculate. Jenna moved to the cabinet, pulling down two mugs. I noticed she was moving normally, no visible limp or hesitation. The ankle seemed better today.

I didn't mention it.

"I'll make us some tea?"

"Okay."

I sat on a counter stool.

"So," she said, filling an electric kettle. "I should probably apologize for Friday."

"You don't need to apologize."

"I kind of do." She kept her back to me, hands busy with tea bags. "I called you weird."

"I was...sort of."

She turned, leaning against the counter. "That's not the point. You were trying to help and I just...reacted. I should have at least listened."

"I told you I'd been calculating the likelihood of you getting hurt. You probably had a normal response to someone giving you the probability of injury from a cheer stunt. Which was weird."

A laugh escaped her. "I guess weird is one way to describe it, but it's not the correct way."

She was silent for a moment, fingers tapping against the counter. "You care Nate, and I know that. Sometimes you show it in a really strange, statistical way."

She smiled at me. The kettle clicked off. She poured hot water, the steam rising between us like a temporary barrier. She handed me a mug, then pulled out a barstool and sat.

I sat, wrapping my hands around the warm ceramic. Finding the words felt like trying to translate from one language to another.

"I see the world in patterns," I said finally. "Numbers, data points, probability calculations. It's just how my brain works.

I notice things other people miss because I'm always analyzing, always processing."

I met her eyes. "I can't turn it off. Even when I probably should."

She was quiet for a moment, studying me with an intensity I hadn't seen before. Not judgment. Something closer to understanding.

"So when you were watching practices..."

"I wasn't trying to be creepy. I saw patterns that indicated problems. Structural instability, timing errors, inadequate supervision. The data suggested high injury probability." I paused. "And then I saw you compensating for all of it."

"Because someone has to." She seemed to hear herself. "That sounds..."

"Like you're holding everything together because no one else will," I finished.

She looked down at her tea, steam curling upward. "Yeah. I guess that's exactly what it is."

The admission hung between us. Something real breaking through the surface.

She stood abruptly, moving to the window. Outside, the perfect suburban landscape stretched out—manicured lawns, tasteful landscaping, everything in its designated place.

"How do you manage to just be yourself? You don't shut off the real you, even though you see the world differently. I don't think I like it anymore," she said, still facing the window. "Cheer. I mean."

"The performing, the constant pressure to be perfect, the way it feels like I'm never actually... me. Just this version of me everyone expects."

I stayed quiet, sensing she needed to say this out loud.

"That's horrible, right?" She turned back to me. "I have this thing that other people would kill for, and I'm complaining about it."

"It's not horrible. It's honest."

"I don't know how to be honest anymore."

I understood that more than she probably realized.

"Maybe I don't shut the real me off, but I pull myself back. It's easier than trying to make myself understood."

She moved back to the island, sitting again but closer this time. "So we're both performing, in way."

"Different performances, same problem."

A small genuine smile crossed her face. "This was a weird bonding moment."

"Statistically unusual," I agreed.

She laughed, and something in my chest loosened at the sound.

"I've never told anyone that," she said. "About not liking cheer."

"Why not?"

"Because then I'd have to do something about it. And I don't know who I am without it." She wrapped both hands around her mug. "Which is terrifying."

"You're still you."

"But what if there's nothing there? What if the cheer is all I am?"

I thought about that. About the girl I'd been observing long before I started seeing safety concerns.

"There's something there," I said. "I've seen it."

She looked up, something shifting in her expression. "When?"

"When you're real with people in the small moments. When you jump in to help, show you care. You're showing the real Jenna."

Pink colored her cheeks. "You really have been paying attention."

"I notice things."

"Why?" she asked softly.

"I don't know. I just do."

We sat there in her bright, perfect kitchen, the afternoon sunlight streaming through the windows.

"This is weird, right?" she said finally. "Us. Talking like this."

"Unusual," I said. "But not necessarily bad."

"No," she agreed. "Not bad."

Her phone buzzed on the counter. She glanced at it, then back at me. I should leave. Give her space to handle whatever she needed to handle. But I didn't want to. Not yet.

"I should probably go," I said anyway.

I stood, and she walked me to the door. The space between us felt different now. Less awkward, more... intentional.

"Thanks," she said at the door. "For returning the notebook. And for... this." She gestured vaguely between us.

"Honest conversation."

"Right. That." She smiled. "I'm not very practiced at those."

"You did fine."

"See you at school."

"See you."

I walked back to my truck, aware that something fundamental had shifted. Not just between us, but in how we saw each other. I'd gone there to return a notebook.

Probability of this being a significant development: 89.4%.

Probability of me overthinking it: 100%.

Jenna

I watched Nate's truck pull away from the curb, my notebook clutched against my chest. The same notebook I'd been frantically searching for since Friday.

The one with all my lists, my plans, my careful documentation of everything I needed to keep track of to maintain the illusion of having it all together.

He'd found it at the practice field. Had it since yesterday. And instead of reading through it, instead of analyzing my desperate organizational systems the way I'd been terrified someone would, he'd just... returned it.

He'd found it yesterday. Had been carrying it around, waiting to return it. Could have given it to Maddie or Emilia. Instead, he'd driven to my house. Sat in my kitchen. Told me things I suspected he didn't tell many people.

I see the world in patterns. Numbers, data points, probability calculations. It's just how my brain works.

The honesty in his voice when he'd said that. The vulnerability underneath the precision.

I notice things other people miss because I'm always analyzing, always processing. I can't turn it off.

And somehow, in the middle of explaining why he was weird, he'd made me feel less alone in my own performance. My own exhaustion from pretending.

I don't think I like it anymore.

I'd said it out loud. My ankle twinged—barely there, just a reminder. Rest had helped. It felt almost normal today. I could go to practice Monday without issue.

Practice. Where I'd keep smiling, keep performing, keep holding the structures together because someone had to. Where I'd keep doing something I wasn't sure I even wanted anymore.

I opened the notebook, flipping through pages of lists and schedules and careful documentation. Everything organized, everything controlled, everything designed to keep the wheels turning smoothly.

And tucked in the back, the list I'd started writing. The one I'd been too afraid to look at again:

Things I Know For Sure:

- I'm tired of performing

- My ankle hurts more than I'm admitting

- I don't know who I am without the cheer smile and I'm scared to find out

- Nate notices things no one else does. That's both terrifying and comforting.

17

Risk Assessment: Critical Violation

Jenna

Cheer practice had a sound. Not music—though that pulsed from the speakers—but a rhythm underneath it. Shoes squeaking on gym floors. Synchronized counts. The soft thud of landings. Breath held, breath released.

Today, it all sounded wrong.

We were halfway through transitions when Coach Marquez clapped her hands and said, "I've got to meet with Ms. Larkin. Casey, you've got the count."

She walked off without waiting for confirmation. Taylor didn't even pretend to be surprised. She just gave Casey a nod, like it was all arranged.

I adjusted my ponytail and tried not to think too hard. Smile. Stretch. Keep the formation moving.

"Let's reset pyramid section three," Casey said, like she was bored.

I stepped into position, past Megan and Sophie, who exchanged the smallest glance. Like they wanted to say something but didn't know what or how. I didn't know either.

I was still icing from last practice. Just a little ankle soreness—nothing major. Nothing that should matter.

Still, something curled in my stomach. A flutter. Not nerves—something colder.

Taylor leaned back on the wall, arms crossed, sipping from her Stanley cup like this was all beneath her. Her eyes never left the mat.

We ran through the formation. Once. Twice. Everything technically correct. Nothing I could point to as wrong.

But the tension wasn't in my shoulders anymore—it was under my skin. Behind my ribs.

When we broke for water, Taylor walked by with a low, "Don't overthink it, Jen. That's when you mess up."

I blinked at her. "Wasn't overthinking. Just tired."

"Right," she said, and walked off.

I sat by the wall, unscrewing my water bottle with fingers that felt slightly numb. My hands were shaking, just a little. Not enough to see. Just enough to feel.

The sounds of practice continued. Shoes. Music. Breath.

But in my head, there was a countdown I couldn't stop.

Five, six, seven—

Something was going to give.

I felt the moment the pyramid shifted and I just knew.

We were supposed to bring Jessie down together—controlled, safe. But Casey's grip released early, and suddenly I had all the weight on one side. I tried to compensate, planted my foot to catch the imbalance. A sharp, tearing twist. My ankle folded underneath me, wrong, and the mat barely softened the fall.

Pain bloomed, hot and fast, then deep and steady.

I stayed down.

Not dramatically—just for a second. Like I was catching my breath. Like it was a normal fall and not what it really was.

Coach Marquez didn't move from the sidelines.

"You good, Jenna?" she called, more out of routine than concern.

I forced a nod. "Yeah. Just missed the timing."

"I felt you shift too early, Jen," Casey said, kneeling beside me with a textbook expression of fake concern.

I bit back the reply in my throat. I didn't trust my voice not to shake.

"I'm fine," I said instead. My favorite lie.

Coach checked her watch. "Stretch and hydrate. I've got a staff meeting."

And just like that, she left. The gym door swung closed behind her, echoing louder than it should have.

The rest of the girls were already drifting toward their bags, chatting like nothing had happened. No one offered a hand. No one asked again if I was okay.

So I pushed myself upright, slowly, carefully.

My right foot braced fine. My left—

The second I put weight on it, pain lanced up through my shin and into my knee.

I inhaled sharply. Not a gasp, not a cry. Just enough to know I couldn't do that again.

I sank back to the mat.

Okay. Fine.

This was fine.

I waited until the others were gone before I tried again. The gym had gone quiet—no music, no counting, no fake energy bouncing off the walls.

I pulled my sweatshirt over my uniform and tried to stand. Again. Even more slowly this time.

It didn't work.

I ended up half-sitting on the edge of the mat, clutching my ankle with one hand, gripping my water bottle with the other like it might anchor me.

I didn't want to cry.

I didn't want anyone to see.

Which is, of course, exactly when the gym doors creaked open again.

Basketballs thudded softly against the hardwood. Sneakers squeaked. Voices echoed.

The boys' team. Late practice. Of course.

I turned my face toward the bleachers, hoping to vanish by sheer willpower.

"Jenna?"

I closed my eyes.

Tyler.

"Hey—uh, why are you still here?" he called, walking closer. "Forgot something? Or just decided the gym floor is a vibe?"

Nate was behind him, slower, quieter. Aiden came in next, gym bag slung over one shoulder, frowning immediately. Dayne followed, taking in the scene with a quick glance.

"I'm fine," I said quickly. "Just wrapping up."

"Uh-huh." Tyler stopped a few feet away. "You're sitting like someone who lost a fight with gravity."

"I twisted my ankle. No big deal."

Aiden's brows pulled together. "You can't walk?"

"I can." I tried again. This time I managed to get upright. I even took a step.

And then I almost fell.

Nate stepped forward, fast, catching my arm before I could fully lose balance. "Easy."

I blinked hard and looked away. "I just need to stretch it out."

"You can't even put weight on it." Aiden's voice was gentle. Steady.

"I'm fine."

Tyler snorted. "You keep saying that like it's gonna make it true."

I hated this.

I hated being the center of attention, the weak link, the problem. I hated the ache climbing my leg and the fear that it might mean something real.

"I just need to get home," I said.

"Call your mom," Nate said. Not loud. Just... final.

"I don't want to worry her."

""Too late," Tyler muttered. "I'm worried and I'm not a parental."

Nate looked at me—not with pity, but something worse. Honesty.

"If you don't call her, I will."

That stopped me. I stared at my phone for a second. The cracked screen, the faint reflection of my own face.

I didn't want to. But I also couldn't stand here any longer. I dialed.

By the time Mom pulled up in front of the school, I was sitting on the bench by the vending machines, ankle propped on my backpack. The boys hadn't left. Tyler leaned against the wall, pretending not to watch me. Aiden stood nearby, arms crossed. Dayne hovered by the door, keeping watch. Nate sat next to me, s till.

I hadn't said much.

Neither had he.

But he hadn't moved.

Mom got out of the car quickly. "Sweetheart—what happened?"

"Just a twist," I said, turning my voice to the breeziest possible setting. "Honestly, it looks worse than it is. I'll ice it at home."

She looked me over, frowning, but not panicking. She trusted me. She always had.

"I don't think it's that bad," I added. "I can just rest tonight. We don't need to—"

"Jenna." Nate's voice was quiet but solid. "You couldn't walk."

I looked at him, willing him to let me off the hook.

"I'm fine," I said again, firmer this time. Brighter. "It's probably a level-one sprain. I read about those. They don't even always need crutches. It'll feel better by morning."

Tyler snorted under his breath. Aiden stayed quiet.

Nate didn't move, but his tone sharpened just enough.

"You wince every time you breathe. You almost fell trying to stand. That's not fine."

Mom looked between us. "Jenna?"

"I don't want to make a big deal."

"You're not," Nate said. "You're hurt. That's the deal."

It didn't sound like judgment. It didn't sound like pressure. Just... fact.

And somehow, that was worse.

Mom stepped forward and gently touched my shoulder. "Let's go. Urgent care's still open."

I didn't argue.

I didn't say fine again.

Nate handed me my bag without a word, and I got in the car.

As Mom pulled away, I kept my eyes forward, refusing to look back.

I felt the moment settle like a weight in my chest.

Not just the pain.

The shift.

Smile-always-smile. That was the first rule I learned when I started cheer. Five years old, bouncing in my sister's hand-me-down uniform. Smile through the hard parts. Smile through the mistakes. Smile so everyone thinks you're fine. I'd said "I'm fine" four times tonight.

And Nate had looked at me and said, "No, you're not."

The smile hadn't worked for the first time since I was five. And it was almost a relief.

18

At Least Six Weeks in a Boot

Jenna

4:32 PM — Exam Room

EMILIA: Tyler just told me what happened.

EMILIA: Are you okay??

IVY: Aiden said you couldn't walk

IVY: and that you're at urgent care

IVY: what did they say??

MADDIE: omg jen are you okay?

MADDIE: Dayne said your ankle looked really bad

ARIA: sending all the good vibes

ARIA: let us know what the doctor says

JENNA: hey

JENNA: yeah im okay

JENNA: just waiting for x-rays to come back

JENNA: moms with me

EMILIA: What happened exactly?

JENNA: pyramid went wrong

JENNA: landed bad

JENNA: twisted my ankle pretty good

IVY: oh no jenna

MADDIE: that sounds awful

MADDIE: does it hurt a lot?

JENNA: yeah but they gave me something for it

JENNA: just waiting to hear how bad it is

7:45 PM

JENNA: ok home from dr.

JENNA: fractured ankle

JENNA: at least 6-8 weeks in a boot

EMILIA: Oh Jenna. I'm so sorry.

IVY: six WEEKS???

MADDIE: omg that's the whole season

ARIA: are you okay???

JENNA: yeah im fine

JENNA: i mean it sucks but it is what it is

IVY: that's so long though

IVY: you must be devastated

JENNA: honestly?

JENNA: not as much as i thought id be

EMILIA: What do you mean?

JENNA: idk like obviously it sucks

JENNA: but also this whole season has felt off

JENNA: so maybe its fine

MADDIE: wait really? I thought you loved cheer

JENNA: I do or I did

JENNA: its just been different this year

JENNA: so being out isnt as tragic as it sounds

ARIA: that makes sense if you weren't loving it anyway

JENNA: exactly super tired now

EMILIA: Of course you are. You're injured and in pain. Do you need anything?

JENNA: no im good moms got it covered

JENNA: doctor gave me the to do list

JENNA: rest ice compression elevation

JENNA: no weight bearing for 2 weeks

JENNA: boot for 4-6 more

JENNA: physical therapy after

JENNA: its a whole thing

MADDIE: that's so much

JENNA: pain meds are kicking in lol

ARIA: text us if you need ANYTHING

ARIA: like literally anything food - homework - junk food

JENNA: be out of school for a few days

JENNA: just gonna focus on healing and sleep

JENNA: and watching all the British Baking Show

ARIA: valid life plan

MADDIE: let me know if you need anything

MADDIE: I can drop stuff off

JENNA: thanks Maddie

JENNA: having you guys helps knowing you dont think im being dramatic

IVY: you're injured, that's the opposite of dramatic

EMILIA: We're here for whatever you need. Even if it's just texting about nothing while you watch bad TV.

JENNA: you guys are the best

JENNA: okay pain meds are really hitting now im gonna pass out

JENNA: talk tomorrow?

ARIA: sleep well!

IVY: feel better!

MADDIE: text if you need anything!

EMILIA: Rest. We've got you chiquita.

19

Awake to the Reality of the Boot

Jenna

I'd woken up an hour ago to the reality of the boot, the pain, and six-plus weeks ahead of me. Mom had left for work—she'd checked on me before leaving, reminding me about ice and meds. Dad was still out of state. My sisters were wherever they always were—busy, texts to be returned much later.

I was curled into the left corner of the couch—blanket bunched behind my back, ankle propped on a pile of pillows, boot on. The remote lay beside me, half-buried in the quilt.

The Great British Bake Off flickered on screen—something about crumb structure and a close up of Paul Hollywood's critical stare. I'd started the episode an hour ago, then restarted it. Twice. I couldn't seem to focus.

My crutches leaned against the armrest. I hadn't touched them in an hour. Everything hurt, even thinking. I felt weird, floaty—like I wasn't supposed to be here. Not at home. Not at school. Not at cheer. Not performing.

My phone buzzed on the cushion beside me.

> NATE: How are you doing?

> ME: alive. medicated. bored.

> NATE: Everything's organized for your homework, since one of us is in each of your classes

> NATE: I'll collect and bring it over after school before practice ME: ok thanks

> NATE: See you around 3:30

Two minutes later, another text.

> EMILIA: Nate is organizing your homework

> EMILIA: I was going to, but he jumped on it

> EMILIA: I'm sure it's just a random act of kindness.

> EMILIA: Nothing having to do with you.

I managed to eat some crackers around noon, took another round of pain meds, and promptly fell asleep with Paul Hollywood mid-critique on the TV, feeding my mind what it needed to create the strangest British Baking Show dream.

Paul Hollywood wore a white doctor's coat over his blue shirt, a stethoscope draped around his neck. Mary Berry stood beside him in a matching coat, holding a clipboard decorated with tiny hand-drawn flowers.

"Let's have a look then," Paul said, his accent crisp and clinical.

They examined my ankle with the same intensity they brought to judging a signature bake. Paul pressed gently on the swelling, frowning. "The structure's compromised. You can see where the ligaments have torn—complete collapse of the foundation."

"Oh dear," Mary said kindly, patting my hand. "But you know, sometimes a good rest is exactly what's needed. Like proving dough. You can't rush it."

Paul crossed his arms. "Six weeks minimum. No weight-bearing for two. The elasticity won't return if you push it too soon."

"Will it heal?" I asked.

Mary smiled warmly. "Of course it will, darling. You just need time and patience. And perhaps a nice cup of tea."

Paul gave one firm nod. "Follow the prescription. Ice, elevation, anti-inflammatories. No shortcuts."

"But what about—"

"No. Shortcuts." He fixed me with that signature stare.

"Otherwise you'll end up with a soggy bottom," Mary added.

The knock woke me. Three soft taps.

I blinked, disoriented. Bake Off had auto-played through two more episodes. My mouth tasted like cotton and stale crackers.

Another knock, this time followed by a cautious voice.

"It's Nate."

I sat up slowly, realizing the ice pack I'd applied earlier had slid off and I was now sitting on it. Which probably explained the soggy bottom comment.

He knocked again, louder. He'd probably figured out the exact pressure to knock to get attention without being obnoxious.

"Come in!" I couldn't get the ice pack out without hurting my ankle. Guess I'd just have a cold butt.

The door opened quietly. Nate stepped inside, holding a manila folder and a grocery bag. His expression was hard to read—like he was both assessing my injury and feeling my pain.

"Hey," I said, suddenly aware of my mismatched socks, ratty sweats and hoodie PJs. Oh, and my morning, noon, and afternoon breath. And my unwashed face. And the messy bun probably turned squirrel's nest on top of my head.

"Homework from everyone." He held out the folder, either not noticing or not caring that I was a complete mess.

I took it. Our fingers brushed. He pulled back like he'd miscalculated the distance.

"Thanks."

He hesitated, then held up the grocery bag. "I got you some tea. I looked up what helps with inflammation and healing. Some of the recommendations weren't available locally, but I got you turmeric ginger blend and green tea. And I ordered chamomile for the inflammation and rooibos for antioxidants—they should arrive in a couple days."

"You researched tea for an ankle fracture?"

He shrugged, then nodded slightly. "You like tea, so it seemed relevant. And I got some cookies because cookies always help, that's basic science. I asked Emilia what your favorite is. She said the snickerdoodles from Main Street Bakery." He paused. "And since these are your favorite, there could be some stress-reduction benefits too."

My throat caught. Not because of the snacks. Because he noticed. Because he remembered. Because he asked. Because he researched stress reduction and thought of cookies.

"You can sit," I said before I thought too hard about it.

He took the armchair but sat forward, like he might need to leave at any second. For a moment, neither of us spoke. The Bake Off soundtrack filled the silence—flutes and gentle narration.

Nate's eyes flicked to the screen.

"You're on episode three. Signature biscuit round?"

"You watch it?" I asked, too surprised to filter my voice.

"Last season. During winter break. It's soothing."

I smiled—small but real. "Right? It's like a hug. But British. And full of sugar."

He didn't laugh, but his mouth twitched.

"I had the weirdest dream," I said. "The pain meds, I think. Paul Hollywood and Mary Berry showed up as doctors to diagnose my ankle. Paul kept talking about compromised structure and Mary said I needed to rest like proving dough and warned me about soggy bottoms."

Nate's eyebrow raised. "That's... oddly accurate medical advice."

"Right? Even my subconscious knows Paul Hollywood doesn't mess around."

"Mary Berry as a doctor makes sense too. Very reassuring bedside manner."

"Exactly!" I shifted on the couch, grinning. "Though I'm pretty sure real doctors don't tell you about soggy bottoms."

We watched in silence for a minute. Then Nate said, "They're not factoring bake time properly. The density's going to be off."

I blinked. "Wait—are you math-analyzing Bake Off?"

"I was just saying," he replied, almost defensively, "if you over-cream your butter, the structural integrity—"

"Stop. This is sacred," I said, mock-serious. "Don't ruin this for me with equations."

He raised an eyebrow. "You love structure. You're basically a walking planner."

"I am not."

"I've seen your color-coded homework charts."

"That's—" I sputtered. "That's unrelated."

We stared at each other. Then, for the first time in days, I laughed. A real laugh. Sharp and surprised and stupid. Nate just watched me, his mouth doing that not-smile again.

I shifted and my blanket slipped off the couch. Nate caught it mid-fall, fingers brushing my ankle boot as he draped it back over my leg. On screen, someone's biscuits collapsed.

"I should go," he said eventually, standing. "I need to get to practice."

"Yeah, you'd better get to practice. Have Coach call me if you're late—I'll give you an excuse." I decided to put it out there. "It was nice having your company. Wish it was longer."

I reached for my crutches.

"Don't get up." He moved closer, gently pushing the crutches back.

He paused, still standing close. "I could come by tomorrow. If you want."

I felt like Paul Hollywood and Mary Berry had just texted me hearts.

"Sure. Bring more notes. Or, you know... ruin a scone's probability curve or something."

"I'll do my best to bring science to the bake," he said, moving to the door.

Then he left so quietly it felt like I'd imagined him, but the tea and snickerdoodles proved he'd been here.

20

Booted and Baking

Nate

Homework had stopped being an excuse—I didn't use an excuse to go see Jenna any more. I still brought homework in neatly labeled folders. I just handed everything over when I walked in and forgot about it. We both did.

That wasn't why I kept showing up.

Another afternoon. Late. The sun was angling through the window beside her couch, casting soft light over the floral blanket bunched at her feet. Her hair was in a top knot. She had a pencil behind one ear and a cup of tea in one hand. There was flour on the counter.

I'd brought it the first time—said I wasn't sure if she had enough for multiple batches. She did. I saw her well-stocked pantry later, but she didn't make it a big deal.

I turned the crank on the sifter. "Why do we bother buying pre-sifted flour when it still needs to be sifted?"

"I think it's the only choice now?"

"It compacts during shipping. The label is pointless."

"So you're mad at the bag."

"I'm frustrated by the misleading terminology." I tapped the sifter. "How many people skip sifting because they trust the label? Their bakes suffer and they don't even know why."

Jenna's smile softened. "You're worried about hypothetical bakers?"

"I'm concerned about misinformation affecting outcomes."

"That's the same thing." She leaned forward, inspecting the dough. "You care about people getting it right."

I didn't respond. I kept sifting.

"That's kind of adorable, Nate."

"Paul Hollywood probably cares, and he's not adorable."

Jenna

Nate Berglund sifting flour and complaining about inaccurate flour bag labeling. Unexpected.

"I've never seen Paul Hollywood wearing a dancing cupcake apron, so maybe he would be adorable. Especially if it contrasted nicely with his blue eyes."

Nate looked up from the sifter. "Paul Hollywood probably has haute couture aprons. And underlings to sift for him."

"You're judging him for hypothetical sifting staff?"

"I'm pointing out that Paul Hollywood is too professional to be adorable."

"If he started a movement to have flour bags factually relabeled and wore an apron that said *Hello Cupcake* there would be adorable potential."

He hmmmed in response. He finished sifting and started measuring out the wet ingredients. I watched him work—methodical, precise, completely focused. And adorable—but I didn't say it out loud this time.

When he mixed everything together, I leaned forward, inspecting the dough.

"It's too dry. Add milk."

"Empirical proof?"

"Vibes."

He gave me a look but complied. Stirred. Adjusted. Waited.

"How's the ankle?" he asked quietly.

I looked down at the boot, then back at him. "Sore. But better than it was."

He nodded, hands stilling in the dough. "You don't have to pretend it's fine... and I don't just mean your ankle."

My throat tightened. "I know."

No sympathy, no "poor Jenna"—just permission to be me. That's what made it feel like care.

Nate

When the timer went off, I pulled the tray from the oven. I made two mugs of tea and brought them into the living room where Jenna had already settled on the couch.

"Be right back."

I returned with a plate of still-warm scones.

"Too dense," she said, breaking one open. "No crumb structure. Despite the perfect sifting technique."

"Clearly there were other variables at play."

"Mary Berry would pat your hand and suggest more leavening."

We watched The Great British Bake Off together in silence that had become easy for us—comfortable and just there. One of the bakers was talking to their cake like it was their baby. Jenna laughed, warm and unguarded.

"You really love this show," I said.

She shrugged. "They're just people making stuff that doesn't matter and being themselves, which somehow makes it all matter...We haven't talked sweetly to any of our bakes. Maybe you should have cooed at the scone dough."

I looked at her, the pain of that possibility on my face. She was trying not to smile. She leaned her head against the back of the couch.

"I used to bake all the time. Before cheer. Before everything had to be performance."

I glanced at her, then back to the screen. "You should keep doing it."

"Not alone." She said it to the TV, not to me. Then, quieter, "Not if I'm the only one eating these scones."

I didn't look at her. Didn't want to spook the moment. "I could keep showing up."

"Yeah," she said. "You could."

Jenna

He stood to go, then pulled a folded slip of paper from his pocket and set it on the coffee table.

"What's this?" I asked.

"Homework," he said. "The kind you might actually like."

He was gone before I could ask what he meant.

After he left, I sat with one of the scones in my hand. I unfolded the note.

"Brené Brown. TED Talks. Start anywhere."

And underneath that, smaller:

"Just in case you don't know how strong you are."

I pulled out my laptop. And I watched.

"The Power of Vulnerability." Twenty minutes of Brené Brown talking about connection and wholehearted living and the courage to let people see you as you really are.

I watched it twice and both times discovered more pieces of myself I thought I'd lost.

Later I texted him: "forgot how strong I was. needed that reminder. thank you" and "thanks 4 noticing what other people miss"

A few seconds later, my phone vibrated.

> Nate: You didn't forget. You just spent a long time trying to fit the average.

I stared at that. He was right. I'd been so busy being "fine"—being what everyone expected—that I forgot I could be more.

I texted back: "so done being average. time to shred the bell curve"

I smiled at the image—me, refusing to be just another data point in the middle.

My phone buzzed again.

> Nate: Already noted. You're an outlier.

I never expected outlier to be the best thing ever said about me.

21

Bakebot Learns to Pin

Jenna

I opened the door wearing a hoodie he'd left one of the first afternoons he'd spent here.

He noticed—the thing was at least two sizes too big. His eyes flicked to the hoodie, then back to my face. "Looks comfortable."

"It is."

We'd been doing this for almost two weeks now. The routine was so established, I didn't even ask if he was staying.

"This is doomed," I said from my stool, boot propped on the chair rung beside me.

Nate glanced up from the counter, where he was weighing flour like he was prepping for a space mission. "You said you wanted to try laminated dough."

"I also said it was irrational and finicky and designed to make me cry."

He carefully added a half gram more to the scale. "You said it would be fun."

I squinted at him. "You're using my words against me. That's cold."

"Room temperature," he corrected. "You said that's ideal for the butter block."

"Okay, BakeBot. Let's see if we can actually laminate anything without tearing it to shreds."

He paused and glanced at me sideways. "Confidence is high."

"You say that now. Let's wait until the third fold."

I liked how quiet the house felt when he was here. Not empty. Just... settled.

"What are you doing?" he asked, setting down the flour.

"Pinterest."

He stared at me. Blank.

"You don't know what Pinterest is?"

"Should I?"

I turned the laptop toward him. "It's where you save images that inspire you or that you want to remember. You collect them and organize them into boards by theme."

"Like a folder system."

"No. Like a vision board."

"What's the function?"

I pulled the laptop back. "There doesn't have to be a function. It's just... something I like. They make me feel things."

He processed this. "So it's aesthetic data aggregation for emotional regulation."

I blinked. "I... guess? But please never say that again."

"Can I see?"

I hesitated, then turned the screen back around.

He sat down next to me, watching as I scrolled through my "Chaos Energy" board. Paint splatters. Wildflowers. Girls mid-laugh.

"This is just pictures," he said.

"Yeah, just pictures, but more."

I clicked to another board. "After."

Dance studios. College campuses. Movement.

He leaned closer, studying each pin like it was data.

Then he paused. Scrolled back up.

"That's a Fibonacci spiral."

"Yeah."

He kept scrolling. "And the golden ratio. And... fractals."

I didn't say anything.

He clicked into the board. "'Math is Beautiful.'"

"It's just—"

"You made a math board." He looked at me.

"I made a 'trying to understand what Nate sees in math' board."

He was quiet for a long moment. Then he scrolled to the next board. Basketball courts at golden hour. Action shots. Vintage gym aesthetics.

"And basketball," he said softly.

He didn't say anything. Just stared at the screen.

"You spent multiple sessions curating visual representations of my interests," he finally said.

"Are you going to make this weird?"

"Wasn't it already bordering on weird?" He looked at me. "It's different from anything anyone's done for me."

I shrugged, trying to play it off. "I just wanted to see what you see."

His expression did something I couldn't read.

"Can I scroll through them?" he asked quietly.

"Yeah. Just... don't judge my pinning skills."

"Pinning? That's how the aggregated aesthetic data is assembled?"

"Never mind."

While the dough proofed, he calculated rise times down to the minute. I told him some things you had to feel.

He didn't argue. Which meant he was listening.

When it was time, he brought the bowl to me. I poked the dough gently. It sprang back.

"Not bad," I said.

"You were right. Feeling it matters."

"Of course I'm right. I'm the boss."

We worked like that for the next hour. I directed. He baked. We debated golden brown versus just-barely-done.

When the pastries came out—slightly lopsided, over-flaked in one corner, perfect in the other—we just stared at them like they were magic.

"Better crumb," I said. "Still a little chaotic."

"Imperfect variables," he said. "High probability of success anyway."

When he left, the laptop stayed open on the couch. My boards were still glowing on the screen—he'd scrolled through every single one before he went home.

He showed up on Friday wearing a different hoodie.

I was still wearing his.

"No baking today?" he asked, looking at the empty counter.

"I go back to school on Monday," I said. "I'm kind of baked out."

"Fair."

He sat down on the couch. Pulled out his phone.

"What are you doing?"

"Downloading Pinterest."

I stared at him. "You're what?"

"You said it's aesthetic data aggregation for emotional regulation. I want to see if it works."

"No, you said it's aesthetic data aggregation for emotional regulation, Nate. I said it's pictures, but more. I don't think you'll just automatically get Pinterest by downloading."

"Why not? You explained the function."

"It's not about function. It's about—" I stopped. "Okay. Fine. Let me help you."

I sat next to him and walked him through setting up an account.

"What do I search for?" he asked.

"Whatever you want. What are you interested in?"

He thought for a second. "Data visualization."

I laughed. "Of course. Okay, search that."

He did. Started scrolling through infographics, chart designs, and creative ways to display complex information.

"This is useful," he said, pinning three in a row.

"Make a board for them."

"A board?"

"To organize them. Like... 'Data Viz' or something."

He created a board. Named it "Visual Information Architecture."

I tried not to smile. "That's very you."

He kept scrolling. Pinning. Organizing.

Then he paused on an image. A basketball court at sunset, empty, the light coming through at a low angle.

He pinned it.

"What board?" I asked.

He hesitated. Created a new one. Didn't show me the name.

"I won't judge," I said.

He turned the phone toward me.

The board was called "Things That Feel Right."

The basketball court was the only pin. I hoped he'd find more.

"That's a good board," I said quietly.

He nodded. Kept scrolling.

Over the next half hour, he added more. A photo of a library. A shot of someone's hands working through a proof on a chalkboard. A recipe with annotations in neat handwriting. The Fibonacci spiral.

And then—he pinned one of a girl laughing, mid-motion, blurred and real.

He glanced at me. "This one reminded me of you."

"You're getting it," I said.

"Getting what?"

"Pinterest. It's not just about collecting things. It's about noticing what makes you feel something."

He looked at his board. Then at me.

"I think I understand now."

Nate

When I left that afternoon, I kept the app open. Sat in my car for a few minutes before starting the engine. Scrolled through her "Chaos Energy" board again. Pinned two images to my own board. I didn't tell her. She'd understand.

22

Back with a Boot

Jenna

I stood in front of my closet for ten full minutes and still ended up in leggings. The boot didn't fit under jeans, and I wasn't about to wear a skirt just to pretend I had it together.

I settled for a long hoodie that covered the top of the brace and a braided headband that I hoped communicated intentional instead of confused.

The result looked like I was trying to cosplay as myself.

At the main office, I handed over a note. "Temporary withdrawal from activities," my mom had written. "Doctor's recommendation: limit activity due to ankle fracture. Reconsider after 8 weeks.

The secretary nodded and stapled it to a form. Just like that, I was officially out—gym, cheer, anything that involved being upright for too long. Not that I minded. The cheer team especially. I was done with that before the injury made it official.

By second period, I remembered exactly why I'd been okay staying home. The hallways moved like stampedes. No one offered space. My boot caught on a locker edge when I turned too fast and sent my water bottle flying. Someone laughed—probably not at me, but I felt it anyway.

People said hi. Asked about my ankle. Then kept walking. I smiled and said "getting better," because "I got injured during an unsafe stunt and the coach ignored it" wasn't exactly hallway-appropriate.

The squad didn't know yet. I didn't feel like telling them.

I passed the gym on the way to lunch.

I heard the counts before I saw the pyramid. "Five, six, seven—up!"

Sophie was flying. Casey had the center base.

I should've kept walking. Turned away before they spotted me.

Too late.

"Jenna!" Taylor's voice cut through the music. "Hold up a sec!"

I stopped. The boot suddenly felt heavier.

Taylor jogged over, Casey right behind her. Both wearing matching practice gear—co-captain tanks, hair identical in high ponytails. They looked coordinated. Intentional.

"Hey," Taylor said, smile bright and sharp. "We didn't know you were coming back today."

"Yeah," I said. "Just... felt ready."

Casey glanced at my boot. "How's the ankle?"

"Getting better."

"That's great." Taylor tilted her head, like she was genuinely concerned. "We've been worried. The whole squad has."

I nodded. Didn't know what to say to that.

"So..." Taylor lowered her voice, stepped closer. "We wanted to check in. About what happened."

My stomach tightened.

"Coach Marquez asked us about it," Casey added. Her smile didn't reach her eyes. "Since we were running practice that day."

There it was. The real reason they'd stopped me.

"We told her it was just a freak accident," Taylor continued. "Wrong landing, you know? Could happen to anyone. Nothing anyone could've prevented."

She wasn't asking if that's what happened. She was telling me what the story was.

"Right," Casey said. "We all know how unpredictable stunts can be. Even when everything's done correctly."

I looked between them. Both smiling. Both waiting.

"Yeah," I managed. "Unpredictable."

"Good." Taylor's smile widened. "We just wanted to make sure we were all on the same page. You know, in case anyone asks. Parents, administration, whatever."

"We're just looking out for the team," Casey added. "Making sure there's no... confusion."

The word landed like a threat.

"Of course," I said.

"Great!" Taylor squeezed my arm—friendly, almost affectionate. "We're so glad you're okay, Jenna. Really. The squad isn't the same without you."

They walked back to practice. Rejoined the formation like nothing had happened.

I stood there for another second, boot anchoring me to the floor.

That room used to be where I knew exactly what to do, how to stand, when to smile. Now it felt empty even when it was full. Like I'd been performing a part so long I forgot there were other ways to be.

But this was different.

This was realizing the people I'd trusted with my safety were more worried about covering their own backs than whether I could walk without a boot.

Lunch was worse than the hallways.

I sat at our usual table—Tyler, Emilia, Maddie, Aria, Aiden, Ivy. The people who actually mattered. Nate slid into the seat across from me, two spots down. Tyler between us like a buffer.

Our eyes met.

He nodded. I smiled.

"How's the ankle?" he asked.

"Fine," I said. "Getting better."

"Good."

The word hung there between us, nowhere to go.

Tyler jumped in with something about basketball conditioning. Emilia asked Maddie about spirit week planning. The table filled with noise.

I picked at my sandwich, appetite gone. The conversation with Taylor and Casey kept replaying. We're all on the same page, right? Like I'd signed a contract I didn't remember agreeing to.

Nate and I kept looking at each other across the space. Like we were speaking different languages now. At my house, we'd spent an hour in silence and it felt full. Here, ten seconds felt like drowning.

I wanted to ask if he'd finished the Great British Bake-Off season. If he'd calculated any steps to improve our laminated dough technique. If he missed the quiet of being busy together too.

Instead I ate my sandwich and nodded when Maddie said something about student council homecoming planning.

Nate looked down at his tray.

I looked at Emilia.

We didn't know how to do this version of us yet.

By last period, the ache in my ankle had spread up my calf. I shifted in my seat and scribbled something in my planner, more out of habit than purpose.

Back to school = reality check.

I added another line beneath it without really meaning to.

Maybe I dreamed him.

That night, I opened our text thread. My last message was from two days ago: a math joke about obtuse angles.

He'd responded with: "Always. Especially before 8 a.m."

I hovered over the keyboard. Typed:

Felt weird seeing you at school. Different from at home.

Then deleted it.

I stared at the screen. Then flipped my phone face-down and turned off the light.

My room felt too quiet. Not the good kind.

23

Translation Errors

Nate

Days since Jenna returned: tracking notation t_1, t_2, t_3... and illogically hoping math helps me out because I think I'm messing up.

t_1

Jenna's first day back. At lunch, she sat two spots down, across from me. Tyler in between like a firewall. I'd sat next to her on her living room floor for hours and never run out of things to say. Now I couldn't think of a single opening that didn't sound like a script.

"How's the ankle?" I asked. "Fine," she said. "Getting better."

I nodded. She smiled.

Tyler filled the space with something about drills. The table buzzed with conversation. Jenna and I kept glancing at each other. Every time our eyes met, I felt the same thing I felt when I touched the flour off her face—like we were close to something real. Here, with everyone watching, it felt impossible.

I wanted to ask if she'd watched another Brené Brown TED Talk. If she had any new recipes she wanted to try. If she felt as lost here as I did. Instead I ate my lunch and listened to Tyler explain another school's zone defense.

She looked at Maddie when Maddie spoke. At Emilia when Emilia laughed. She didn't look at me again until I wasn't looking. I felt it anyway.

t₂

Tyler noticed during study hall. "You okay, Berglund? You've been solving the same equation for six minutes."

"It has multiple steps."

"Right. And your pen's upside down."

I looked down. He was right.

In math class, Jenna sat three rows ahead. I watched the back of her head, the way she tucked her hair behind her ear when she was concentrating. She didn't turn around once.

Or maybe she did when I wasn't watching.

After lunch, I passed her in the hallway.

She was digging something out of her locker, one hand braced against the metal door for balance. Her hair was pulled back. Her shoulders were tight.

"Hey," I said.

"Hey." She glanced up, smiled quickly.

I was three feet away. Close enough to touch. Close enough to say I miss the version of you that doesn't have to smile on command.

Instead: "How's your history project going?"

"Fine. Almost done."

"Good."

She shifted her weight, the boot making a small sound against the floor. The moment stretched, then snapped.

"See you," she said.

"Yeah. See you."

We both kept walking.

That night, I opened our text thread. The last message was from two days ago—her math joke about obtuse angles.

I'd responded with: "Always. Especially before 8 a.m."

t₃

Tyler cornered me on the walk to last period.

"You gonna actually talk to her, or just keep doing the sad-math-genius thing?"

"I don't know what to say."

"Try anything. You two are doing this weird long-distance staring contest and it's painful to watch."

"It's different here," I said. "Everything's... louder."

Tyler stopped walking. Looked at me. "So say it quieter. In your way."

He clapped me on the shoulder. "You're overthinking it, man. Just talk to her like you do at her house."

"What if she doesn't want me to?"

"Then she'll tell you. But right now, you're both just stuck."

I'd been watching Jenna for years. Noticing patterns. Cataloging smiles. Because she'd always pulled me in, but I'd remained on the fringes. In the past two weeks, something had changed. I wasn't just watching anymore.

I missed her. Not her laugh. Not the baking. Her. I missed watching her realize she didn't have to filter herself to matter. I didn't know how to say that in a hallway between classes.

t₄ — Study Hall

Tyler threw a balled-up paper at my head.

"Dude, you're being so extra right now."

"Extra what? I'm just sitting here."

"Exactly."

He sat across from me and rested his chin on his hand like he was about to deliver a speech. "You're doing that thing again. The one where you pretend you're above emotional panic because you know how to spell probability."

"I'm not panicking."

"You're completely panicking."

I adjusted my pen. "She hasn't texted either."

"Which means she's probably panicking too. Or she thinks you've moved on. Or—crazy thought—she doesn't know what any of it meant to you."

I blinked.

Tyler smirked. "You're smart, but you're bad at people. Which is why I appointed myself your STATS coach." He peeled the wrapper off a granola bar like he was about to order me to run ten suicides and he was settling in to watch.

"Okay, I've let you mope long enough. Make the spreadsheet."

I frowned. "What spreadsheet?"

"The one that says You're the Muffin of My Heart. Chart her smile to your rising heart rate. Rank which baking spice she most reminds you of. I don't care—just do something that sounds like you."

I didn't answer.

Tyler leaned in, quieter now.

"You don't have to say it like anyone else would. Just say it."

Friday Night

That night, I made the spreadsheet and sent it.

I labeled it:

Bakebot Emotional Data Points from Jenna Lundquist Exposure Experience.

I didn't expect a reply right away. But five minutes later, I got:

> Jenna: You just sent me an adorable spreadsheet

I didn't calculate what that meant.

I just smiled.

Jenna

My phone buzzed at 9:47 PM.

I'd been lying in bed, scrolling through nothing, trying not to think about how quiet the house felt. How quiet everything felt without him.

The notification said: "Nate Berglund sent you a file."

I sat up.

The file name made me blink twice:

Bakebot Emotional Data Points from Jenna Lundquist Exposure Experience.

I opened it.

Oh.

Oh.

I pressed my hand to my chest as my own hearts tried to make what he'd recorded.

Cinnamon reminds me of her. Not because she's sweet. Because she lingers.

I read it twice. Three times. The words blurred slightly.

Her laugh after she said 'BakeBot'—I think that was the first time I wanted to say I liked her out loud.

Oh.

She looks different when she's not performing. Not dimmer. Quieter. But brighter somehow. Realer. I like that version best."

I set the phone down. Picked it back up. Read it again. He saw me. And he liked what he saw. My hands shook a little as I scrolled.

> If time spent together increases: Laughter frequency rises Emotional masking decreases Probability of deeper connection = statistically significant

> Current status: Probability of me being able to explain how I feel in words = currently low Probability that I'll keep trying anyway = extremely high Margin of error = irrelevant

> Conclusion: Urgently recommend further testing. At least daily. More often if conditions allow.

I laughed. Then I might have cried a little. Then I laughed again, because Nate Berglund had just asked told me he felt something using a spreadsheet and it was the most perfect thing I'd ever seen. The most perfect, because is was so perfectly him.

My fingers hovered over the keyboard. I wanted to say something that matched what he'd just given me—something honest and vulnerable and exactly right.

But all I could manage was:

Me: You just sent me an adorable spreadsheet.

Me: Why are graphs adorable when you created them for me?

I watched the typing bubble appear. Disappear. Appear again.

Then I kept typing before he could respond:

Me: Nate Berglund you made a data spreadsheet about us baking together

Me: "Cinnamon reminds me of her because she lingers"???

Me: This is the most ridiculous thing anyone has ever done for me.

Me: Also the sweetest. And Most Adorable.

Nate: So… recommend further testing?

My heart did something complicated and wonderful.

Me: Yes. Daily. Starting tomorrow if you want.

Me: I really miss our test kitchen.

Nate: Me too.

I waited, smiling at my phone like an absolute disaster of a person.

Another message came through:

Nate: One more thing. Check the Aggregated Emotional Data when you get a chance.

Me: Already did. All 23 pins. You updated your emotional regulation data.

Nate: Aesthetic data aggregation for emotional regulation.

Nate: You taught me that.

Me: I taught you well.

Me: Also you're kind of killing me right now.

Nate: In a good way?

Me: Such a good way. See you tomorrow.

Nate: Text when you're ready for me to come over.

I set my phone on my nightstand and stared at the ceiling. My room didn't feel too quiet anymore.

It felt full of possibility. Full of cinnamon and spreadsheets and a boy who noticed everything about me and decided I was worth 23 Pinterest pins and a hypothesis about deeper connection.

I fell asleep smiling, the spreadsheet still open on my phone.

"I like that version best."

Me too.

Bakebot Emotional Data Points from Jenna
Lundquist Exposure Experience.
Compiled only for the eyes of Jenna Lundquist
Introduction-Data Points

SHEET TWO: SUBJECTIVE NOTES

Cinnamon reminds me of her. Not because she's sweet. Because she lingers.

Her laugh after she said 'BakeBot'—I think that was the first time I wanted to say I liked her out loud.

She looks different when she's not performing. Not dimmer. Quieter. But brighter somehow. Realer. I like that version best.

Historical Data Point:

Her laugh after she said 'BakeBot'—I think that was the first time I wanted to say I liked her out loud.

Hypothesis

If time spent together increases: → Laughter frequency rises → Emotional masking decreases → Probability of deeper connection = statistically significant

Venn Diagram

Circle A: People I feel comfortable around

Circle B: People who make me laugh

Circle C: People I miss when I'm not near them

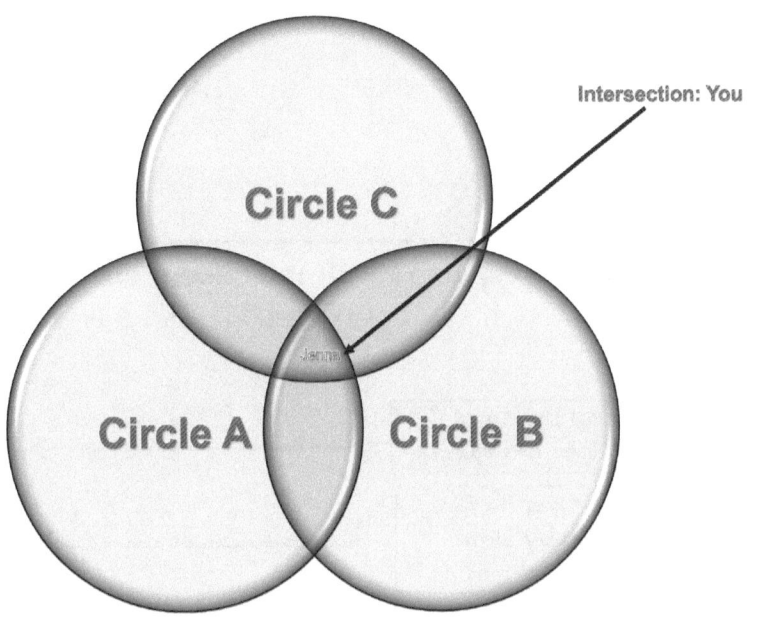

Intersection: You

Intersection: You

Circle C

Circle A   Circle B

Jenna

Circle A: People I feel comfortable around
Circle B: People who make me laugh
Circle C: People I miss when I'm not near them

Line Graph of Nate's Mathematically Impossible to Measure Emotional Reactions

251

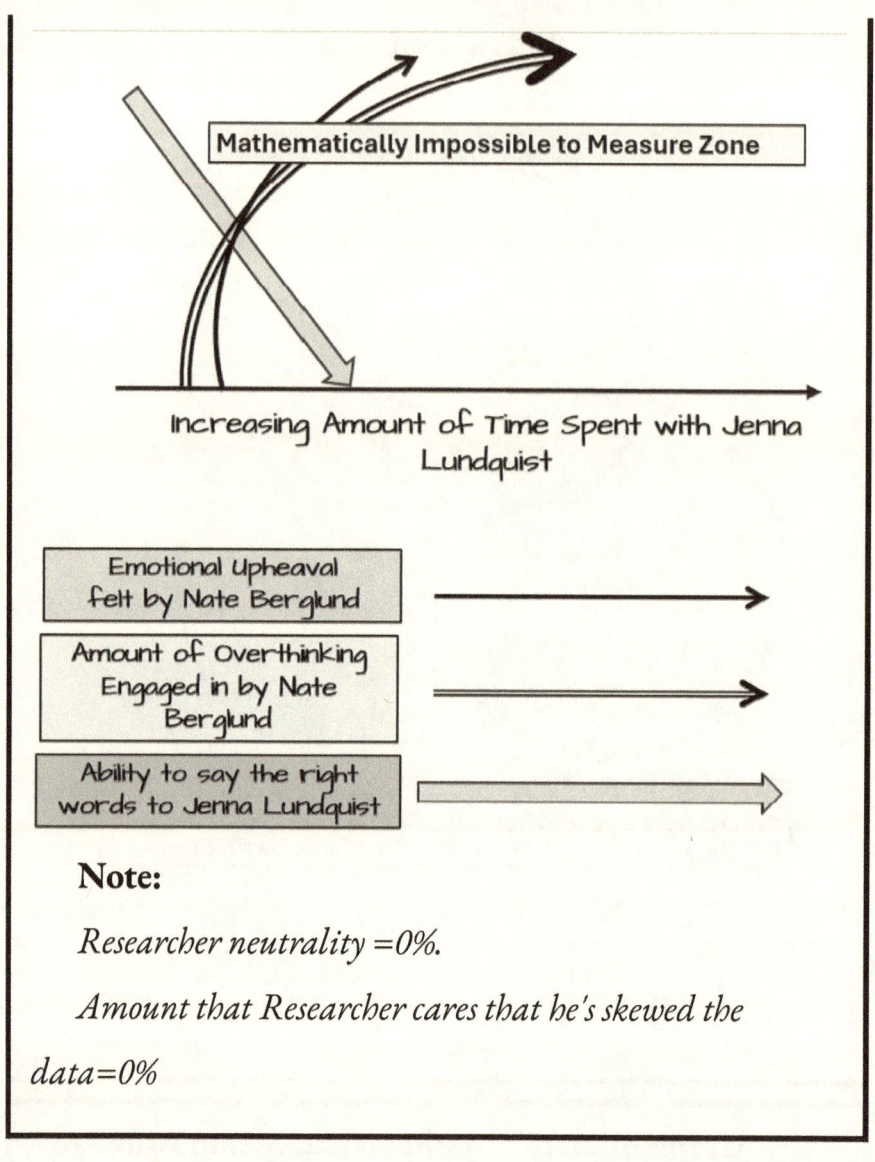

Note:

Researcher neutrality =0%.

Amount that Researcher cares that he's skewed the data=0%

Line Graph – the Spice Chart of Jenna Lundquist

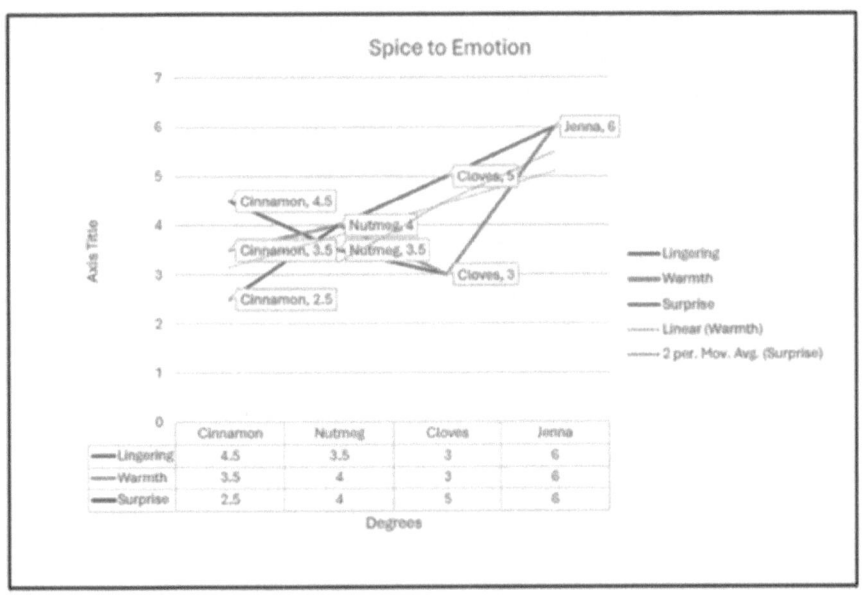

Spice to Emotion

	Cinnamon	Nutmeg	Cloves	Jenna
Lingering	4.5	3.5	3	6
Warmth	3.5	4	3	6
Surprise	2.5	4	5	6

Degrees

Emotion to Bake Chart

The Day's Bake	Jenna's Action or Reaction	Nate's Emotional Response
Underbaked Banana Muffins	Disgust at the unbaked goo inside the muffin.	Heart rate increased significantly when Jenna's disgusted expression was seen to be unbelievably cute.
Laminated Dough	Called Nate's flour bag rant adorable.	Wanted to tell her to say it again.
Croissant Crisis	Covered in flour	Could hardly look at her because of her glow.
Burned Scones	Laughing so hard she couldn't talke.	Stunned by how musical her laughter sounded.

Notes: Control variables included sarcasm, British narration, and crutch location. Conclusion: Highest stability observed when both parties are in the same room. Recommend further testing.

Current status: Probability of me being able to explain how I feel in words = currently low Probability that I'll keep trying anyway = extremely high Margin of error = irrelevant.

Conclusion: Urgently recommend further testing. At least daily. More often if conditions allow.

24

Flour Wars and Peace

Jenna

We agreed on challah.

Well—technically I said, "Let's make something we can braid," and Nate said, "That makes a subset of one bread," and I said, "Perfect. Let's do that one."

We didn't call it a date, didn't call it anything. He showed up with a fresh bag of flour, and I was wearing the hoodie he'd left here last week. He noticed. Didn't comment. Just got a look—soft around the edges—then set the flour on the counter and draped another hoodie he'd brought across the back of the sofa.

The kitchen was warm, just-right warmth. Saturday morning light came in soft and wide through the window over the sink. I sat on the stool, boot still on. He stood at the counter, rolling up his sleeves.

"Your ankle doing okay?"

"It's okay for now."

He gave me a look but didn't push.

"Do you want to start the dough?" he asked.

"No," I said. "That part's yours. I'll handle the aesthetics of the braiding."

He nodded. "Fair division of labor."

He was being so careful. Not with the flour—with me.

"Should I be nervous?" I asked after a few minutes of him silently measuring yeast.

He paused. "Are you?"

"A little."

He looked up. "Why?"

I didn't answer. Not directly.

"Because if this goes badly," I said, "I won't be able to pretend I didn't care."

He folded in the yeast like a secret.

"It won't go badly."

"You sound sure."

"I'm not."

I smiled. "Good. That makes two of us."

We kneaded in shifts. I joked that it was emotional processing. He didn't argue. Flour got everywhere—mostly on Nate. He was being so careful not to get any on me or near my boot. Measuring and mixing with precision, even as I kept reaching over to mess with him. I swiped a streak across his cheek.

He raised an eyebrow. "You keep claiming it's accidental."

"It absolutely was."

"At least own up to your flour crimes."

I grinned and reached for the flour bag. He caught my wrist before I could get to it.

"I don't think so."

"You're no fun."

"I'm being strategic." He was almost smiling, and he hadn't let go of my wrist.

"Strategic how?"

He dusted his flour-covered fingers across my nose. "Like that."

"Nate Berglund, did you just—"

Before I could finish my protest, he stepped closer, still holding my wrist gently, and we were close enough that I could see the different shades of blue in his eyes. We both froze.

His thumb traced a small circle against the inside of my wrist. My other hand had somehow ended up flat against his chest. I could feel his heartbeat under my palm.

"Your eyes are a nicer blue than Paul Hollywood's," I said, because apparently my brain had stopped working.

His brows lifted slightly. "What?"

"Great British Bake-Off. He's got blue eyes. Yours are better."

Something in his expression shifted—softer, surprised, like he didn't know what to do with that information.

"I can't believe I just said that out loud," I muttered.

"I'm glad you did."

I looked up at him. He was still close enough that I could see flour caught in his eyelashes. Close enough that I could feel the warmth radiating from him. Close enough that I could make a choice.

So I did.

I leaned up and kissed him. Just once. Soft. Brief. Like a question. He went very still. Then his hand—the one that had been tracing circles on my wrist—slid up to cup my jaw.

He kissed me back like he was solving an equation. Methodical. Careful. Testing variables. Except the variable was me, and the equation was complex and he was paying attention to every outcome. He pulled back just enough to breathe.

"Was that—"

"Yes," I said.

"Can I—"

"Yes."

This time when he kissed me, it wasn't careful. It was sure. His other hand joined the first, framing my face, thumbs gentle against my cheekbones. My hands fisted in the front of his flour-covered sweatshirt, anchoring myself to something solid while everything else felt impossibly light.

He kissed me like I was the most important piece of data he'd ever collected. Like he was memorizing the angle, the pressure, the exact way I tilted my head to get closer. Like he'd been calculating this moment for years and now that it was happening, he wasn't going to miss a single detail.

When we finally pulled apart, we were both breathing harder. His forehead rested against mine.

"You're covered in flour," he said quietly.

"So are you."

"Yeah." His thumb brushed across my cheekbone. "But you look... good like this."

"Like a disaster?"

"Like yourself." His voice was quiet, serious. "You're always pretty, but you're beautiful when you don't curate yourself."

"Flour truce?" I whispered.

"Truce," he said.

But neither of us moved. Not yet.

He stepped back slowly, like he was giving me time to say something. I didn't know what to say. My brain was still catching up to the fact that Nate Berglund had just kissed me like I was the answer to every unsolved equation.

We were both covered in flour. The kitchen looked like a snowstorm had hit it.

He cleared his throat. "We should probably clean up before the dough rises."

"Probably," I agreed, not moving.

Neither did he. Not right away.

After the dough rose, I hobbled over to the counter. He didn't tell me to sit back down, just shifted to make room beside me. We braided practice pieces out of leftover dough strips. One turned out even. One collapsed halfway through. One looked like a tragic pretzel.

Nate lined them up on the counter like evidence. "We're getting better."

"Or worse in interesting ways," I said.

We did the real braid together, his fingers mirroring mine, folding under and over without needing instructions. At one point our hands bumped. Neither of us pulled away.

I made my way to the table, boot clunking against the floor. He pulled out a chair for me without asking. We sat while everything baked—both the practice pieces and the real challah.

No homework. No planning. Just quiet, tired satisfaction.

When the timer dinged, the whole kitchen smelled like warm sugar and trust.

He pulled everything out—the practice pieces golden and imperfect, the challah beautifully braided. He set them on a trivet in the center of the table.

I picked up the challah/pretzel disaster, turning it over in my hands. "That one's us," I said.

Nate looked at it, then at me. "No. That's us if we make assumptions about data and don't talk."

He was right.

I pulled off a twisted piece. "This part is me thinking you didn't want to talk to me at school."

He pulled off another piece. "This part is me not knowing how to be the same person at school that I am here."

"This part," I said, breaking off another chunk, "is me almost texting you and deleting it."

"This part is me making a spreadsheet instead of just saying what I meant."

"That part wasn't bad though."

"No," he agreed. "That part worked."

I held up the last piece—the center where everything had twisted together into a knot. "This part is us not saying what we actually want."

He took it from my hand. Set it down on the table between us.

"So... we're...?" I asked.

He didn't pretend not to know what I meant.

"Yes. We're official. Together. Dating. A couple." He paused, like he was running through a mental checklist. "Boyfriend and girlfriend, if you want to use traditional labels. Exclusive. Committed to further testing of the—"

I laughed. "Nate."

"I'm just making sure we're clear on all variables."

"We're clear," I said. "Very clear."

"Good." He looked directly at me. "Because I want all of those things. With you."

"Me too," I said. "All of them."

His hand covered mine on the table. Not just pinkies this time. Full hand. Deliberate.

I turned my palm up and our fingers laced together.

The challah hadn't collapsed.

Neither had we.

25

Peer Reviewed

Jenna

I got to the cafeteria first. It felt weirdly significant.

Usually Emilia or Aria claimed the table. Sometimes Tyler arrived early to stake out extra chairs with dramatic flair. But today it was just me, the low roar of lunch chatter bouncing off concrete walls, and the smell of French fries and whatever the cafeteria was calling "pizza" today.

I sat in my usual spot—boot propped on the crossbar under the table, Nate's hoodie sleeves covering my hands. The fabric still smelled like his laundry detergent and something else I couldn't name but that made my chest feel less tight.

I wasn't hiding. I wasn't performing. I was sitting. Present. But also... nervous.

This was the first time our friend group would see us together as an actual couple. The first time Nate would have to decide where to sit. The first time I'd have to navigate being "Nate's girlfriend" in public instead of just in my kitchen.

Emilia slid into the seat across from me a minute later, eyeing the hoodie like it had something to say.

"So," she said.

I sipped my tea. "So?"

"That's new." She nodded at the hoodie.

"Is it?"

"Jenna." Her voice was patient but amused. "I've known you since third grade. You rarely wear giant size clothing."

Before I could respond, Nate arrived. He stopped at the end of the table, backpack over one shoulder, lunch tray in hand. His eyes met mine for a second—just long enough for me to see the question there.

I shifted slightly, making room beside me. He sat down. Not across from me where he used to sit. Not two spots away with Tyler as a buffer. Right beside me.

Emilia's eyebrows went up.

Nate set a granola bar on the table in front of me without comment—the kind I actually liked, not the cafeteria's cardboard-flavored version.

"Thanks," I said quietly.

"You're welcome."

Emilia was staring at us like we'd just confirmed a major scientific theory.

"Em," I started.

"Oh, no worries. Carry on. No comments, I'm just... observing."

Aiden and Ivy showed up next, fingers laced, mid-argument about whether a song Ivy liked "slapped" or was "mid at best." Drew trailed behind them with his usual quiet nod.

"Wait."

Ivy stopped mid-sentence when she saw us. Saw Nate sitting beside me. Saw the granola bar. Saw my hand resting near his on the table.

"Finally," Ivy said, taking her seat.

"Finally what?" I asked innocently.

"Don't even," Ivy said, grinning. "You two are SITTING NEXT TO EACH OTHER."

"We sit at the same table every day," Nate said.

"Not like THAT you don't."

Maddie appeared with Dayne, both laughing about something. She took one look at our seating arrangement and grabbed Dayne's arm.

"Oh my god," she whispered, but not quietly enough.

"What?" Dayne looked confused.

"LOOK." Maddie pointed.

Dayne's face lit up with understanding. "Ohhhhh. Okay. Respect, Berglund."

Tyler and Aria were last. Tyler was mid-rant about someone stealing his parking spot when he reached the table, but he stopped dead when he actually looked at us.

His face transformed into pure satisfaction.

"NO. WAY."

"What?" Aria asked, setting down her tray.

"LOOK." Tyler pointed at us like we were evidence in a criminal trial. "Operation S.T.A.T.S. is COMPLETE. The spreadsheet WORKED."

Nate's ears went red. "Tyler—"

"I TOLD you the spreadsheet would work! I SAID 'make something that sounds like you' and you DID and now LOOK!" Tyler was practically vibrating with victory. "I'm a GENIUS. I'm the STATS coach of the CENTURY."

"You gave him some good advice?" Emilia asked, smiling.

"I COACHED him. For WEEKS. This is MY success story."

"It's really not," Nate muttered.

"It absolutely is. You sent the spreadsheet Friday night, right? And now it's Monday and you're sitting NEXT to her instead of awkwardly across from her pretending you don't have feelings."

"Wait, what spreadsheet?" Maddie asked.

Tyler leaned back in his chair, clearly ready to hold court. "Oh, let me tell you about the spreadsheet. It had DATA. It had ANALYSIS. It had a conclusion that said 'recommend further testing.' It was PEAK Nate. And I TOLD him to do it."

"You told me to be myself," Nate said. "The spreadsheet was my idea."

"Yeah, but who COACHED you to be yourself? Who sat through WEEKS of you calculating smile variations? Who gave you the pep talk about aesthetic data aggregation?"

"I'm sorry, smile variations?" Drew asked.

"He has a numbering system," Tyler said proudly. "I've been coaching him for like a month. This is my victory."

Ivy was practically bouncing. "Okay but ARE you guys together? Like officially?"

I looked at Nate. He looked at me.

"Yes," I said.

"We're together," Nate added. "Dating. Official. Boyfriend and girlfriend if we're using traditional labels. Exclusive. Committed to—"

"Nate," I laughed, squeezing his hand under the table. "They get it."

Tyler threw both hands in the air. "THIS IS THE BEST DAY OF MY LIFE. My coaching WORKED. I'm putting this on my résumé under Leadership Experience."

"Tyler," Emilia said, voice dangerously calm. "The best day of your life? Of your entire life?"

He froze. "Uh—"

"Because I would've thought," she leaned in and whispered something in his ear.

"Okay, yes, that was definitely better than this," Tyler said quickly.

She whispered again.

"And that day too, obviously—"

She whispered a third time.

"Yeah, for sure better."

She whispered again.

Tyler's face went slightly red. "Okay, that one DEFINITELY beats this."

"Mmhmm." Emilia looked entirely too pleased with herself and gave him a side-eye.

"FINE. Can't top anything in my life since sophomore year, but definitely a great day for YOU and definitely highlights my coaching. And it's been a good coaching year."

Emilia sat back, satisfied. "That's what I thought."

Aiden was grinning. "Smooth recovery, man."

Tyler threw his hands up. "THIS is what happens when you date someone smarter than you. They weaponize data."

"You just took credit for teaching me to do that," Nate said.

"I'm just saying," Dayne jumped in, "I had plans. Was working up my nerve. But you snooze, you lose." He shook his head. "Berglund swooped in with DATA. Can't compete with that."

"I didn't swoop," Nate said.

"You absolutely swooped," Tyler corrected. "With graphs and everything. It was a statistical swoop."

"That's not a thing."

"It is now."

The table dissolved into laughter and overlapping conversations. Tyler kept taking credit for the coaching. Ivy wanted to know every detail about the spreadsheet.

I sat there, Nate's hand near mine, surrounded by friends who were genuinely happy for us, and something that had been tight in my chest for weeks loosened just slightly.

Then I saw her.

Casey. Across the cafeteria, talking to Taylor and a couple other girls from the squad. She glanced over, caught my eye.

She didn't smile. Just... looked. Like she was taking note.

My stomach tightened.

"Jenna?" Nate's voice was quiet, just for me. "You okay?"

I looked back at him. At the table full of friends. At Tyler still narrating his coaching success story.

"Yeah," I said. And for right now, in this moment, it was true. "I'm good."

26

Precious Cargo Delivery Routes

Jenna

By Friday, the granola bars had become routine.

Nate would arrive at lunch, sit beside me, and slide one across the table without comment. Something small. Something that said I'm paying attention.

Today when he sat down, I started picking at the wrapper, not because I was hungry but because I needed something to do with my hands.

"Hey," he said quietly.

"Hey."

He studied me for a second too long. "Rough day?"

"It's fine."

The thing was—it wasn't fine. It had been four days of not-fine.

Monday had been good—our friends finding out, Tyler's victory lap, everyone happy for us. But Tuesday, Casey had "accidentally" bumped me hard enough into my locker that I'd dropped my books.

Wednesday, someone sent me screenshots of a group chat where they discussed how I "couldn't handle varsity." Thursday, no one would partner with me in Bio.

And today, I'd spent the entire morning checking over my shoulder.

Emilia arrived and immediately clocked my expression. She looked at Nate, who gave a small shrug that clearly meant I don't know either.

The rest of the group filtered in—Aiden and Ivy, Drew, Maddie and Dayne, Tyler and Aria. Normal lunch-table chaos. Tyler was mid-story about something, Ivy was showing Aria her phone, everyone settling into their usual spots.

But Maddie was watching me.

She waited until the table noise hit a comfortable level, then leaned in.

"Jenna. What's going on?"

Not are you okay. Not how are you feeling. Just—what's going on.

Like she already knew I wasn't okay and just needed me to say it out loud. My throat went tight.

"I'm fine," I started.

"Jenna." Emilia's voice joined, gentle but firm.

Nate's hand moved slightly on the table. Not touching mine. Just... there. The table hadn't gone completely quiet, but the people nearest us had stopped talking. Tyler. Aria. Ivy.

I traced the edge of my tea bottle with my thumb. "They've been... it's been weird. Since I came back."

"Weird how?" Ivy asked quietly.

I took a breath. "Getting bumped in the hall and not seeing who it was. On Tuesday Casey 'accidentally' bumped me into the lockers. Hard enough that I dropped my books. She apologized really loud so everyone could hear, but her eyes were—" I stopped. "She wasn't sorry."

No one said anything.

"And it's been like that all week. Not just her. Taylor. Some of the other girls." I couldn't look at them. "Wednesday someone screenshot a group chat and sent it to me. They were talking about me. About how I 'couldn't handle varsity' and that's why I quit."

"That's bullshit," Tyler said flatly.

"I know. But it's not just online. Yesterday Taylor cornered me in the bathroom and said she hoped I was 'being smart' about what I told people. That the team needed to 'stay unified' and 'protect the program.' She made it sound like concern, but it was a warning."

My voice was getting smaller and I hated it. "And in Bio, no one would partner with me for the lab. Mr. Danning asked if I was 'feeling up to participating' or if I needed to 'take it easy.' In front of everyone."

Aria's expression went dark. "He said that?"

"He thought he was being nice. Like I'm fragile or something." I finally looked up. "And maybe I am. Maybe they're right and I just—"

"Stop." Nate's voice was quiet but absolute. "They're not right."

"They corner me between classes," I said, the words coming faster now. "Not every time. But enough that I'm always watching for them. Always checking over my shoulder. I'm not even on cheer anymore, I don't understand why they'd start acting like this. They're—"

My voice cracked.

"And I can't even walk away from them fast enough when they corner me." I gestured at my boot. "Doctor said six weeks minimum, then PT. So when they decide to follow me, I just have to... take it."

Emilia reached across the table. "They're going after you because you made them look bad."

I nodded, throat closed, no words getting out. That's when Nate spoke again, low and deliberate.

"We can fix part of this," he said. "You shouldn't be walking alone."

Tyler looked up. "What do you mean?"

"Between classes, there's overlap. We figure out everyone's routes and make sure she's never by herself. Doesn't have to look obvious—just covered."

"Okay, so we're building a friends as bodyguards schedule?" Tyler asked.

Nate nodded. "Something like that. We'll rotate. Make it casual."

Maddie leaned closer. "What do you actually need from us?"

I pulled Nate's hoodie sleeves over my hands. "I just... I need people around. Between classes. So they can't corner me alone."

"Done," Tyler said, flipping open his notebook. "Okay, everyone call out your periods."

Voices overlapped—Aiden claiming mornings, Emilia offering second, Maddie volunteering the choir-to-cafeteria route, Ivy third.

"Back stairwell," Drew said quietly. "End of sixth."

Tyler was scribbling furiously. "We're doing this, taking action against the garbage people."

Nate glanced at his notes. "I'll put the full schedule together tonight—rotations, overlap times. We can test it Monday."

"Good," Tyler said. "I'll double-check everyone's schedules and make sure we didn't miss a gap."

"Are we starting a task force?" Ivy asked hopefully.

"God, no," Aria said.

"Too late, I'm writing it down—"

"Tyler—"

Despite everything, I almost laughed.

"Wait, wait." Tyler held up one hand. "Important boundary question before we go further."

Everyone stopped.

"All boyfriend stuff is Nate's department, right? Like, hand-holding, hoodie situations, general romantic gestures—that's all him. The rest of us are strictly professional?"

Nate's ears went red. "Tyler."

"I'm establishing boundaries! This is a security detail, not a rom-com. Plus I already successfully coached you through getting the relationship. I'm not doing BOTH jobs."

He paused, then looked around the table. "Although—there's still a couple of single dudes in this group, and well, if you need coaching I'm available. Track record speaks for itself. Just remember with Lundquist here, it's too late. You snooze, you lose."

Dayne snorted into his water bottle.

"Office hours are Tuesdays and Thursdays," Tyler said without missing a beat.

Ivy was laughing. "Are you actually starting a consulting business?"

"I'm just saying—results-oriented approach, proven success rate—"

"I'm putting it in the official notes," Tyler said, writing. "Professional boundaries. Romantic duties remain with N.B., courtesy of T.A.'s excellent prior coaching. Coaching services available to qualified candidates upon request."

"Tyler," Emilia said quietly and pulled him closer to whisper in her ear again.

He looked kind of shell shocked. "Okay, business plan revised- Relationship Coach Consulting is on hold. I'm going to be too busy in the near future to invest the needed human capital - which is me."

Emilia smiled smugly and rolled her eyes, then Tyler leaned and whispered something into her ear and she flushed tomato red.

The table settled into planning mode—who had which period, what routes made sense, how to make it look casual.

I sat there listening, and something in my chest that had been clenched all week finally loosened.

Sixth period ended early. I had a follow-up checkup for my ankle, which meant getting signed out and leaving before the final bell. Everyone else was still in class.

The hallway was half-empty, the kind of quiet that makes your footsteps sound too loud. I should've texted someone to walk with me—but it was just the parking lot.

Bright sun, open space. Safe enough. Or so I thought.

Then I heard footsteps behind me. Too close. Too deliberate.

"Jenna!"

I knew that voice. My stomach dropped.

I kept walking, boot clunking against asphalt, trying to move faster without looking like I was running.

"Jenna, wait up!" Casey's voice, bright and false. "We just want to talk."

They were flanking me now. Herding me toward the gap between the gym and the portables where there were no cameras.

My ankle throbbed. The boot made running impossible.

"I'm fine," I said, hating how small my voice sounded. "I have an appointment—"

"This'll just take a second." Taylor moved to block my path. Her smile was bright. Friendly. "We've been worried about you."

Casey nodded. "The squad misses you. We all do."

I tried to step around them. Taylor shifted with me.

"We heard some things," Taylor continued, voice soft. Concerned. "About you talking to people. About what happened at practice."

My stomach dropped.

"We just want to make sure you remember it correctly," Casey said. "You know, what actually happened with the injury."

"I know what happened."

"Do you?" Taylor's smile never wavered. "Because we remember you shifting early during the dismount. We all felt it. That's what caused the fall."

"You let go—"

"You shifted early," Casey repeated, like I hadn't spoken. "Coach Marquez saw it too. That's why she didn't make a big deal about it—because everyone knows pyramid work is unpredictable when someone's timing is off."

My throat went tight.

"We're co-captains," Taylor added. "Which means people come to us when they have questions. And if someone started asking about that practice—about supervision or safety protocols or anything like that—we'd have to tell them the truth. That you shifted early. That the fall was on you."

"We're just trying to protect you," Casey said, saccharine sweet. "If this becomes a thing, if administration gets involved, everyone's going to remember what really happened. How you lost focus. How it wasn't anyone's fault but your own."

"We wouldn't want you to embarrass yourself," Taylor said. "Or make Coach Marquez look bad by spreading a confused version of events. She's been nothing but supportive of you."

My heart was pounding. The boot felt like it weighed a hundred pounds.

Casey stepped closer. "So we just wanted to check in. Make sure we're all remembering the same thing. That we're all clear on what actually happened."

"And if we hear you've been telling people a different story," Taylor said quietly, "we'll have to correct that. For the team. For the program. You understand."

She let that sit for a second.

"We'd hate for there to be any... confusion that needs clearing up."

"Jenna! Hold up there, girl."

Dayne appeared from between two parked cars, grinning like he'd just found exactly who he was looking for. "It's a pain being stuck in that boot, huh? I had one freshman year—sprained ankle. Hard to get anywhere fast."

He gave Casey and Taylor a pointed look. "Crutches were better for one thing, though."

Taylor frowned. "Yeah? What's that?"

"You could at least take someone out at the knees with them."

Casey's smile froze. Taylor's eyes narrowed.

"We were actually talking," Taylor said.

"Cool, cool." Dayne didn't miss a beat, still casual. "Anyway, I just wanted to say—I gotta admit, I had plans, Lundquist. I knew you were single, I was working up my nerve, and then—" He snapped his fingers. "You snooze, you lose. Berglund swooped right in."

A surprised laugh escaped me. Casey made a small, disgusted sound.

"Seriously though," Dayne continued, like Taylor and Casey weren't even there. "Happy for you guys. He's good people. Intense, but good people."

We'd reached the main parking lot. Casey and Taylor had stopped following. I glanced back. They were standing by the gym, watching.

Dayne waited while I unlocked my car. His casual expression shifted—just slightly, just enough.

"Tyler texted the group. Said you signed out early for your appointment and were heading out alone. Figured I was closest."

"Thanks, for showing."

He smiled, softer this time. "We're friends, Jenna. That's kind of the whole deal."

"Yeah," I said quietly. "It really is."

"Anyway." He knocked once on the roof of my car. "See you, Jenna. Stay safe."

He walked away, hands in pockets, like this was the most normal interaction in the world. I sat in my car for a full minute before my hands stopped shaking enough to start the engine.

I pulled Nate's hoodie tighter around me and draped another blanket across my lap. I tossed the box of Cheez-Its off my legs and pushed my homework to the side. I channel-surfed until I found an episode of The Great British Bake Off. I tried to focus on the bakers and their quirks. Everything kept blurring together.

Lunch and my friends rallying, making plans—it had all been good. Better than good. I'd felt like maybe things would be okay. That feeling had been missing for a long time.

Then sixth period hit. Hopefulness from lunch made me careless—let my guard down—and they ambushed me. Casey and Taylor waiting, trailing me into the parking lot. Doubt crept back in. Hoping had made it all feel worse.

My phone buzzed.

Phone in hand, I stared at the message.

His truck pulled up less than ten minutes later. His familiar footsteps and polite knock—he never just walked in—halted my spiral.

"Come in," I called.

Seeing him framed in the doorway, backpack slung over one shoulder, let me take my first full breath since the parking lot.

"Hi," he said.

"Hi."

He took in the scene—me buried in his hoodie, homework on the floor, Cheez-Its tossed aside. Without a word, he sat down and pulled me into his arms.

I went still, then gave him all my weight, pressing my face into his side. Steadiness, warmth, and strength wove around me. My tension started to crack, became less stifling.

"I'm tired and cold," I said, voice muffled against his sweatshirt. "And scared. Casey and Taylor ambushed me in the parking lot and I... if Dayne hadn't—"

His arms tightened. "I know. Dayne texted after."

We stayed like that for a while—his chin resting on top of my head, my face pressed against his shoulder. His arms banded around me. His heartbeat under my ear was slow and even. I matched my breathing to it.

"I really was scared," I whispered. "Not just today. All week. I keep waiting for them to corner me, knowing—" my voice cracked "—knowing I'd be trapped. That I couldn't get away fast enough. And I felt like I should've been braver. Tougher."

His arms tightened again. "You won't have to worry about running from them now. You're not facing them alone anymore. Okay?"

He went quiet for a moment. "I should've known sooner. How bad it was."

"You couldn't have—"

"That first week you came back—before Saturday—I saw things. The way you'd check over your shoulder, how you'd tense when certain people walked by. The way Taylor and Casey would position themselves near you in the halls, like they were making sure you saw them."

His voice dropped. "But I didn't know what to do about it. I wanted to ask, to help, but we could barely talk at school and I thought maybe you regretted letting me in. I thought maybe it was just a moment."

"Oh." Every part of me understood that fear.

He kept going. "So I just watched, tried to figure out the right thing to say. Then Saturday happened and I thought maybe things would get better. That we'd figured it out. But they didn't stop. It got worse. And even after we were together, you didn't tell me about the lockers, the bathroom—"

"Nate." I touched his arm. "Stop."

He looked at me, startled.

"You don't have to keep apologizing for what you didn't know," I said quietly. "You saw more than anyone else did. You helped me breathe again. That's what matters."

He exhaled, some of the tension leaving his shoulders.

"You're here now," I added, firmer this time. "Right here. With me."

My phone buzzed on the coffee table. Emilia's name on the screen.

> EMILIA: Miggy and Sofía made you something. You need to see this.

I opened the video.

MIGGY (on video):

He was wearing a paper crown, holding a spatula like a sword, standing in the Prestons' kitchen.

"Jenna. I heard you got hurt because of cheer betrayal."

He paused, face very serious.

"That's when someone has a smiley face but mean stuff in their brain. I learned that from Emilia when she was talking to Farm Guy, but I wasn't spying on purpose. Oh, and cheer betrayal is in the Bible."

He raised the spatula and shouted:

"THIS IS A CHEER. READY OKAY!"

"Gimme a J!" (He high-kneed in a circle)

"Gimme an E!" (He dropped the spatula, picked up a Nerf dart)

"Gimme another N, then a different N, THEN AN A!"

"What's that spell?? JENNA!

And she was STRONG!

And she was GOOD!

And her smile was REAL not mean-fake!"

He pointed the Nerf dart at the camera.

"And if you're mean to Jenna again, I'll never ever let you pet my cows."

He paused, winded.

"Also you're turning into a bad dizzy chicken."

Miggy straightened his crown with great dignity.

"You didn't quit. You just left un-good people behind. That was smart. And if you need backup, I have Nerf weapons and three battle capes."

He ran offscreen, yelling something about "justice toast."

Then the camera panned.

SOFÍA:

She wore a tutu over her overalls, one shoe on, and what might have been a sticker crown. She was holding a half-eaten slice of bread like a trophy.

"JENNA!" she yelled.

"NO BAD GIRLS!

YOU! STRONG GIRL!

YOU! SHINE!

RAHHHHHHHHHHHH!"

She spun in a circle, dropped the bread, picked up a hairbrush, and launched into freestyle choreography:

"Go, Jenna, GO!

You NICE!

You PINK!

YOU BITE BAD GIRLS!"

EMILIA (offscreen): "Sofía. We do not bite people."

SOFÍA (glaring at camera): "BITE bad ones."

She gave a final stomp, pumped one fist in the air, and shouted:

"YOU GO! JENNA WIN!"

Then she tripped over nothing, stood up immediately, yelled "ME OKAY!" and ran offscreen screaming "CHEER MORE LATER!"

The video ended.

I was crying and laughing at the same time, and I didn't care that Nate was watching.

"Miggy has three battle capes," I managed.

Nate's mouth twitched. "He's very serious about backup."

"And Sofía wants me to bite people."

"Only the bad ones," he said. "She was very specific."

I wiped my eyes, still smiling. The fear from the parking lot felt smaller now. Not gone—but manageable.

Nate reached for his backpack.

"I got everyone's schedules—and yours—figured out. There's someone with you during every class change, every hallway transition, any time you're not in class. You're not going to be alone. I've got it typed up."

He held it out. I took it, unfolding it slowly.

Typed. Color-coded. Names in neat columns, time slots, hallway routes mapped like battle plans. My name at the top in bold:

JENNA – HALLWAY COVERAGE (ALPHA DRAFT, LIVE)

I scanned the list:

E.P. – Locker area, after 1st period A.C. – Library hallway, 3rd to 4th period transition I.H. – Choir wing to English D.T. – Back stairwell, end of 6th period T.A. – Cafeteria to parking lot N.B. – Always

I kept reading. Every period. Every transition. Someone's initials next to each time slot.

Then I hit the bottom.

In a different font, clearly added later:

AMENDMENT (added by T.A.): All hand-holding, hoodie-sharing, and romantic gestures remain exclusive to N.B. Other coverage personnel will maintain appropriate professional boundaries. This is a SECURITY DETAIL, people.

A laugh burst out of me before I could stop it.

Nate looked pained. "Tyler said he was proofreading."

"I think every document should get a Tyler amendment added."

"That actually frightens me."

"This is the best thing I've seen all week." I was still smiling. "Did you try to delete it?"

"He threatened to rewrite the entire schedule in Chiller."

I laughed harder. Nate's mouth twitched despite himself.

The smile faded as I looked back at the schedule—at all the names, all the time slots. The sheer amount of organization this must have taken.

"You built this," I said quietly. "All of it." I kept my eyes on the paper. "At lunch it felt impossible—everyone's different classes, all the transitions. How did you make all the connections?"

He shifted on the couch. "It's just... pattern matching. I already knew most people's schedules from being around campus. Then it was mapping your route against theirs, finding overlaps."

He gestured at the paper. "Tyler has English with you second period, so he's got first-to-second transition. Ivy's choir is near your third, so she takes that one. It's like solving for variables."

"You make it sound simple."

"Maybe not simple, but solvable. We had all the variables—we just had to put them into the equation correctly." He paused. "Everyone wanted to help. We just needed to coordinate. We were covering you all afternoon. You just didn't know it yet."

I looked up. "Dayne."

"Yeah. He was closest when you left sixth period."

I looked at the schedule one more time. My name at the top. Everyone else's lined up beneath it. Every minute accounted for. A network made of people who saw me.

"Okay," I said quietly.

"Okay?"

"Okay." I touched the paper. "I'll keep it in my binder for Monday."

Something in his posture relaxed. Just slightly.

"And Jenna?"

"Yeah?"

"If something happens and you don't have anyone walking with you, call me. I don't care what class I'm in—I'll be there."

I nodded, not trusting my voice.

"Thank you. For organizing all of this."

"Everyone wanted to help. We just needed a system."

"Still." I looked at him. "You made it happen."

He started to stand, then stopped when I reached for his hand.

"Can't you stay?" I asked.

He looked at me for a long moment.

"You can always assume I'll want your company, Nate. And if I need space, I'll tell you. I know we confused each other at the beginning, but I won't play games with you."

He sat back down—closer this time. Close enough that when I shifted over an inch, and I could rest my head on his shoulder.

We sat like that—quiet, comfortable, the schedule on the coffee table and the evening light fading through the windows. He shifted slightly, and I looked up. And the second time Nate Berglund kissed me, I felt like I was a precious element he was learning.

27

Permission to Not Cheer

Jenna

Amber and Hailey were home for the weekend, which meant the house smelled like decisive opinions and expensive peppermint shampoo, the distinct scent of thinking highly of myself wove through it all.

By Saturday morning she'd already cleaned out the coat closet and alphabetized the tea drawer. I stayed upstairs. Not hiding, exactly. Just... holding still.

It was Hailey who came first.

She slipped into my room without knocking, kicked off her boots, and flopped across my bed like she lived here.

"So," she said.

I looked up from my laptop. "So?"

"Nate Berglund is apparently now a one-man emotional reconnaissance team."

My eyebrows lifted. "What?"

"He texted me Friday. Very calm. Very serious. Asked if I'd talked to you lately. Said if I hadn't, I probably should."

She tilted her head. "And then signed off like some kind of mystery character."

I groaned into my sleeve. "Of course he did."

Hailey smirked. "Not the vibe I expected from Math Nate."

"Me either."

Then her voice gentled. "So... what's going on?"

I told her a little. Enough to draw a map. She listened with her whole face—elbows on her knees, eyebrows furrowed, heart in her eyes.

When Amber came in with tea a few minutes later, I felt the air shift. She didn't ask questions. Just sat on the edge of the bed, offered me a mug, and waited.

Eventually, I gave them the whole story. Cheer. Taylor. The locker bumps. The slow unraveling of everything I thought I could handle.

Amber listened like she was composing a speech. Hailey listened like she was ready to yell at someone.

I took a breath. "And there's something else."

They both looked at me.

"I don't think I want to go back."

Silence.

"To cheer," I clarified, even though they knew. "When the boot comes off. When I'm cleared. I don't think I want to go back at all."

My voice got smaller. "And I know you guys loved it. I know it was this huge part of who you were in high school, and Mom still has all your trophies and photos everywhere, and I just—" I stopped. "I don't want to disappoint you."

Hailey blinked. "Disappoint us?"

"You were both so good at it. You thrived. And I thought I was supposed to—" My throat closed. "I thought if I did cheer like you did, I'd finally be... like you."

Amber's expression cracked. "Oh, Jenna."

"I'm not saying I hated all of it," I said quickly. "I liked parts. The routines, the precision, learning new skills. But the culture, the politics, the constant performance—" I shook my head. "I don't think I ever loved it. I think I just loved the idea of being the kind of person who could love it."

Hailey leaned forward. "Jenna. You know I quit, right?"

I froze. "What?"

"Senior year. Halfway through. I quit the team."

"You—what? No you didn't. You were captain. You were at nationals—"

"Nationals was fall semester," Hailey said. "I quit in January. Told Coach I needed to focus on college apps, but really?" She looked at Amber. "I was exhausted. The drama, the pressure, the way Taylor's older sister ran that team like a dictatorship—I couldn't do it anymore."

Amber nodded. "And I almost quit sophomore year. I stuck it out because I'd already committed to it, but there were days I wished I'd had the guts to walk away."

I stared at them. "But you both always talked about it like it was the best thing—"

"It was good for us in some ways," Amber said carefully. "The discipline, the teamwork, the physical challenge. But that doesn't mean it was easy. Or always healthy."

"I loved the sport," Hailey added. "I didn't always love the culture. There's a difference."

"And you," Amber looked at me directly, "don't have to do something just because we did it. You're not us, Jenna. You're you. And if cheer isn't for you? That's completely okay."

"More than okay," Hailey said firmly. "It's right. You're allowed to choose something different."

My eyes burned. "I feel like I failed."

"Failed what?" Amber asked gently.

"Being... enough. Being like you."

Hailey moved closer, taking my hand. "Jenna. You don't need to be like us. You never did. That was never the assignment."

"And honestly?" Amber's voice was soft. "Watching you these past few months, trying to force yourself into something that wasn't working—that's what hurt to see. Not you quitting cheer. You being miserable."

I wiped my eyes. "I kept thinking if I just tried harder, smiled more, was a better teammate—"

"Stop," Hailey said. "That's the same thinking that kept you being the 'easy kid' who never asked for anything. You don't have to earn the right to make choices for yourself."

"What do you even want to do instead?" Amber asked. "If cheer's not it, what is?"

I hesitated. "I don't know yet. Maybe nothing for a while. Maybe just... figure out what actually feels like me instead of what I think I should be doing."

"That," Hailey said, "sounds really healthy actually."

"And you know what?" Amber added. "Mom and Dad will be fine with it. They might need some explanation, but they'll understand. Especially once we talk to them."

I looked between them. "You'd do that?"

"Of course," Hailey said. "That's what I meant about helping them catch up. Part of that is helping them understand that you leaving cheer isn't a failure—it's you taking care of yourself."

"You know what you're really good at?" Amber asked.

I shook my head.

"Being the kind of person people feel safe around. Making spaces feel like home. Noticing what people need before they ask." She smiled. "That's your thing. That's what makes you you. Not how high you can throw someone in the air."

"And that tall math genius?" Hailey grinned. "He figured that out way before we did."

"You know what's weird?" I said. "People always called me the easy kid."

Hailey nodded slowly. "Because you didn't scream during road trips or get detention."

Amber added, "Because you passed your classes, kept your room clean, and said thank you without being asked. But being kind, generous, and caring—that's what made you easy. Your big heart. Not easy to ignore—easy to trust. Easy to appreciate. And we haven't always done that enough."

"I think I started believing it meant invisible," I said quietly. "Like if I didn't need anything, they didn't have to see me."

Amber's face shifted.

"Jenna," she said, setting her mug down. "You weren't the easy kid. You were the heart."

I didn't say anything.

"You know that, right?" Hailey pressed. "You're the one who made holidays feel like holidays. You made birthday cards. You reminded Mom to pack Dad's lunch."

"That's just stuff," I said.

"No," Amber said gently. "It's the rhythm of our house. The little glue."

I looked down at the blanket between us. Then said, almost too softly, "I remember once when I was little—Amber had strep and Hailey was grounded, and Mom was overwhelmed. I helped make dinner, set the table, got drinks, took a plate to both of you in your rooms. Mom said I was such a help. But then Dad took his dinner to his office, and Mom kept answering texts and phone calls. I sat at the table by myself and ate my dinner."

I shrugged.

"I wasn't sad. Not really. I just remember thinking... if I didn't need anything, it made everything easier."

Neither of them spoke right away.

Then Hailey leaned her head against my shoulder. "That shouldn't have been your job."

Amber reached over and squeezed my hand. "You're not just the helper. You're the heartbeat."

Later, when things felt less fragile, Hailey said, "So, Nate?"

"Oh no."

Amber grinned. "He's been making math-heart eyes at you since our families went camping together. We've been waiting for you to catch up."

I groaned. "Can we not."

Hailey nudged me. "He's a spreadsheet looking for his perfect data."

"And you like him," Amber added, "because you've never not been seen by him."

I didn't answer. But I didn't deny it.

They didn't promise to fix it.

But they promised they were in it with me.

And that was enough for now.

It was Sunday night when they sat me down.

Amber's duffel was packed, coat folded neatly over the arm of the couch. Hailey had made popcorn like it was casual—like they weren't about to drop something carefully coordinated.

I knew that look. The sister look. The "we already did something" look.

"You held everything together," she said. "Too tightly sometimes. But you kept the pieces in place."

Hailey grinned. "She's got a tall, cute math genius looking out for her now. We might have to share the job."

Amber hugged me. "Our family's not the best about saying it, but I love you, little glue gun." She grabbed her duffel and headed for the door. Hailey stood, stretched, and followed her out to the car—probably to finish some big-sister gossip.

Amber crossed one leg over the other. "Okay. Before I head back—just want to let you know we reached out to someone."

I frowned. "What kind of someone?"

"Our old cheer coach," Hailey said. "Mrs. Wexler. Remember her? She's at the junior high now, guidance counselor. She knows how cheer culture works, and she knows how to ask the right questions without tipping anyone off."

"She's going to call you," Amber added. "She's asking questions. Discreetly. She knows what to look for."

Amber leaned forward. "In the meantime, stick to Nate's schedule. Let the people who've already shown up... keep showing up."

I nodded, the lump in my throat climbing fast.

Then Amber added, "And heads up—next time I come home, I'm bringing someone with me."

That got a look from Hailey. "Finally?"

Amber smirked. "Maybe."

She stood and was already at the door when she turned back one last time.

"You know we used to call you our little Glue Gun, right?"

I frowned. "What?"

28

Safe Passages

Jenna

When Mom asked if I needed a ride to school, I told her a friend was picking me up. She hadn't said anything about the bullying yet, so I guessed Hailey hadn't found the right moment. But Mom wasn't oblivious.

After I yelled, "Bye, Mom," she followed me to the front door and looked out.

"Oh. Nate Berglund. Hmmm. Not surprised."

I got to his truck as fast as my boot would allow. He came around to help me in, and when I saw him wave toward the house, I realized she was still watching.□

Once we were driving, he reached over and laced his fingers through mine on the console between us. Natural. Easy.

"Ready?" he asked.

"As I'll ever be."

At school, I didn't ask for another copy of the schedule, but I got one—an aesthetically upgraded version printed on blue graph paper, tiny checkboxes beside every period. Across the top, in small handwriting, he'd added a quote:□

You don't have to be fearless. Just don't let fear stop you. — Serena Williams

Monday to Friday. Between every class. Never alone. Nate had mapped it out and handed it to me like it was just another stat sheet. No big talk. No dramatic pause. Just, "If anyone's late, text me first. Then Tyler."

I held the paper a second too long. He noticed.

"This doesn't mean you're weak," he said, voice low but steady. "It means everything else is too messed up."□

I nodded, folded the schedule, and slipped it into my back pocket.

Week One

First Period → Second

Nate was waiting just outside the classroom when the bell rang.

He didn't say much—just fell into step beside me as I gathered my things. I moved slower than usual, but he matched my pace without comment.☐

When we got to my locker, he leaned against the one next to mine. Hoodie, backpack, silent presence.☐

I shoved my books in with a little more force than necessary.

"I'm not fragile," I muttered, then felt guilty for complaining.☐

"Only Casey and Taylor think you're fragile," he said. "I just can't stand to see you get hurt anymore while proving how strong you are."

Before we started walking again, he handed me a folded sticky note. I opened it:☐

"Your real self is allowed to take up space. — Emilia"

We walked without talking. With Nate, that always felt fine. Halfway down the hall, he reached for my hand. He cut a diagonal path through the traffic jam by the science wing. I noticed people looking. They didn't say anything.☐

When we reached my next class, he squeezed my hand once before letting go. "See you at lunch."

Second → Third

Tyler appeared like a border collie on caffeine. "Guard Formation Alpha, in motion!" He saluted me with a spiral notebook.□

Drew followed behind him—less border collie, more sentry tower. Silent. Solid. Unmissable.

We passed Taylor near the stairwell. She didn't say anything at first—just narrowed her eyes and made a sharp little sniff like something smelled off. Casey trailed behind her, fake-laughing at something no one said.□

"She needs a whole parade now?" Casey muttered as we passed.

Drew didn't even flinch. He just stepped wider, blocking their line of sight like a moving wall. Tyler launched into a fake monologue about hallway detours due to "excessive emotional toxicity."

Before I reached my classroom, Tyler slipped me a card:□ "They don't decide who you are. — Aria"

I laughed. I turned back and caught the look on Taylor's face—tight-lipped, unsure. The smirk was gone.

Third → Fourth

Ivy flanked me on one side, Aiden on the other.□

Ivy pointed at a homecoming poster with TASTE THE TRADITION in block letters. "If that doesn't sound like a threat, I don't know what does."□

"Maybe it's a promise?" I offered.

"Of what—cafeteria lasagna? Worse, lutefisk?" She was warming to her topic now. "What if tradition tastes like stale fish paste and cardboard? My grandma makes lutefisk pudding—seriously—and loves it. What if tradition IS lutefisk pudding? Count me out."□

Aiden shook his head but smiled as he listened.

At English, Ivy squeezed my arm and handed me a pink note:□

"You shine bright even when you're quiet. — Ivy"

Lunch

I sat between Nate and Emilia. Tyler was across from us with a spiral notebook open, scribbling furiously. Drew mostly just raised his eyebrows and shook his head at whatever Tyler was plotting.

Ivy pointed toward the TASTE THE TRADITION poster visible through the cafeteria windows. "Okay, but seriously, what IS the tradition they want us to taste? Because if we're talking actual North Dakota heritage foods, I have CONCERNS."□

"Your grandma's lefse is good," Aiden said.□

"Lefse is fine. Lefse is the gateway drug. I'm talking about the REAL stuff." Ivy pulled out her phone. "Lutefisk. Fish soaked in LYE until it's basically jelly that smells like ammonia and sadness."

"My grandpa loves that," Maddie said. "Christmas isn't Christmas without the lutefisk smell making everyone gag."□

"EXACTLY." Ivy was on a roll now. "Or how about rakfisk? Fermented trout. You just leave it rotting for MONTHS and then eat it RAW."

Tyler looked up from his notebook. "Wait, say that again."□

"Rakfisk. Fermented for months. Eaten raw. Why?"

"Because that's HORRIFYING and I'm writing it down." Tyler was scribbling faster now.

"Writing what down?"

"Screenplay. Teen horror movie. Homecoming: A Traditional

Terror. This is GOLD."

"You're writing a horror movie about fermented fish?" Drew said flatly.

"About ALL of it. The lutefisk, the rakfisk, everything. Think about it—unsuspecting high schoolers forced to confront their ancestors' culinary nightmares at homecoming."□

"That's the worst movie pitch I've ever heard," Emilia said.□

"You say that NOW. But wait until Act Three when the—"

"Don't finish that sentence," I warned.□

Tyler grinned and kept writing.

"Blodpølse," Ivy continued. "Blood sausage. With syrup. BLOOD. WITH. SYRUP."□

"That's actually pretty common in a lot of cultures," Emilia said.□

"Doesn't make it less horrifying when you're twelve and your grandma tells you what you just ate."

"What about the German-Russian stuff?" Aria asked. "My family's got some weird ones too."

"Like Fleischkuekle?" Ivy said. "Which literally translates to FLESH CAKE?"

"It's good though," Aria protested. "It's like a fried meat pie."□

"It's called FLESH CAKE, Aria."

I was laughing now, and Nate's hand found mine under the table, his thumb tracing small circles against my palm.

"Head cheese," Drew said quietly.□

Everyone turned to look at him.

"Not cheese. Pig's head in gelatin."

There was a beat of horrified silence.

"Drew wins," Tyler declared, writing furiously. "That's the worst one. Definitely the mid-boss of my screenplay."□

"Your WHAT?" Emilia asked.

"The rakfisk is the final boss, obviously. But head cheese is the mid-movie twist villain."□

"You're actually doing this," Maddie said.□

"I'm COMMITTED. This is art." Tyler kept writing. "Wait, wait, wait. What about prairie oysters?"

Everyone groaned.

"What are prairie oysters?" I asked.

There was a pause. Aiden said carefully, "Rocky Mountain oysters. It's... ranch food."□

"It's bull testicles," Drew said flatly.□

"DREW," Ivy yelled.□

"She asked. They're deep-fried. A useful by-product of castrating young cattle, about four months old."□

"Poor babies!" Ivy cried.

I nearly choked on my water.

"A delicacy," Tyler added. "Perfect for the jump-scare in Act One."

Tyler was still scribbling. "Okay, I'm documenting all of this for the screenplay. You're all going to be characters. Drew, you're dying first—you're the hero who investigates the smell."□

"Why do I die first?"

"Because you're brave and noble. It's very Obi-Wan."

"That doesn't make me feel better."

"It should! Obi-Wan is iconic."

"Oh, don't forget about Surmelksuppe," Ivy said. "SOUR MILK SOUP. You take milk, let it go bad, and make SOUP out of it."□

"My great-grandma made that," Maddie said. "With raisins."□

"WHY WOULD YOU RUIN RAISINS LIKE THAT?"

Tyler's pen was almost a blur. "This is incredible. The smell... it's coming from the cafeteria. Cut to: screaming. Blood sausage everywhere. A single pickled herring sitting ominously on a lunch tray."

"You're really committing to this," Aria said.□

"I'm the group historian. Someone has to document these moments."

"You're not the group historian," Drew said.□

"I am—it's a volunteer position."

Conversation kept bouncing—pickled pig's feet, knoephla soup ("boiled biscuit gravy")—while Tyler added to his notes.□ Somewhere in the middle of it all, I realized something.□ Tradition was only good if you wanted it. If it was forced on you—if you were told you had to swallow it just because it had always been done that way—it was just lutefisk. Something that looked harmless but made you gag.

Nate squeezed my hand under the table like he knew exactly what I was thinking.

The room was still loud. But today it sounded like normal.

Sixth Period

I was halfway to class—my bodyguard for the route was Aria—when I heard, "Wait up?"□

It was one of the JV girls—Hallie, maybe? She was clutching a water bottle like it might protect her.□

"Can I walk with you?"

I nodded. "Yeah. Of course."

We walked in silence. Just before we reached the door, she added, "You look strong again."□

I didn't correct her.

"Jessie wanted me to give this to you." She handed me a wrinkled note before disappearing down the opposite hall: "You're not the only one. You're just the only one who held onto her brave. — Jessie"

Final Bell

Nate was there again.

"Made it," he said.□

"I feel like myself, but..." I started, then stopped. "Not."□

He shrugged. "You're always you, even when you've hidden yourself deep down."

I didn't say anything. I just let him take my hand as we walked out the doors together.

After a day of walking the hallways with bodyguards, I felt stronger than I had in weeks.

At his truck, I asked, "Okay, simple word problem. If Jenna's going home and Nate's with her in the parking lot... where's Nate going to spend the afternoon?"□

"Home. With Jenna."

He didn't hesitate. Didn't even pause.

"That one's been solved for a while."

He opened my door, waited while I climbed in, then leaned in to kiss my forehead before closing it.

On the drive home, I realized the schedule had done something bigger than keep me safe—it had built a rhythm.□ Different people, same routes, same quiet protection.□ It would keep going—until it didn't need to.

Until I didn't.

***

Week 2 The schedule continued—different people, same routes, same quiet protection.

Tuesday, Dayne walked me to second period and told me about his fear of death by ND windchill and how Ivy had TED talked him about way North Dakotans deal with blizzards. By the time we reached my classroom, I'd almost forgotten why he was there.

Wednesday, Maddie linked her arm through mine between third and fourth, chatting about the homecoming dance like it was the most normal thing in the world. When we passed a group of cheerleaders, she didn't break stride—just kept talking.

Thursday at lunch, Tyler arrived with stapled packets labeled **HOMECOMING: A TRADITIONAL TERROR** and performed his twenty-page "screenplay" about haunted lutefisk.

By the time he reached the part where Drew died heroically and Ivy weaponized lefse, everyone was crying from laughter.□

It was absurd.

Exactly what I needed.

Because after weeks of real fear—real isolation, real pain—laughing at flying pickled herring was almost comforting.□

We could make jokes about haunted food.

We could do it together.

Friday Afternoon

I noticed something shift. Taylor walked past me—no words, no glance.□

Maybe she'd been told to back off. Maybe she was just tired of the game.

Either way, I didn't flinch.

When Nate picked me up after last period, I leaned into him as we walked to the parking lot, his arm around my shoulders.

Week Three

Somewhere between the second and third week, the tension in my shoulders began to fade.□

I wasn't checking over my shoulder anymore.

Wasn't tensing when footsteps came up behind me.

The hallways felt different—emptier in certain places, but safer.

"You okay?" Nate asked, noticing my pause between classes.□

"Yeah," I said. And meant it. "I think I am."

The schedule quietly loosened after that.

Not abandoned—just relaxed.

Nate still walked me between most classes. Sometimes I'd wave him off, tell him I was fine, and he'd let me go. Tyler still showed up between second and third, but mostly to complain about his English essay.

The notes kept coming, though—little reminders slipped into my locker or handed off between classes:□

You're doing great. — Emilia

Still here. Still you. — Ivy

Math isn't the only thing that adds up. — Nate

It went on quietly—no fanfare, no announcement.□

Just steady presence, shrinking as I grew stronger.□

Until the day I realized I didn't need it anymore.

29

Can You Repeat that Please?

Jenna

The cafeteria was loud the way it always was at lunch—hundreds of conversations layering over each other, the clatter of trays, the squeak of chairs dragged across the linoleum.

Our usual table was packed: Emilia, Tyler, Ivy, Aiden, Aria, Drew, Maddie, Dayne, Nate. All of us crammed together, the way we'd been doing since the school year started.

I was halfway through explaining my English paper to Maddie when the PA system crackled to life.

Everyone groaned. Announcements during lunch were never good news—usually something about parking violations or a reminder about an assembly no one wanted to attend.

"Good afternoon, Riverbend High." Mrs. Anderson's cheerful voice. "Just a quick announcement about homecoming court nominations."

The cafeteria noise dropped a few decibels. People were actually listening now.

"For junior court, we have the following nominees. Princes: Tyler Alred, Nate Berglund, and Aiden Pedersen."

Tyler's fork clattered to his tray. "YES."

"What?" Emilia muttered. She looked around the table. "What did she say?"

Aiden's head fell back and he groaned. Ivy immediately reached for his hand under the table.

"Princesses: Jenna Lundquist, Aria Cooper, and Emilia Preston."

The world tilted slightly.

My name. Out loud. Over the PA system. In front of the entire school.

Around our table, reactions happened all at once:

Tyler jumped up. "I TOLD you guys I had charisma!"

Emilia was still looking around in confusion. "No, this isn't real, right? I'm dreaming. It's a nightmare. Please tell me this isn't happening."

Aria set down her sandwich. "Okay, then. It's a thing, isn't it."

Aiden let out a quiet sigh. "Okay."

Then he looked at Ivy and said, "You should be a Princess, Princess."

Ivy's cheeks went pink. "Stop," she said, but she was smiling, squeezing his hand tighter.

And me? I just sat there, fork suspended halfway to my mouth, processing.

Six months ago, I would've been thrilled, it would've been part of THE path, the one I was supposed to be following. Homecoming court was something to check off. One of the checkboxes that proved I was doing everything right. Now? I felt... nothing. Maybe, nothing that I would have expected.

"Jenna?" Ivy's voice cut through my thoughts. "You okay?"

"Yeah," I said automatically. "Just surprised."

"I'm so sorry," Ivy said to Aiden, squeezing his hand. "You can do it. You'll be okay."

"It's fine," Aiden sighed, though his shoulders slumped.

"At least you don't have to give a speech or anything," Aria said.

"Just wave and smile," Ivy added.

"I can do that," Aiden said. "Probably."

Drew looked visibly relieved. "Dude, sorry, but thank God that's not me."

"Right?" Dayne grinned. "Guess the new kid mystique wore off."

"You're not that new anymore," Maddie pointed out.

"New enough to dodge this bullet, apparently." Dayne grinned at the nominees. "You have my thoughts and prayers."

"Very helpful," Aria said.

"I could also offer memes for moral support?"

"Now we're talking," Tyler said.

Maddie was staring at the three of us girls. "Wait, so you all—"

"Apparently," Aria said.

Tyler was still standing, hands raised like he'd just won a championship. "This is DESTINY. I'm going to need to plan my wave pattern—"

"Tyler," Emilia said through her teeth. "Sit down."

"Can't. Too busy basking in the glory of—"

Emilia grabbed his sleeve and yanked. He sat, but immediately turned to her with the biggest puppy-dog eyes I'd ever seen.

"Em," he said, voice going soft. "Please. Be happy. Like this much happy." He held his fingers an inch apart. "I get to do this with you. That's the best part."

Emilia's expression flickered—annoyance giving way to something softer before she rolled her eyes. "You're impossible."

"But you love me anyway."

"I'm not sure right now."

"Yes, you are one hundred percent sure," Tyler said, grinning. Then quieter, just for her: "Come on. It'll be fun. I promise."

She sighed. "It's objectively a waste of time."

"But you'll look amazing in that dress you haven't bought yet, and I'll be right there with you, and we'll make your mom and mine happy, and then we can go eat fries and forget it ever happened."

"Fine," Emilia said. "But I'm not waving more than once."

"I'll take it." Tyler beamed like she'd just agreed to marry him.

"Somehow this is all your fault," Emilia added.

Nate, who'd been silent this whole time, was staring at his lunch tray like it contained a complex math problem. I could see him calculating something—probably the statistical probability of this being a mistake.

Tyler leaned over. "Nate. Buddy. You're going to be fine. We'll coordinate. I'm thinking synchronized waves—"

"No," Nate said flatly.

"You haven't even heard my full vision—"

"Still no."

"Calculating the statistical probability this is a mistake," Nate muttered.

"It's not a mistake," Tyler said. "The people have spoken!"

"The people," Nate said, "are wrong."

Our eyes met across the table. His expression was a mix of confusion and mild horror.

A laugh bubbled up before I could stop it. Of all the people who'd hate this attention, Nate Berglund was probably at the top of the list.

I watched them bicker, watched Ivy comfort Aiden, watched Aria calmly return to her sandwich like this was just another Tuesday. Around us, the cafeteria buzzed—people whispering, staring, probably already posting about it.

And somewhere in the middle of that noise, I realized something:

I was nominated. And I didn't need it.

Six months ago, this would've felt like proof I was doing everything right. Now it just felt like acknowledgment. Nice, but not necessary. Not the thing that made me matter.

But here's what did: my friends were nominated too. The people I actually cared about would be standing on that field with me—Emilia, who hated the spotlight; Nate, who'd rather solve equations than wave at crowds; Tyler, who was genuinely thrilled just to share it with the person he loved.

That meant something. Not because of the recognition, but because I wouldn't be performing alone anymore.

I'd be standing there with people who actually knew me.

And even if I didn't care about this for myself anymore, I could still make it good for them.

I pulled out my phone and opened a new note.

"Okay," I said, loud enough to cut through the chaos. "Logistics."

Everyone turned to look at me.

"Friday night game—we all go together. I'll coordinate snacks. They'll pull us down to the field around halftime for introductions. Wave, smile, done."

"Then Saturday is the dance. That's when they announce the results and do the crowning thing." I kept typing. "We should all go together to that too. Do something after?"

"Obviously," Tyler said, eyes lighting up. "I have plans."

"No choreography," Emilia warned.

"I was going to say dinner reservations, but sure—ruin my creative vision."

"Your creative vision always ends with someone getting embarrassed," Aria said.

"Only sometimes," Tyler protested. "And it's usually me."

Nate was watching me with that look again—the one that saw through the organizational mode to whatever was underneath.

"You don't have to organize everything," he said quietly.

"I know," I said. "But left to his own devices, Tyler will try to choreograph an entrance, and we'll all suffer."

"I was thinking about a coordinated arrival sequence—" Tyler began.

"NO," everyone said at once.

Tyler put his hands up. "Fine. Fine! We'll just walk in like normal people. But I'm doing it with enthusiasm."

"Of course you are," Emilia said giving him an indulgent look.

Maddie watched me with a thoughtful expression. "You're really good at this, you know. The organizing thing."

Something about the way she said it warmed me. It wasn't you're perfect, not you always know what to do. Just recognition. That I was good at something I'd always done, but now for the right reasons. Not performing. Just helping.

The bell rang. Everyone started gathering their things, still talking about Friday, still processing. I stood, grabbed my tray, and felt Nate fall into step beside me as we headed toward the trash cans.

"You okay?" he asked, voice low enough that only I could hear.

"Yeah, I am," I said. And surprisingly, it was true. "It's weird. A couple months agot I'd have felt more...validated? Maybe?"

"What do you feel?"

"Like it doesn't matter as much as I thought it would. Like it's just... a thing that's happening. Not the thing that defines me."

He nodded slowly. "That's probably healthy."

"Probably." I dumped my tray. "You're going to hate every second of it, aren't you?"

"Absolutely."

"But you'll do it anyway."

"Unfortunately."

I smiled. "Tyler really will try to choreograph something."

"Grab me when you make a run for it."

"Already calculating optimal escape routes and I've got you slotted into my plans."

We stood there for a moment in the cafeteria chaos, people flowing around us toward their next classes.

"Hey," Nate said, quieter. "For what it's worth... I'm glad I get to do this with you."

Something warm settled in my chest. Not the validation I used to crave from being nominated. Just... this. Standing next to someone who saw the real me and didn't need me to be anything else.

"Yeah," I said. "Me too."

"See you after school?"

"Yeah."

30

The Normalcy of a Nomination

Nate

I got home after practice and both Mom and Dad were already seated at the dinner table. Not strange, but the way they were sitting—straight-backed, smiling, waiting—set off a quiet alarm in my mind.

"Hey," I said, dropping my backpack by the door.

"Hey, honey." Mom gestured to my chair. "Come sit. Dinner's ready."

Dad was already serving himself from the casserole dish. "How was school?"

"Fine." I slid into my seat and reached for the serving spoon.

"Just fine?" Mom's smile widened. "We heard some interesting news today."

I paused mid-scoop. "What news?"

"Homecoming court," Dad said, like he was announcing I'd won a scholarship. "Junior prince nominee. That's a big deal, Nate."

Oh.

"Lindy Pedersen mentioned it when I ran into her at the bank," Mom continued. "Said Aiden's on the ballot too. She was so excited."

"It's not a big deal," I said. "They nominate a bunch of people. Most of them don't win."

"Still," Dad said. "It means people like you. Respect you."

I focused on my plate, cutting chicken into precise squares.

"And Tyler's on there too, right?" Mom asked. "You three—that's half the basketball team."

"Tyler, Aiden, and me," I confirmed. "And three girls from our friend group."

Mom's expression brightened. "Emilia?"

"And Jenna Lundquist. And Aria Cooper."

There was a pause. A specific kind of pause I'd learned to recognize over the years.

"Jenna," Mom repeated, smiling. "Oh, I haven't seen her mom in ages. We used to do everything together—cookouts, camping trips, mini-golf tournaments that got way too competitive."

Dad laughed. "Her dad and I still talk about the year we lost the grill lid to the wind at Lake Sakakawea. Good family."

Mom's smile turned soft. "You and Jenna were inseparable on those trips. Always collecting rocks or inventing games by the campfire."

"Yeah," I said.

Mom's eyes warmed. "And now you're spending time together again?"

I hesitated. "Yeah."

Her eyebrows lifted. "And now you're—?"

I sighed. "Yes, Mom."

Dad smiled. "So... together?"

"Apparently," I said, stabbing at my chicken.

Mom beamed. "That's wonderful, Nate. We're so happy for you."

"See?" Dad added. "Basketball. Friends. A girlfriend. Homecoming court." He looked at Mom, then back at me. "You're thriving, honey. You really are."

I set down my fork.

"Finally doing all the normal high school things," Dad continued, not noticing my expression. "It's good to see."

Something in my chest tightened.

"Normal," I said quietly.

"Well, yes." Mom nodded, missing my tone. "You know—friends, activities, dating. The whole experience."

I pushed food around my plate. "So you think I'm normal now?"

The words came out more flat than I'd intended. Both parents went still.

"What do you mean?" Mom asked carefully.

"Homecoming court. Basketball. Girlfriend. Friends." I looked between them. "Is this what normal looks like? Because that's what you wanted, right? For me to be normal?"

They exchanged a glance. Not the united front look. Something else. Uncomfortable realization.

Dad set down his fork. "Is that what you think we wanted?"

"Isn't it?"

Mom's smile had faded completely. "Nate—"

"You've also been worried about me, about what I was like. What I did. Like if only I was more normal, then you could take a breath. Relax."

I took a breath. "So I tried. Did the things you wanted. And now I'm... what? Normal enough?"

The silence stretched.

Finally, Mom set down her fork. Her expression had shifted—no longer surprised, but sad. Understanding.

"The social skills classes," she said quietly. "You hated those, didn't you?"

I didn't answer.

"We knew," Dad said. "We could tell."

I looked up, startled.

"You never complained," Mom continued. "Not once. You went every week, came home, said they were fine. But we saw your face when we mentioned them. The way you'd go quiet."

"We should've stopped them," Dad said. "But we didn't know what else to do."

Mom leaned forward slightly. "Nate, do you remember second grade? When we got the call from Mrs. Henderson?"

I remembered. Sort of. The details were fuzzy.

"You'd been eating lunch alone for weeks," Mom said.
"Every day. In the same spot by the windows. And when she
asked if you wanted to sit with the other kids, you said no. You
said they were too loud and you liked being alone."

"Which was probably true," Dad added. "But Mrs.
Henderson was worried. And so were we."

"Why?"

Mom's voice was gentle. "Because you were seven. And
seven-year-olds aren't supposed to want to be alone all the time.
Then you'd go quiet, not even talking about the things that
fascinated you."

"So you figured something was wrong with me."

"No." Dad's voice was firm. "Wrong with how things were
going for you. You were brilliant and curious and you saw the
world in ways other kids didn't. But you were also... lonely.
And you were starting to hide the things that made you excited
because other kids didn't understand them."

Mom reached across the table but didn't quite touch my
hand. "The social skills classes weren't about making you
normal, Nate. They were about giving you tools to connect with
people. So you wouldn't have to hide."

"But you kept hiding anyway," Dad said. "You got very good at it."

"We made mistakes," Mom said. "We worried too much about whether you were fitting in, and not enough about whether you were happy. We should've asked better questions. Should've listened better."

"But we weren't trying to change you," Dad added. "We were just scared. Because you were so convinced that you had to keep people at a distance to protect yourself. And we didn't know how to tell you that wasn't true."

The tightness in my chest was back, but different now.

"Then third grade, you and Tyler became friends, then Aiden." Mom continued, "You found a place, other kids who let you be you."

"And you seemed lighter," Dad said. "Like you'd finally found people who made sense to you. Who you didn't have to perform for."

Mom's eyes were bright. "So when we heard about homecoming court, we were happy. Not because you were doing normal things, but because it meant you'd found your people and they're still there. That you weren't eating lunch alone by the windows anymore."

I looked down at my plate. At the chicken I'd cut into precise squares. At the table where I'd eaten dinner every night for seventeen years.

"I thought you wanted me to be different," I said quietly.

"We wanted you to be happy," Mom said. "And we're sorry we made you think those were the same thing."

Dad cleared his throat. "For what it's worth, we never wanted you to be normal. Normal kids don't teach themselves algebra in sixth grade. Normal kids don't make thirty-page binders about anything. Normal kids don't see patterns nobody else sees."

"You're not normal," Mom agreed. "You're extraordinary. We always knew that. We just wanted you to know it too."

Something in my chest cracked open.

"Okay," I managed.

"Okay?"

I nodded. "Yeah. Okay."

Mom reached across the table and squeezed my hand. For real this time.

"Finish your dinner," she said gently. "And tell us more about this homecoming thing. Are you nervous?"

"Terrified," I admitted.

"Good," Dad said. "That means it matters."

"And Jenna will be there with you," Mom added. "Right?"

"Yeah."

"Then you'll be fine." Her smile was warm. Real. "You've always been fine when you had the right people beside you."

After dinner, I went upstairs and dropped onto the floor, leaning against my bed frame.

The conversation kept replaying. Not because it was bad, but because of what I'd learned.

They wanted my happiness, not my normalcy.

And they'd given me something I hadn't known I needed—context. A reason behind the worry that wasn't about changing me at all.

I pulled out my phone. Found her name. Hit call.

She picked up on the second ring.

"Hey," she said.

"Do you think I'm normal?"

A pause. Then: "No. I think you're better."

She paused again. "But I'm a girl who was hiding behind her cheerleader smile and saying I'm fine to get through life, so... I really hope you're not normal."

I smiled despite myself. "My parents said something similar. Kind of."

"Smart parents."

"Sometimes." I leaned back against my bed. "They told me about things I'd forgotten. From when I was younger."

"Like what?"

"Like how I used to eat lunch alone in second grade because the other kids were too loud. Or how I threw away a project I loved because nobody else cared about it."

She was quiet for a moment. "That sounds really lonely."

"It was," I said. "I'd just gotten good at pretending it wasn't."

"Tyler snared you in his conspiracy in third grade and the rest of us wandered in. And you kept us."

I thought about Tyler stealing my fries at lunch. About making terrible baking show commentary with Jenna. About the coverage schedule and the folder she'd made and the way Miggy called me his best tall person.

"Now I have people who don't make me pretend," I said.

"Yeah," she said softly. "You do."

"So do you."

"I know." I could hear her smile. "Took me a while to figure that out. But I know."

We were quiet for a moment. Comfortable silence.

"I though cheerleading was my normal , was what my parents expected of me," she said . "Turns out they just wanted me to be okay and to truly figure out what I want."

"Are you? Okay?"

"Getting there," she said. "Better every day."

"Good."

"What about you?" she asked. "Are you happy?"

I thought about it. About the friends I had now. About being captain. About her.

"Yeah," I said. "Actually, I am."

"Good." Her voice went softer. "Then your parents got what they wanted. And so did mine."

31

The Listener

Jenna

The clink of mugs and the low hum of conversation filled
Brew & Bean, but at our little table by the window, everything
felt hushed.

I sat up straight, hands wrapped around a mug I hadn't
touched yet. Nate sat beside me, close enough that our
shoulders almost touched.

Across from us, Mrs. Wexler sipped something that smelled
faintly of cinnamon. She didn't say much—not yet—but her
eyes were kind. Alert. Present.

"Thanks for meeting us," Nate said quietly.

I nodded. "My sisters said you'd listen."

"I will," Mrs. Wexler said. "I promise I'm not here to play devil's advocate or protect a program. Just tell me what you need me to know."

I took a breath. My hands tightened around the mug.

"I don't really know where to start," I admitted.

"Start wherever feels right," she said gently. "I'm not in a hurry."

So I did.

I told her about the pyramid formation—how they'd changed it without enough practice time, how unstable it felt. About being at the top and feeling the bases shift beneath me. About the fall. About my ankle.

I told her about coming back to school after my injury—how Casey and Taylor cornered me between classes, how the harassment got worse instead of better, how I couldn't even walk to my locker without checking over my shoulder.

I told her about the parking lot. About them following me, blocking my path, telling me I shifted early. That the fall was my fault. That if I told anyone a different story, they'd make sure everyone knew the "truth."

Nate stayed quiet beside me, but I could feel his presence—steady, supportive, letting me tell my story.

When I finished, Mrs. Wexler leaned forward slightly. "Can I ask a few questions?"

I nodded.

"Who was there when you got injured? Who was spotting?"

"Casey and Taylor were my bases. There were two other girls—backspots. And the rest of the squad was there, I think. Maybe fifteen people total?"

"And Coach Marquez?"

I hesitated. "She wasn't there. She'd left Casey in charge—went to meet with Ms. Larkin or something. She does that a lot."

Mrs. Wexler made a small note on a napkin. "And after the injury—what kind of follow-up did she do?"

"She—" I stopped. "She wasn't there when I fell. She came back before practice ended, and I was still on the mat. She asked if I was good from across the gym. Didn't even come over. Just told me to stretch and hydrate, then left for a staff meeting. She walked out while I was still sitting there."

Mrs. Wexler's pen paused. "She left while you were injured?"

"I couldn't even stand up. The boys' basketball team came in for their practice and found me sitting there. One of them had to call my mom because I couldn't walk to my car."

"And when you came back to school after that?"

"She never asked what happened. Never reviewed the formation. Just said to take it easy when she saw me in the boot."

Mrs. Wexler looked at Nate. "You're on the basketball team, right? I remember your name from the program."

"Yes, ma'am."

"Have you observed cheer practices? Seen how things are run?"

Nate shifted slightly. "Yeah. The gym schedules overlap sometimes—we're warming up while they're finishing. Coach Marquez is barely there. She shows up at the start, then disappears. Usually to her office. The captains run everything."

"How often would you say she's actually supervising?"

"Maybe fifteen minutes out of a ninety-minute practice," Nate said. "If that."

Mrs. Wexler's expression didn't change, but something in her eyes sharpened. She looked back at me.

"You said Casey and Taylor tried to convince you it was your fault. That you shifted early."

"They've been saying that since it happened. But I didn't. I know I didn't." My voice cracked. "And then someone sent me—"

I pulled out my phone. My hands were shaking.

"Someone on the squad sent this to me. Anonymous AirDrop. I don't know who."

I opened the video and slid the phone across the table.

Mrs. Wexler watched it once. Then watched it again.

Fifteen seconds. Casey and Taylor in the locker room. Audio scratchy but clear enough.

"She's lucky it was just her ankle."

"She'd better keep her mouth shut about it. Not make a big deal."

"It was just a stupid accident. Probably her mistake anyway."

Laughter.

Mrs. Wexler set the phone down carefully. "Can you send this to me?"

"Yeah." I AirDropped it to her immediately. "Is that—is that enough?"

"It's evidence of harassment," she said. "Clear evidence. Combined with what you've told me about the coaching situation, the lack of supervision, the unsafe practices—" She paused. "Jenna, this is serious. The school has a responsibility to provide safe athletic environments and to address harassment. They didn't do either."

Something in my chest loosened.

"What happens now?" I asked.

"Now I take this to the administration. They'll need to investigate. Interview people. Review the coaching practices and supervision protocols." She looked at me directly. "I can't promise it'll be fast, and I can't tell you what the outcome will be. But I can promise they'll take this seriously."

I nodded. Didn't trust my voice.

"Jenna," she said, and I looked up. "Thank you for bringing this to me. I know it wasn't easy."

"It wasn't," I admitted. "But someone had to."

"You're right. Someone did." She stood, tucking her phone into her pocket. "I'll be in touch soon. And if you need anything in the meantime—if Casey and Taylor approach you again, if anything happens—you call me immediately. Okay?"

"Okay."

"And Nate?" She looked at him. "Thank you for being here. For supporting her through this."

"Of course," Nate said quietly.

When we stepped outside, the air was crisp and cold. I let out a breath I hadn't realized I was holding.

"She believed me," I said.

"She did," Nate said.

For the first time in weeks, I felt like I could actually breathe all the way in. The cold air filled my lungs, sharp and clean.

We stood there by his truck for a moment, not quite ready to leave yet.

"You okay?" he asked quietly.

"I think so." I looked up at him. "I don't know what happens next. But at least someone's listening now."

"Yeah." He opened the passenger door for me. "Come on. Let's get you home."

A little bit broken. A little bit braver.

And somehow, okay.

32

Pieces of Nate

Nate

Coach cancelled practice.

The text came through during last period: *No practice today. Film review rescheduled. See you tomorrow.*

I stared at my phone for a second, recalculating my afternoon. Then I texted her.

> **ME: Practice cancelled. Want to just sit in my truck for a bit? Talk?**

Three dots appeared. Disappeared. Reappeared.

> **JENNA: Yeah. Meet you there after last bell?**

> **ME: Sounds good.**

The parking lot was nearly empty by the time she made it out—most people gone within minutes of the final bell. I'd parked toward the back, away from the stragglers.

She opened the passenger door and climbed in, dropping her backpack at her feet.

"Hi," she said.

"Hi." I started the truck so the heater would run. October afternoons got cold fast. "Didn't feel like going home yet."

"Me either." She tucked her hands into the hoodie pockets—my hoodie pockets. "Your house or mine?"

"Thought maybe we could just sit here for a bit. If that's okay."

She studied me for a second. "Yeah. That's okay."

She slid over to tuck herself into my side. We sat in comfortable silence for a minute. The heater kicked on full blast, filling the cab with warm air. Outside, a few remaining cars pulled out of the lot.

"You okay?" she asked finally.

"Yeah."

"Nate."

I looked at her. She'd shifted slightly to see my face better, still close.

"You texted me specifically to talk," she said gently. "So talk."

I took a breath.

"I started dating Jenny sort of by accident. Well, not sort of. Really by accident. Our moms worked together and are friends. They thought we'd be cute together. Jenny's sweet, quiet, likes math and science. They kept putting us together. Here's $20, see if Jenny wants to go see that new Marvel movie, stuff like that."

Jenna stayed quiet, listening.

"And it was fine. Easy. We'd go to movies, study together, do the things you're supposed to do when you're dating. But the whole time, I felt like I was following a script someone else wrote."

"What do you mean?"

I looked out the windshield. "Like there was a checklist. Date every two weeks. Text good morning. Hold hands at school. And if I did all the things on the list correctly, I'd feel what I was supposed to feel."

"But you didn't."

"No." I paused. "And I kept thinking maybe I was broken. Like everyone else could just naturally know how to do this, but I needed instructions."

She shifted closer. "You're not broken."

"Jenny said that too. When we broke up." I smiled slightly. "She was really nice about it. Said we were better as friends. That she could tell I was trying too hard to be what I thought a boyfriend should be instead of just being myself with her."

"She sounds smart."

"She really is. Pretty sure she'll get a full-ride scholarship to an Ivy League school of her choice."

"Good for her." Jenna squeezed my hand. "But I'm guessing this isn't just about Jenny."

"No." I took a breath. "When I was younger—kindergarten, early elementary—my parents put me in social skills classes."

She didn't react with surprise or pity. Just waited.

"They were worried. I didn't make friends easily. Didn't understand jokes. Took everything literally. Got upset when routines changed. Liked the quiet. Liked alone time." I drummed my fingers once on the steering wheel. "The teacher would have us practice things. How to start conversations. How to tell if someone was joking. How to know when it was your turn to talk."

"Did it help?"

"Some. I learned the patterns. The scripts. But it always felt like I was translating from a language everyone else spoke natively." I paused. "There was this one time—I was five. My parents had me in soccer, trying to help me be more social, I guess."

"Okay..."

"I walked away from practice. It was so boring and the kids weren't listening to the coach. Then I saw a flock of geese flying south. I was fascinated by how they kept their V formation going."

"I love hearing the geese honking overhead when they're flying south."

"I followed them. Left the field, crossed a stream. Saw them land in a field, which was really cool. I decided to sit down and watch them. Meanwhile, no one knew where I was. I was fine sitting there, just watching and listening. But my parents were freaking out."

"I bet they were terrified."

"I understand that now. But back then?" I shook my head. "They decided to keep me busy after that. Put me in activity after activity. Keep me occupied with normal kid stuff, and then came the social skills classes and a therapist."

Jenna reached over to turn the heat down. "They were scared they might lose you for real. I kinda get that."

"Me too. But back then I thought they just wanted me to be like other people's kids. It seemed like they couldn't understand me the way I was, so there were times I just stopped trying to make myself understood. Not depression really, but I just didn't want to try so hard anymore. Those times scared them more, so the busyness continued."

I looked down at our joined hands.

"And what I started to think was that being myself wasn't good enough. That I needed to translate everything into something other people could understand, even if it meant erasing what I actually cared about."

She was quiet for a moment. "Do you still feel that way?"

"Sometimes." I looked out at the empty parking lot. "Like I'm different people in different places. At school I'm Math Nate. The quiet stats guy. At home I'm supposed to be Normal Nate—the kid who wants what they wanted. And here—"

"You're just you," she finished softly.

"Yeah. But I don't know which one is real anymore. Or if any of them are."

"What if they're all real?" She shifted to face me more fully. "What if those versions aren't separate people? What if they're just different parts of the same person responding to different contexts?"

"That's not how it feels."

"I know. It feels like you're performing different versions. Trust me, I get that." She squeezed my hand. "But here's the thing. When you're doing math or organizing schedules—that's really you. When you're trying to make your parents happy—that's really you too, even if it doesn't fit right. You're not fragmented. You're multifaceted."

"Multifaceted sounds better than broken."

"Because you're not broken." She said it like a fact. "You're just trying to fit into spaces that weren't designed for someone like you."

I sat with that for a moment..

"There's something else."

"Okay."

"Coach said, I was nominated for team captain this year. I have to let him know my answer soon."

She went still. "What?"

"The team voted."

"Nate." Her voice was full of something I couldn't quite name. "That's—that's huge."

"I don't think I should do it."

"Why not?"

"Because captains are the guys who rally the team. Who give speeches. Who lead by being visible and vocal." I looked down. "That's not me."

"Who says that's what a captain has to be?"

"Everyone. That's what captains do."

"Or that's what some captains do." She turned more fully toward me. "The team voted for you. Not Tyler. Not Drew. You. They picked the guy who shows up, does the work, and sees what needs fixing before anyone else does."

"That's not leadership."

"That's exactly leadership." She took both my hands now. "You notice what people need before they ask. You help half the team with homework. You organized an entire coverage schedule so I wouldn't be alone between classes. You make people feel like they matter." She paused. "That's not leadership?"

I didn't answer.

"You don't have to give speeches or pump people up," she continued. "You just have to be you. The version of you who notices what needs doing and does it. That's what they voted for."

"What if that's not enough?"

"What if it's exactly what they need?" She tilted her head. "You spent years learning social scripts and trying to translate yourself for other people. Maybe this is the first time someone's asking you not to. Maybe they want the actual you, not the performed version."

I turned that over, like a theorem I couldn't quite solve.

"I don't know how to be the same person everywhere," I admitted.

"Maybe you're not supposed to be." She said it gently. "Maybe you just need to stop apologizing for being different depending on where you are."

Outside, the sun was dropping lower, shadows lengthening across the parking lot.

"Thanks," I said quietly.

"For what?"

"For listening. For getting it. For not thinking I'm broken."

"You're not broken," she said again. "You're Nate. And that's more than enough."

She leaned her head against my shoulder, and we sat in comfortable quiet for a few minutes.

Then her phone buzzed.

She glanced at it, then went still.

"What?" I asked.

She stared at her screen. "AirDrop notification."

"Okay?"

"From an unknown sender." She looked up at me, something shifting in her expression. "The filename says T_and_C_locker_room.mov."

T and C.

Taylor and Casey.

"You don't have to open it," I said.

"What if someone's trying to help?" Her finger hovered over the screen. "What if someone finally saw enough?"

She pressed accept.

I watched her face as the video played. Watched the color drain. Watched her hand tighten around her phone.

When it ended, she just sat there.

"Jenna—"

"She's lucky it was just her ankle," she said quietly, repeating what she'd just heard. "She'd better keep her mouth shut about it. Not make a big deal. It was just a stupid accident, probably her mistake anyway." She paused, eyes filling. "And then they laughed."

She looked up at me. "It's like they just hate me for being me. Why?"

I took both her hands. "They don't hate you. They're protecting themselves. Coach Marquez leaves them in charge when she shouldn't—that's negligence. They messed up, and now they're trying to make sure no one looks too closely."

"Can I see it?" I asked gently.

She handed me the phone without a word.

Fifteen seconds. Shaky footage. Audio scratchy but clear enough. The words she'd repeated, then laughter. Then it cut off.

I handed the phone back carefully.

"Who sent it?" I asked.

"I don't know. Unknown sender."

"Someone on the squad," I said. "Someone who finally saw enough."

She nodded, quiet, still processing.

"I don't think Coach Marquez even cares about us all that much anymore," she said. "That's hard to take. She's supposed to care."

Around us, the parking lot continued—a few cars driving past, someone locking up a building, the wind picking up slightly. Normal. While Jenna's world had just shifted.

She looked down at her phone again. "I need to show someone. Mrs. Wexler, maybe. And my parents. And—" She stopped. "I don't even know where to start."

"Start with saving the video," I said. "Make sure you have it backed up. Then we figure out next steps. Mrs. Wexler will probably call soon, and we'll have what we need to give her. Okay?"

She nodded, already moving—air-dropping it to herself, saving it to cloud storage, making sure it couldn't disappear.

When she looked up again, something in her expression had changed. Not broken. Resolved.

We sat there for another few minutes, neither of us ready to leave yet.

Eventually we had to go. The sun was setting properly now, the parking lot nearly dark.

I drove her home, the truck cab warm and quiet. She kept her hand in mine the whole way, and we didn't need to fill the silence with anything else.

At her house, I jumped out and came around the front of my truck to help her out.

"Thank you," she said after I kissed her softly for a moment.

"For kissing you?"

Jenna gave me a playful shove.

"For telling me about you. For being here for me."

"Thanks for letting me go off script."

33

Baked Goods Dating

Nate

I'd spent days trying to figure out where to take Jenna on an actual date—something that wasn't hanging out at her house or talking in my truck. Not the usual Riverbend spots. Not a movie. Not the mall in Dickinson—definitely not the mall.

There were good restaurants but none of them felt right. I wanted us to breathe, be together without interruptions, in a place that felt like us.

So I landed on Easy Sweets, a bakery I found while scrolling through restaurant reviews. Good reviews, a straightforward menu. An us kind of place.

I picked her up and didn't say where we were going—just somewhere in Dickinson. We listened to a The Things Bakers Know podcast while we drove.

"A bakery?"

"Is this okay?"

"It's perfect. It's kind of us—and kind of adorable of you to think of it."

I wasn't sure how to respond to adorable again, so I just got out and opened her door.

We ended up in a corner booth with cinnamon rolls the size of dinner plates and tea that actually tasted like tea instead of hot brown water. Jenna insisted we split one because there's no way I can eat this whole thing—reasonable, since the roll could've fed a small family.

She pulled off a piece and popped it into her mouth. "Oh. Oh wow."

"Good?"

"Really good." She pushed the plate toward me. "Try it."

I did. She was right.

"Wow, that is really good."

"It's nice to just eat something delicious and not think about technique or structure."

"Technique and structure are why the bakes turn out well. The challah turned out well because we followed proper technique."

"The challah turned out well because we stopped overthinking and just braided it." She took another bite. "Also because you're secretly good at baking and won't admit it."

"I'm adequate at following instructions."

"You sifted flour for twenty minutes and gave a lecture about misleading bag labels."

"That was factual information."

"That was you caring about hypothetical bakers." She smiled. "Which again was adorable."

I pushed away the warm feeling that followed every time she said that.

"What do you think about trying cinnamon rolls or caramel rolls sometime—when we're not baked out?"

I pulled out my phone and opened Pinterest to show her the pastry-recipe board I'd made. She laughed when she realized what it was.

The bakery hummed around us—quiet conversations, the hiss of the espresso machine, soft music I couldn't name.

Jenna wrapped her hands around her mug and gave me a look that was half-smile, half-knowing.

"So," she said. "Homecoming Junior Court. You and me both nominated."

I groaned.

She took a sip of her tea. "Emilia's disgusted. Tyler's already campaigning."

She laughed—soft and real. "And I bet a homecoming court nomination is something that's never crossed your mind."

"It's not funny."

"It's a little funny." She leaned forward slightly. "You realize you could win, right? You're a varsity athlete. You're nice to everyone. The female half of the school thinks you're mysterious and cute. You're quiet, but that helps your mystique. And then there's the blue eyes—better blue eyes than Paul Hollywood."

I took a drink of coffee to avoid responding.

She tilted her head, eyes bright with mischief. "So... did you want to plan your homecoming court campaign? I could help. Make posters. Write a speech. A joint campaign?"

"Absolutely not."

"'Vote Nate: He's Already Done the Math'?"

"Jenna."

"'Berglund for Junior Court: Silently Judging Your Poor Life Choices Since Kindergarten.'"

Despite myself, I almost smiled. "You're enjoying this."

"I really am." She took another sip of tea, then her expression shifted—mock-suspicious. "Wait. Is that why you wanted to date me? Strategic homecoming court positioning?"

I blinked. "What?"

"Think about it. You start dating the former cheerleader who got injured and quit. Suddenly you're nominated for junior court." She gestured dramatically. "Not very Prince Charming. More like a charming anti-hero using the princess for social advancement."

"That's not—"

"I'm onto your scheme." She was trying not to laugh. "What's next? Do you have a math proof for picking my dress to make your eyes look bluer? Make you stand out in the photos?"

I paused. "You're messing with me, but I could use math to steal the nomination if I cared about it at all."

"True." She grinned. "But seriously, the fairy tale-ish-ness of it all is kind of ridiculous. Basketball guy. Former cheerleader. Homecoming court. We're like a cheesy movie."

"I refuse the label cheesy."

She settled back in her seat. "I need to warn you—if you were strategically dating me for social advancement, you picked the wrong girl. I quit the squad, remember? I'm probably hurting your chances."

"You're not hurting anything."

She looked at me for a beat, something softer in her expression. "Okay."

We sat in comfortable silence for a moment, the bakery warm around us.

"So," I said. Then stopped.

She looked up. "So?"

I cleared my throat. "Homecoming. The dance."

"Yeah?"

"Do you... I mean, would you..." I stopped. This was terrible. "Are you planning to go?"

"Probably? Everyone goes." She tilted her head. "Why?"

"Because." Deep breath. "Would you want to go with me? Officially. Like—" Why was I still talking? "As a date. Together."

The silence lasted approximately three seconds but felt like an hour.

Then she smiled—soft and real, not performed. "Nate Berglund. Are you asking me to homecoming?"

"Yes." My face was definitely red. "Badly. But yes."

"That was pretty bad," she agreed. "But sweet. And cheesy." She was still smiling. "But yes. I'll go with you."

"Yeah?"

"Yeah." She reached across the table and took my hand. "Although now I'm reconsidering the whole 'strategic dating for homecoming court' theory."

"I wasn't even hoping for a nomination," more firmly this time. "And you know it."

"I know." Her eyes were warm. "That's what makes it sweet."

I took a long drink of coffee to give myself something to do that wasn't staring at her like an idiot.

34

The Case for Nate Berglund

Jenna

I couldn't stop thinking about what he'd said about being team captain. Not the part where he didn't feel captain-y. I got that.

But the part that stuck—the part that made my stomach twist—was how he talked about what captains were supposed to be. Loud. Visible. The kind of leader who rallied people with speeches.

And he was so sure that wasn't him.

He didn't say it to get attention. He believed it.

And I realized something.

If I told him he mattered, he'd smile and change the subject.

If I told him he led people quietly, he'd find a way to argue it with logic.

If I told him I believed in him, he'd thank me and still feel alone.

So I wasn't going to make a speech.

I was going to build a case.

Maddie was the first person I asked.

We were in the library during study hall, and I kept it casual. "Remember last spring when you had the flu?"

She looked up from her laptop. "Yeah. Why?"

"What happened with your library shift?"

"Oh." Her expression softened. "Nate showed up. I didn't even ask. He just... knew I couldn't make it."

She told me he'd updated the inventory tracker and left her a note about the new labeling system so she wouldn't be lost when she came back.

"Try Aria," she said. "She's got one too."

Aria told me how Nate proofread her astronomy presentation and actually listened when she talked about space.

"It's not that he got it," she said. "It's that he didn't fake it. He asked real questions. Made me feel like what I was saying mattered."

Tyler was next: the reluctant sentimentalist.

"Nate helped me pass Pre-Calc. Brought flashcards. Made me use them. Didn't make it weird when I kept getting the same problems wrong."

He paused, then added, "He could've made me feel stupid. He didn't."

I was building a list. Names. Quotes. Patterns.

Emma from the stat crew told me how Nate taught her Excel formatting during her first week and made her feel like she belonged in the gym.

"He treated me like I knew what I was doing," she said. "Even when I didn't."

She told me to talk to Marcus.

Marcus Lee, who plays pickup ball after school and uses a wheelchair, told me about the jammed gym door that made it nearly impossible for him to get in independently.

"I never even mentioned it to him," Marcus said. "He just noticed. And the next day it was fixed."

He looked at me, then added, "Sometimes being seen is the whole thing."

I kept going.

Talia, a freshman who'd cried over a history paper, ended up with Nate's annotated notes from the year before. "He didn't treat me like a little kid," she said. "He just helped."

Back at our lunch table, I was sorting through it all when Emilia looked up and said, "You should talk to Miggy."

"Why?"

"Because Miggy talks about Nate like he's a superhero. And Sofía lights up when he's around. They're small, but they're not wrong."

So I did.

Miggy had turned the living room into a craft explosion.

Markers, stickers, and construction paper were scattered like confetti. His tongue was sticking out the side of his mouth while he drew what might've been a dinosaur in a basketball jersey.

Sofía was in her high chair with a crushed graham cracker, humming to herself and smearing applesauce in expert swirls.

I sat cross-legged on the floor. "Hey Miggy," I said casually, "can I ask you something?"

He didn't look up. "You want to know my top three monster trucks or my bottom three?"

"Neither, surprisingly."

"Then it must be about Nate."

I blinked. "Why would you say that?"

"Because he's your boyfriend. And your face got soft."

"My face got—?"

Miggy waved his marker like a wand. "Girls get soft face when they think about their boyfriend."

I opened my mouth. Closed it. "Okay, fair."

He pointed at his drawing. "This is Nate as a basketball robot."

"Cool. Can I write down some things you remember about him?"

Miggy nodded, thoughtful now. "Nate always helps me find my stuff. One time my shoe was under the couch for a thousand years and he found it. And he says 'Good job' even I'm just being me, like he already knows I'll do it good later. And when Sofía cried because she didn't want her banana cut, he held her and said, 'You're allowed to feel your feelings.'"

I stared at him. "He said that?"

Miggy nodded, like duh. "He's very wise."

Sofía perked up at the sound of Nate's name. "Nay-nay?" she said, twisting in her seat.

"Yeah," I said gently. "Nate."

She kicked her legs and clapped her sticky hands. "Nay-nay my up! Up!"

Miggy translated with great authority. "She means Nate is the best shoulder ride. She calls it up."

I wrote that down too. Carefully. Like it was sacred.

Miggy leaned over and whispered, "You should tell him he's my best tall person. That's different than a best friend. It means extra."

I smiled and pulled him into a hug. "Thanks, Miggs."

He hugged back tight, then added, "When you give this to him, are you gonna cry?"

"I don't cry."

"You probably will. But it's okay. You're allowed to feel your feelings."

Later, I transcribed Miggy's contribution into my notes, but I kept his original crayon masterpiece with all its all-caps truths:

NATE KNOWS THINGS. HE HELPED ME FIND MY SHOE.

HE CARRIED SOFÍA WHEN SHE WAS MAD.

HE SAYS 'GOOD JOB' EVEN WHEN I AM JUST BEING.

Sofía just babbled "Nay! Up!" and slapped her spoon like it was a vote.

The next day, I tracked down the guys on the team.

Drew told me how Nate talked him down after a bad pass at Regionals.

"He didn't yell. Didn't even flinch. Just told me what I did right and moved on."

Tyler said Nate ran drills with a new player after practice. Quiet. No spotlight.

"Nobody noticed until the kid got better," Tyler said. "That's when I realized Nate had been working with him the whole time."

Aiden told me Nate managed spacing and adjustments without anyone noticing—"until you realize everything stayed together because of him."

"He makes people play smarter," Drew said. "That's captain stuff. Has been since last year."

That night, I sat at my desk with everything spread out in front of me—printouts, quotes, scribbled notes, even Miggy's green crayon thunderstorm of appreciation.

I tried to make it neat. Make it logical. Make it Nate-friendly.

I titled the folder: Observational Data: The Case for Nate Berglund

Inside:

Section 1: Peer Reports

Section 2: On-Court Analysis

Section 3: Community Impact

Section 4: The Younger Observers

And then, at the very back, I clipped in a handwritten note:

Nate,

I didn't write this because I think you need a pep talk.

I wrote it because you deserve to see what everyone else sees.

You think being quiet means being invisible.

But I think it's what makes you extraordinary.

This isn't a list of compliments.

It's proof.

I've never trusted someone the way I trust you. Not because you say the right thing, but because you notice.

You noticed me when I was falling apart.

You still do.

And I noticed you, too.

—J

I closed the folder and held it for a second before tucking it in my bag.

He might brush it off. He might pretend it didn't matter.

But I knew better.

And now—so would he.

35

Captain

Nate

I found Coach in his office after practice, going through plays on his tablet.

He looked up when I knocked. "Berglund. Come in."

I stepped inside. The office smelled like coffee and old leather, the same as always. Coach's desk was organized chaos—clipboard stacks, a water bottle collection that should've been recycled weeks ago, game schedules pinned to a corkboard.

"Got an answer for me?" he asked.

"Yeah." I stayed standing. "I want to accept."

Coach set down his tablet. Leaned back in his chair. "You sure?"

"I'm sure."

He studied me for a moment, doing his own calculation—checking if I meant it, if I was ready.

"What changed? When I first asked, you looked like I'd asked you to calculate pi to the last digit."

"I thought about it."

"And?"

I thought about Jenna's folder. About Miggy's crayon declaration. About Tyler's vote, and Drew's, and all the others who apparently saw something I couldn't see in myself.

"And someone showed me that I was already doing parts of the job—leading without the title," I said.

Coach nodded slowly. He stood, walked around the desk, leaned against it. Less formal now. More like he was talking to a player, not interviewing one.

"You know what this means, right? It's not just wearing the C on your jersey. It's setting the tone. Making sure everyone's locked in. Being the one the team looks at when things get hard."

"I know."

"You'll need to talk more. Not constantly—that's not your style and it shouldn't be. But when you talk, they need to hear you."

I nodded.

"And you'll need to handle conflicts. Mediate when Tyler and Drew get into it about defensive rotations. Keep morale up during a losing streak. Be present."

"I can do that."

Coach crossed his arms. "I know you can. That's why I brought it up in the first place." He paused. "Your leadership doesn't look like everyone else's. That's not a problem. That's an asset."

Something in my chest loosened.

"We'll announce it Monday after break," Coach said. "Give you Thanksgiving to process. First game as captain is November 30th. Home game against Dickinson."

"Okay."

"Any questions?"

I thought about it. "What if I mess up?"

"You will," Coach said simply. "Everyone does. The question is what you do after."

Fair.

He held out his hand. I shook it.

"Congratulations, Captain."

The word settled over me. Not heavy. Just... real.

"Thanks, Coach."

"Get out of here. Enjoy your break."

Ten minutes later, I was halfway to my truck when I pulled out my phone.

Me: Can I come over?

Three dots appeared immediately.

Jenna: Yes. Always yes.

Jenna: Everything okay?

Me: Yeah. I have news.

Jenna: Good news or captain news?

Me: Same thing.

Jenna: GET OVER HERE

Twenty minutes later, I was standing on her porch.

She opened the door before I could knock. Still in her school clothes, hair pulled back, smiling like she already knew but wanted to hear it anyway.

"Well?" she said.

"I told Coach yes."

The smile went full voltage. "Nate!"

She pulled me inside, closed the door, then just stood there looking at me like I'd done something remarkable.

"I'm really proud of you," she said.

We moved to the living room. She sat on the couch. I sat beside her, closer than I would've a few months ago. Close enough that our shoulders touched.

"How do you feel?" she asked.

I considered it. "Like I finally answered a question I've been avoiding."

"Good answer or bad answer?"

"Good." I paused. "Scary, but good."

"Scary how?"

"What if I'm not what they think I am?"

She tilted her head. "What do you think you are?"

"Someone who notices patterns. Who shows up. Who cares about the details."

"That's exactly what they need," she said. "You don't have to be Tyler. You don't have to be loud or flashy. You just have to be you."

The folder had said the same thing. In testimonials and crayon and careful documentation. But hearing it from her made it land differently.

"Coach announces Monday," I said. "After break."

"So you get Thanksgiving to sit with it."

"Yeah."

She leaned against my shoulder.

"You're going to be a really good captain," she said quietly.

"I hope so."

"You will be." She squeezed my hand. "I don't need a file of evidence to know that about you."

I thought about the folder in my backpack. About all the things I hadn't seen until she showed me.

"Thank you," I said. "For that. For all of it."

"Pick me up Saturday at ten. We'll celebrate somewhere."

"Saturday at ten."

She was still looking at me. Something shifted in her expression—softer, more certain.

She reached up slowly, her hand gentle against my jaw. Her thumb traced along my cheekbone.

"I'm really proud of you," she said again. Quieter this time.

Then she leaned in and kissed me.

Soft at first. Gentle. But then her other hand came up to my shoulder, anchoring herself, and the kiss deepened. Not rushed. Certain. Present. My hand found her waist. The fabric of her shirt was warm under my palm. She shifted closer, and I could feel her smile against my mouth before she pulled back just enough to look at me.

"Congratulations, Captain Berglund," she whispered.

My heart was doing something irregular. Statistically improbable but undeniably real.

"Thank you," I managed.

"For the kiss or the folder?"

"Both."

She laughed softly, her forehead resting against mine for a moment before she settled back into the couch, still close. Her hand found mine, fingers lacing together. We sat like that for a while. Not talking. Just breathing. The living room quiet around us, the last of the daylight fading through the windows.

"You okay?" she asked eventually.

"Yeah." I looked at our joined hands. "More than okay."

"Good."

I stayed another twenty minutes after that. We didn't talk about much—school, Thanksgiving plans, normal things. Easy things. But my hand stayed in hers the whole time. And that felt normal too.

When I finally stood to leave, she walked me to the door.

"Text me when you get home?" she said.

"It's a ten-minute drive."

"Still."

"Okay."

She kissed me again at the door. Briefer this time, but just as certain. When I left, the night air was cold and clear. Stars overhead. Everything the same as it had been this morning. Except I was captain now. And somehow, that felt exactly right.

I sat in my truck for a moment before starting the engine. I felt proud. Proud in a way different from understanding discrete calculus or solving a problem no one else in class could figure out. This was something else. About being chosen.

36

Bake Sale Dating

Jenna

I found the bake sale online Thursday night. Trinity Lutheran, forty minutes west. Lefse, rosettes, krumkake, sandbakkels—all the Norwegian standards.

Saturday morning, I directed him west out of town.

"You're really not going to tell me," he said.

"Nope."

The fields rolled by—brown and flat, hay bales scattered like punctuation. I found a playlist on his phone and watched the horizon.

Thirty minutes in, he tried again. "Food-related?"

"Maybe."

"Baking-related?"

"You'll see."

Trinity Lutheran was a small white church with a gravel parking lot. A hand-painted sign read: ANNUAL BAKE SALE — ALL WELCOME.

Nate looked at me.

"Norwegian grandmas," I said. "Family recipes. I thought you'd like it."

"I do like it."

"I know."

Inside, the basement smelled like butter and cardamom and coffee. Folding tables lined the walls, loaded with baked goods. Four women—all somewhere between sixty and eighty—watched us come down the stairs.

"Well, hello there," said the one nearest the door. White hair, name tag that said AGNES. "We don't get many young people."

"We drove from Riverbend," I said.

"Riverbend! That's quite a drive for cookies."

"We heard you have the best."

She laughed and waved us toward the tables.

We moved along, and I asked questions. Every cookie had a history. Every recipe had been passed down.

Mildred—shorter, glasses—explained rosette technique. I nodded like I was memorizing it.

"You bake?" she asked.

"We do," I said. "Together."

She looked at Nate, then back at me. "You two dating?"

Nate's ears went red.

"Yes," I said.

"Good." She said it like that settled something. "You should bake together. Best way to test compatibility. Survive laminated dough, you can survive anything."

"We haven't tried laminated dough yet."

"You will." She patted my arm. "And when you do, call Agnes."

Agnes appeared with a plate of samples. "On the house. You drove all this way."

The krumkake was thin and crisp. The rosettes were delicate. The lefse was soft with cinnamon sugar.

"These are incredible," I said.

"My grandmother made krumkake," Nate said. "I haven't had it since she passed."

The women exchanged a look.

"Then you should come back," Agnes said gently. "Phyllis can teach you."

We bought a box of everything. They wouldn't let us pay full price.

Agnes wrote her number on a napkin. "Call me before Christmas. We'll make proper krumkake together."

"We will," I said.

"You're Mr. Olson's student," Mildred said to Nate suddenly. "Physics, yes?"

He blinked. "Yes. How did you—"

"He's my nephew. Says you're one of the bright ones." She paused. "Tell him his aunt says hello. And that he needs to call his mother more often."

I bit my lip to keep from laughing.

Back in the truck, the box sat between us.

"So," I said. "We got adopted."

"Apparently."

"Four Norwegian grandmas. That's efficient."

He almost smiled. "Good celebration?"

"The best." I reached over and squeezed his hand. "Better than a movie."

"Much better."

The drive back was quiet—not empty, just settled. Halfway home, I realized I was still smiling.

37

Already Beautiful Girls

Jenna

The Preston minivan smelled like coffee and the faint sweetness of whatever air freshener hung from the rearview mirror. I sat in the back seat between Aria and Ivy while Emilia rode shotgun with her mom. Mrs. Preston had one hand on the wheel, the other gesturing as she talked.

"Ivy, how's your mamá doing? Haven't seen her in a few weeks."

"Good! She said to tell you she'll call about Thanksgiving planning."

The highway stretched out ahead. I smiled remembering driving the same route with Nate for our first real date.

"So," Mariella said, eyes flicking to the rearview mirror to catch all of us, "homecoming court. When Robbie and I were juniors, we were on it together."

Emilia groaned. "Mamá, please—"

"Very romantic," Mariella continued, ignoring her daughter's protest. "He couldn't get his tie to look right. I had to fix it for him right before we walked out."

"That's adorable," Ivy said.

"That's embarrassing," Emilia added.

Kirkwood Mall on a Saturday morning was busy but not overwhelming. Mariella gave us space as we headed toward the clothing stores, but I could see her following at a comfortable distance, ready if we needed her.

"Okay," Emilia said, stopping outside Maurices. "Let's make this efficient."

"Em, you can't efficiency your way through dress shopping," Ivy said.

"Watch me."

And fifteen minutes later, Emilia stood in front of a three-way mirror in a burgundy dress that somehow managed to be both elegant and practical, and even she couldn't hide the small smile tugging at her lips.

"It has pockets," she announced, demonstrating.

"It's perfect on you," I said.

Aria nodded. "That's the one."

"Ay, mija," Mariella said from nearby, "that's perfect on you."

"Yeah, it's not bad," Emilia said, but she smoothed the fabric, checking her reflection from another angle.

"It's beautiful and you know it. Humor your mamá."

Something passed between them—a quiet understanding. Then Mariella added, "And Tyler will lose his mind when he sees you in it."

"Mamá—"

"I'm just saying what's true, mija."

Ivy caught my eye and grinned. Even Emilia couldn't fight the smile anymore.

I tried on six dresses before I found it.

The walking boot made everything complicated. Too short looked awkward. Too long felt like I was hiding. I needed something that flowed past the boot without calling attention to it, something sparkly enough to feel special but not like I was performing.

The seventh dress was soft blue-gray, hitting just below the knee with delicate beading along the neckline. I stepped out of the dressing room, wobbling slightly on the boot.

"That's it," Ivy said immediately.

"It doesn't look like I'm trying too hard, right?" I asked, checking the mirror.

"It looks like you," Ivy said. "The real you."

That was exactly what I needed to hear.

Aria emerged next, holding two dresses on hangers. "Okay, I need help. Navy or this one?" She held up a deep emerald green that caught the light.

"Try them both on," Ivy said. "We can't tell from the hangers."

Aria disappeared into the dressing room. She came out first in the navy—classic, safe, perfectly fine.

"It's nice," I said.

"Very nice," Ivy agreed.

"But?" Aria prompted, reading our faces.

"Try the other one," Emilia said, leaning against the wall near the dressing rooms.

Aria went back in. When she emerged in the emerald dress, the difference was immediate. The color made her eyes brighter, and something about the cut made her look confident in a way the navy hadn't.

"Oh," Ivy said. "That one."

"The navy is nice," I said. "But this one is stunning on you."

Emilia straightened. "You don't only stand out on the basketball court, you know."

Aria paused, studying her reflection. A moment of recognition crossed her face—she could be this version of herself too.

"Okay," she said. "Yeah. This one."

"Told you," Emilia said, satisfied.

Ivy had tried on three dresses already, standing in front of the mirror in a soft rose color that made her look older, more sophisticated.

"I know I'm not walking," she said quietly, "but I still want to feel—"

"Special," I finished. "You should."

"Aiden's going to forget how to form sentences," Aria observed.

Ivy bit her lip, trying not to smile. "You think?"

"We know," I said.

She turned back to the mirror, and this time when she looked at her reflection, she didn't second-guess.

We stood together in front of the three-way mirror—all four of us in our dresses. The fluorescent lighting wasn't flattering, and we were all still in our regular shoes, but somehow it didn't matter.

We looked good.

Not in the cheerleader perfect smile way I had gotten used to. Just... genuinely pretty. Happy. Real.

Ivy reached for my hand. Aria bumped Emilia's shoulder. And for a moment, we just stood there, four girls about to have a memory worth keeping.

The food court was packed with Saturday shoppers, but we claimed a table near the windows. Mariella insisted on treating us to lunch.

"It's not every day my daughter gets nominated for homecoming court. Let me enjoy this."

I picked at my french fries, still processing the morning. The shopping bags sat at our feet—evidence that this was really happening. Something I would have wanted fiercely when I was mostly the cheerleader version of myself.

"You know," Mariella said, a smile playing at her lips, "homecoming court night was when Robbie first told me he loved me."

Emilia put her face in her hands. "Mamá, no—"

"He said he was going to marry me one day." Mariella's eyes were warm with the memory. "Right there on the football field under the bright lights, in front of everyone."

"What did you say?" Ivy asked, leaning forward.

"I told him I was going to college, so I didn't want to be rushed." Mariella took a sip of her drink. "And that he had to be able to handle spicier food first."

Aria choked on her water. "You what?"

"He couldn't handle jalapeños," Mariella said matter-of-factly. "How was he going to marry into my family if he couldn't eat my mamá's cooking?"

Emilia was shaking her head, but she was smiling. "Did he?"

"Spent the next six months building up his tolerance. By senior year, he could handle serrano peppers." She looked at her daughter fondly. "Sometimes the good ones prove themselves."

The table went quiet for a moment, all of us processing that—the sweetness of it, the realness.

"I called Luz last night," Mariella added, her tone shifting to something softer. "Told her about Tyler being on the court. She was so proud. So happy for him."

Something passed across Emilia's face—understanding, maybe sadness.

"She wishes she could be here to see it," Mariella continued. "But I promised I'd video everything on my phone and send it to her. Every moment." She smiled.

"I guarantee Tyler will have his own blooper reel or music video to send her," Emilia said fondly.

That got a small laugh from around the table. It sounded exactly like something Tyler would do.

"Luz said she's going to watch everything a hundred times," Mariella added softly.

Then she looked around at all of us, her expression shifting to something between amused and firm. "Now, I know what I said about Robbie proposing that night. But for you girls? No talking about marriage. You're seventeen. Enjoy homecoming. Enjoy being young."

"I'm serious," Mariella continued. "If any of those boys start talking about forever, you tell them to learn to handle jalapeños first. And if they're really serious, maybe a serrano. Or a ghost pepper."

Aria snorted into her drink. Ivy was grinning.

"Aria?" Mariella asked. "Who's your date?"

"Not really a date," Aria said. "Just going with Marcus from basketball. We're friends."

"Friends is a good place to start," Mariella said.

She glanced at me, and I knew what was coming. But instead of asking, she just smiled. "And Jenna is going with Nate. That boy has a good heart. Very patient with the little ones."

"He has a beautiful heart," I said, then immediately wished I could take it back when Emilia smirked at me from across the table.

"That's a good thing be sure about," Mariella added, her eyes twinkling.

"Are we getting ready together on Saturday?" Ivy asked.

"My house," Emilia said. "Mamá already offered. She wants to help with hair and makeup."

"And take a million photos," Ivy added.

"For Luz," Mariella said simply. "She'll want to see everything."

"What time?" Aria asked.

"Four?" Emilia looked at her mom for confirmation.

Mariella nodded. "That gives us plenty of time."

The drive back was quieter.

The garment bags hung carefully in the back, and everyone was tired but satisfied. Emilia had her head tilted against the window, watching the farmland pass. Ivy scrolled through photos on her phone—probably already planning outfit details. Aria dozed in the seat next to me.

The afternoon sun slanted across the fields, turning everything golden. In a few days, we'd be standing under stadium lights in these dresses, walking across that field while the whole town watched.

The thought should have terrified me. The old me would have been planning every step, every smile, every moment of the performance.

But now? I just felt... ready.

Mariella caught my eye in the rearview mirror.

"You girls are going to be beautiful for the dance," she said softly. "But you already are. Remember that part too."

I didn't know if I should say something back, but that was okay. I just let the moment be what it was.

Real. Warm. Enough.

38

What Justice Looks Like

Jenna

Mrs. Wexler called on a Wednesday.

"Jenna, I've spoken with the administration. They'd like to meet with you and your parents. Tomorrow morning, before first period."

My stomach dropped. "What kind of meeting?"

"The kind where they listen," she said. "And where things start to change."

The assistant principal's office smelled like coffee and old carpet.

Mr. Hendricks sat behind his desk, hands folded. Mrs. Wexler sat to the side, present but quiet. Mom and Dad flanked me, close enough that I could feel their solidarity even without looking.

"Thank you for coming in," Mr. Hendricks said. "We've completed our initial investigation based on the documentation you provided through Mrs. Wexler."

Initial investigation. Like there might be more.

He cleared his throat. "I want you to know we take these allegations very seriously. Bullying and unsafe athletic environments are not tolerated at Riverbend High."

My dad leaned forward slightly. "What does that mean? Specifically?"

"We've taken appropriate action," Mr. Hendricks said. The phrase sounded rehearsed. "However, due to student privacy laws, I can't share details about disciplinary measures involving other students."

"So we're just supposed to trust that something happened?" Mom's voice was calm but pointed.

"I understand your frustration," he said. "But yes. I can tell you that the students involved will not be in contact with Jenna. And that we're reviewing our athletic department's response protocols."

"What about Coach Marquez?" Dad asked.

A pause. "Coach Marquez is on administrative leave pending further review."

The words hung there. Administrative leave. Not fired. Not reassigned. Just... on leave.

"And cheer?" I asked quietly.

"The program is on hiatus while we conduct a more comprehensive review of team culture and safety protocols. We'll be bringing in a new coach when it resumes."

When. Not if. When.

"Jenna," Mr. Hendricks said, looking directly at me now. "I want to acknowledge your courage in bringing this forward. And I want to assure you that we're committed to making sure you feel safe here."

I nodded. Didn't trust my voice.

"We do need to ask," he continued, "that you refrain from discussing the specifics of this situation with other students. For everyone's privacy and to allow the process to proceed appropriately."

"You're asking her to keep quiet?" Mom's tone sharpened.

"We're asking for discretion," he clarified. "Not silence. Jenna can talk to her friends, to you, to Mrs. Wexler. We're just requesting she not share details about disciplinary actions or name specific students involved."

Translation: Don't post on social media. Don't gossip. Let us control the narrative.

Dad looked at me. "Jenna? How do you feel about that?"

I thought about it. About Taylor and Casey. About whether I even wanted to talk about them anymore.

"I can do that," I said finally. "As long as I can tell people I'm okay."

"Of course," Mr. Hendricks said. "We want you to be okay."

The meeting ended with handshakes and a printed copy of the school's anti-bullying policy that I was pretty sure hadn't been followed at all.

As we left the office, Mom squeezed my shoulder. "You okay?"

"I don't know," I said honestly. "They believed me. But I still don't know what actually happened. To them. To Coach."

"Sometimes justice looks like this," Dad said. "Messy. Incomplete. But still justice."

I wanted to believe him.

They walked me to my locker. Mom hugged me, Dad squeezed my shoulder, and then they left for work

Nate

I think I noticed the absence before most people did. Coach Marquez's office had been dark. Her name was still on the door, but lights were off and the blinds were closed.

Word was spreading that a substitute had taken over girls' PE. By lunch, rumors were circulating that cheer practice was cancelled.

No explanation. No announcement. Just... gone.

I was already at our usual table when Jenna arrived, moving slower than normal. Not from the book, but from something heavier. She slid into the seat beside me instead of across. Close enough that our shoulders touched.

"Hey," she said quietly.

I reached for her hand under the table. "Hey."

Tyler arrived next, took one look at us, and immediately pivoted to the other side. "I'm sitting over here. You two look like you need space."

"We don't need space," Jenna said.

"Yeah, but I need space from whatever emotional processing is about to happen." He grinned. "I'll provide commentary from a safe distance."

Emilia showed up with Ivy and Aria. They took their usual spots, but the energy was different. Quieter. Watchful.

"Meeting went okay?" Emilia asked carefully.

Jenna nodded. "They believed me. Took action. Won't tell me what action." She squeezed my hand. "Coach is on leave. Cheer's on hiatus. Casey and Taylor haven't been here all week."

"Suspended?" Aria asked.

"Maybe. Or they transferred. Or their parents pulled them out. I don't know."

I could feel the tension in her hand. "You did everything right," I said quietly. "The fact that you don't get to see what happened next—that's on them, not you."

She leaned slightly against my shoulder. Just for a moment.

Tyler cleared his throat. "So we're just not gonna talk about how they're gone and you're still here and that's actually a good thing?"

"I'm trying to," Jenna said. "It's just weird."

"Weird is allowed," Ivy said gently.

Jenna

Friday, the hallways felt different.

Not louder or quieter. Just... emptier in specific places.

The bathroom where Casey used to hold court between classes—empty.

The corner by the gym where Taylor would lean with her friends—empty.

Nate walked with me between fourth and fifth period, his hand warm in mine. We didn't talk much. Didn't need to.

I was at my locker when they approached.

Megan and Sophie. Two JV girls who'd always been quiet around me. The ones who'd watched everything but never said anything.

They stopped a few feet away, glancing at each other like they were deciding who should speak first.

"Jenna?" Megan's voice was soft. Nervous.

I turned. "Hey."

"We just wanted to say..." Sophie looked down, then back up. "Thank you."

I blinked. "For what?"

"For speaking up." Megan stepped closer. "We were relieved when we heard. That it's finally done. At least for now."

"You were brave," Sophie added quickly. "And someone else was going to get hurt. So please don't feel guilty about any of it."

The words hit me harder than I expected. I'd been carrying so much weight—wondering if I'd overreacted, if I'd ruined everything, if I should've just handled it differently.

"I don't—" I stopped. "I didn't know if I did the right thing."

"You did," Megan said firmly. "Jessie—one of the sophomores—left because of them. You got hurt because of them. And we were next."

Sophie nodded. "They were already starting. Little comments. 'Fixing' our formations. We just didn't know what to do about it."

"So you did it for us too," Megan said. "And we wanted you to know that."

My throat went tight. I managed to nod.

They both gave small, awkward smiles and walked away before I could figure out what else to say.

Nate appeared beside me, having given us space. "You okay?"

I nodded, blinking hard. "They said I was brave."

"You are."

"They said someone else would've gotten hurt."

"They're right."

I closed my locker, leaning against it for a second. "I keep thinking I messed everything up. Ended the program. Hurt people's seasons."

"You didn't end anything," Nate said quietly. "You stopped something that was already broken."

I looked at him. Really looked at him.

"They thanked me," I said.

"Because you protected them." His hand found mine again. "That's what you do. Even when it costs you."

At lunch, the cheer table had scattered. Some girls sat with other groups. Some ate quickly and left. Megan and Sophie sat together at the far end, and when they caught my eye, they both smiled.

Real smiles. Not performance. Not fear.

Just... relief.

I picked at my sandwich without much interest.

Nate noticed. He always noticed. "You okay?"

"It's weird," I said. "They're just... gone. No explanation. No closure."

"Do you want closure?" Aria asked. "Or do you want them gone?"

I thought about it. "Both. Neither. I don't know."

"Well," Tyler said, "at least you don't have to look over your shoulder anymore."

He was right. I realized I hadn't checked behind me once today. Hadn't tensed when someone walked too close. Hadn't braced for a hallway bump or a whispered insult.

They were gone.

And I was still here.

Nate's thumb traced small circles on the back of my hand under the table. A quiet reminder that I wasn't just here—I was here with people who saw me.

Nate

I watched her laugh at something Maddie said, her whole face lighting up in a way I hadn't seen in weeks.

No shadows under her eyes. No constant vigilance. No performance.

Just Jenna. Lighter. Freer.

Tyler leaned over. "You're doing that thing again."

"What thing?"

"The thing where you look at her like she just proved a theorem you've been working on for years."

I didn't respond, but Jenna caught my eye and smiled. Real. Unfiltered. Hers.

"I'm just saying," Tyler continued, "you can relax now. She's okay. The bad guys are gone. Crisis averted."

"Temporarily gone," I corrected. "We don't know if it's permanent."

"Dude." Tyler turned to face me fully. "Let yourself be relieved. Just for like, five minutes. She's okay. You helped make that happen. That's allowed to feel good."

Maybe he was right.

Jenna reached for my hand again, lacing our fingers together on top of the table this time. Public. Intentional.

Maybe I could let myself feel relieved.

Jenna

The Week After

By Monday, everyone knew something had happened, even if no one knew exactly what.

Coach Marquez's office stayed dark. The cheer schedule board in the gym hallway had been taken down. Practice slots were reassigned to other activities.

No formal announcement. No assembly. Just the quiet reshuffling of a program on pause.

In the hallways, people stared. Some gave me sympathetic looks. Others avoided eye contact entirely. A few whispered when I passed.

I didn't care as much as I thought I would.

The coverage schedule was still technically in place, but it felt different now. Less like protection and more like friends just walking together. Between classes, Nate was there. Hand in mine, steady presence, asking nothing except "You good?"

Usually, I was.

By midweek, the tension I'd been carrying for weeks had finally eased. I wasn't tensing when footsteps came up behind me. Wasn't bracing for a comment or a bump or something worse.

The hallways felt like they belonged to me again.

Ivy mentioned homecoming at lunch. "The game's Friday. Dance is Saturday. We're all still going, right?"

"Obviously," Tyler said. "I have a vision."

"No, visions Tyler," Emilia told him, "You can show controlled enthusiasm like we've talked about."

"A modest vision. A humble vision."

"Still no."

I looked at Nate. "Are we still doing this?"

His hand tightened around mine. "With great reluctance, but yes. We're doing this."

39

Homecoming Game

Jenna

The parking lot was already half full when we arrived, cars lined up in neat rows under the stadium lights. I could see my breath in the cold air, and the marching band's warm-up drifted from the field—their uniforms flashing purple and gray.

Nate pulled into a spot near the back. I grabbed my beanie from my lap and tugged it on. Late October in North Dakota meant layers, usually, it also could be shorts and T-shirts. I wore Nate's school hoodie over my shirt with my heavy coat layered on top, mittens shoved in my pockets until I needed them. The hoodie was dark purple with gray lettering across the chest: RIVERBEND MUSTANGS.

"You're wearing that," he said. Not a question.

"It's warm." I met his eyes. "And it's yours."

Something flickered across his face—pleased, shy.

We met the rest of the group near the ticket booth. Tyler was impossible to miss—letterman jacket, face painted in purple and silver stripes, wearing a purple foam finger.

Ivy and Aiden arrived, looking cold but content. Aria showed up in a white Riverbend hoodie and practical puffer coat, y shaking her head at Tyler's foam finger.

Maddie, Drew, and Dayne joined us, bundled in various shades of purple and gray. We moved toward the bleachers, tickets in hand, the smell of popcorn and hot chocolate drifting from the concession stand.

The stands were packed—a sea of purple and gray, people in Mustangs gear, faces painted, foam fingers waving. We claimed a section near the fifty-yard line, high enough to see but not so high that getting down for halftime would be a climb.

I settled onto the cold metal, the boot sticking out awkwardly, and Nate sat beside me, close enough that our shoulders touched. His jacket was warm against my side.

"LADIES AND GENTLEMEN—"

Tyler stood, waving his foam finger. Emilia yanked his arm, laughing. "You're worse than Miggy, sit."

The game started, and I relaxed into the rhythm of it—the band's fight songs, the student section leading chants from the bleachers, the comfortable chaos of our group. Without the cheer squad, the student section had gotten louder, filling the space themselves, and the pep band played more frequently between plays. It felt scrappier, less polished, but the energy was still there.

Nate bought hot chocolate and handed me one without asking.

"Thanks."

"You were about to ask."

"Was I?"

"Your hands were getting cold. You do this thing where you tuck them into your sleeves."

I looked down. My hands were, in fact, tucked into my sleeves.

By the end of the first quarter, I'd forgotten about the boot, about halftime, about everything except being here.

Halfway through the second quarter, the loudspeaker crackled:

"At halftime, we'll be introducing our Junior Homecoming Court nominees. Princes Tyler Alred, Nate Berglund, and Aiden Pedersen. Princesses Jenna Lundquist, Aria Cooper, and Emilia Preston."

The section around us erupted—pom-poms waving, people cheering. Tyler stood, arms raised.

"THAT'S US."

"We're aware," Emilia said.

Maddie leaned over. "Nominees, how are we feeling?"

"Terrified," Aiden muttered.

"Vindicated," Tyler said.

"Resigned," Aria added.

I caught Nate's eye. He looked like he was solving a particularly difficult equation.

"Stop planning your escape," I said.

"Too late. I've mapped three routes."

"You're coming with me," I squeezed his hand. "We're doing this."

He didn't let go.

Halftime came fast.

We made our way down the bleachers. The field was damp and cold. The stadium lights made everything too bright and exposed. The crowd was a blur of purple and gray, phones out.

A teacher waved us toward the sideline. The band finished their show, purple plumes bobbing as they marched off.

"When they call your names, walk to the center. Wave, smile, walk off. That's it."

Tyler vibrated with energy. Emilia was trying to turn invisible. Aiden kept his hands buried in his pockets. Aria stood calm. Nate was still—the kind of still that meant he was uncomfortable but committed.

"Junior Court nominees," the announcer boomed.

"Tyler Alred."

Tyler sprinted onto the field, arms up, wearing his foam finger, working the crowd.

"Nate Berglund."

He walked like he was headed to the free-throw line. Steady. Focused.

"Aiden Pedersen."

Aiden gave a small wave and looked relieved it was almost over.

"Jenna Lundquist."

I took a breath and walked out. The boot made my gait uneven, but I kept going. Waved once and kept walking.

The cheers felt distant.

"Aria Cooper."

Graceful, calm, like this was routine.

"Emilia Preston."

Emilia walked out like she was facing a firing squad, waved once—exactly once—looked like she would bolt.

Tyler hooked his arm through hers and tugged her to his side. She looked glad to have an anchor.

We stood there together, six of us under the lights. We walked off together—Tyler still waving, Nate looking like he'd survived something—and I realized standing there hadn't felt like validation. It felt like a footnote, then it was over.

The real moment was walking back with Nate's hand finding mine, Tyler's arm around Emilia, our friends waiting with hot chocolate and commentary.

That mattered.

The rest of the game blurred—our team won, Tyler was unbearable about it—and by the time we reached the parking lot, the cold had seeped through every layer.

"My place," Ivy said. "Fire pit's going. There's cider."

"Sold," Tyler said.

We caravaned to Ivy's house. Her backyard opened to fields, and the fire pit was already crackling, flames bright against the October dark.

Ivy's mom brought thermoses of cider and bags of marshmallows, then disappeared inside.

We settled into mismatched chairs with old blankets. The fire threw orange light across everyone's faces—Tyler still streaked in glitter paint, Emilia wearing his beanie, Nate's collar turned up against the cold.

"So," Tyler said, skewering three marshmallows at once, "I'm winning tomorrow."

"You campaigned with glitter," Emilia said. "There's still some in your hair."

"Commitment to the brand."

Aiden rotated his marshmallow with surgical precision. "At least the field part's done."

"The worst part," Nate said.

"The best part," Tyler countered. "Aria, you looked great out there."

"I walked twenty feet and waved."

"With style."

"Thanks, Tyler."

I watched my marshmallow catch fire, then blew it out—burned outside, melted middle.

"That's on purpose?" Nate asked.

"Yep. British Bake-Off method."

"Oh, really? Paul Hollywood likes his marshmallows burnt?"

"Paul Hollywood probably makes his own marshmallows and uses a special flame for toasting."

Tyler's marshmallows were actively flaming until Emilia grabbed his wrist.

"Tyler, you're going to set yourself on fire. And no, being on fire won't improve your chances of winning."

The fire crackled. Someone's phone buzzed. The air smelled like woodsmoke and sugar.

"This is nice," Maddie said. "Better than the field part."

"Way better," Dayne agreed.

Drew nodded. "This is the part we'll remember."

He was right. Sitting there in Ivy's backyard, faces lit by firelight, marshmallow sticky on my fingers, Nate's shoulder warm against mine—this was what mattered.

Not the spotlights, the announcements.

This.

We stayed until the fire burned low and the cold drove us to our vehicles. Nate drove me home, heat blasting. He helped me maneuver out from the front seat and walked me to the door.

His expression was tender, a smile in his eyes. "Pick you up at the Preston's tomorrow?"

"Yep. Glad it's over?"

"Half over. You made it so much better, Jenna. Everything's better with you."

I smiled at him and rose up to meet his lips.

40

I Told You I Had Charisma

Jenna

Getting ready at the Preston farmhouse was organized chaos.

The kitchen table had been transformed into a
salon station—curling irons plugged in, makeup scattered
everywhere. Mrs. Preston's phone was propped up so Tyler's
mom, Luz, could join on FaceTime.

Sofía and Miggy were being corralled by Mr. Preston, but
made occasional escapes into the beauty madness—only to be
recaptured and hauled off laughing by their daddy. His gaze
softened every time he looked around. When he saw Emilia, the
love was unmistakable.

Five of us had taken over the living room—me, Emilia, Ivy,
Aria, and Maddie. Dresses hung carefully on hangers, makeup

scattered across every surface, the air thick with hairspray and nervous energy.

"Mija, tilt your head," Mrs. Preston said, pinning another section of Emilia's hair.

On the phone screen, Luz was grinning. "Oh, Emilia, you look—she looks beautiful, Mariella. Mija, my son better have pretty words for you. Show me Ivy next."

Ivy waved. "Hola, Tía Luz."

"Ay, Ivy, Mija. Stunning. You'd better hear some pretty words from Aiden too."

I sat on the couch in my blue-gray dress, the boot still on, watching the controlled chaos with something warm in my chest. Maddie sat beside me in her dress—a deep plum color that made her look older, sophisticated—scrolling through her phone absently.

Miggy appeared in the doorway, clutching his stuffed dinosaur. "Are you princesses now?"

"Not yet," Aria said. "Just possible princesses."

"You look like princesses already." He climbed onto the couch beside me, studying my dress seriously. "Jenna, is Nate going to be a prince?"

"Maybe, Miggy—but then Tyler or Aiden might be too."

"Hmmm." He frowned thoughtfully. "Nate should win. He's most like a prince. He could rule a country 'cause he knows enough things."

I chuckled. "I'll let him know you said that."

Mrs. Preston finished Emilia's hair—elegant and simple, pulled back so her face was fully visible. Emilia turned her head as Mrs. Preston held up the mirror.

"It's perfect, Mamá."

"So beautiful,Mija," Mrs. Preston said, then kissed the top of her head. "Luz, you see?"

"She's beautiful. Enséñame a todas las guapas cuando termines."

(Show me all the pretty girls when you're done.)

Ivy was next, her rose-colored dress catching the last of the afternoon light. Mrs. Preston pinned her hair into something soft and romantic that made her look older, but still fresh and sweet.

Aria went after Ivy, her dark hair swept up in an elegant twist that showed off the emerald dress perfectly.

By the time Mrs. Preston got to me, I was full of feelings—not about the dance, or the possibility of a crown. Feelings about this, right here. Friends who cared and moments that felt real.

"Jenna, Mija, sit." Mrs. Preston gestured to the chair.

I sat, careful with the boot.

She worked quietly, her hands gentle and efficient. On the phone, Tyler's mom made approving sounds.

"Ay Jenna, so beautiful. Mariella. Look at those eyes."

"Lovely," Mariella agreed. She stepped back, tilting her head. "Natural. You don't need much, Jenna—just enough to highlight."

When she finished, I looked in the mirror and saw a different girl. I looked like me, but more real, even with the hair and makeup. I was more myself.

"Thank you," I said quietly.

Luz's voice came through the phone again, teasing: "¿Y con quién va nuestra guapa Jenna esta noche?"

Mariella laughed. "Con Nate Berglund. You remember him?"

"¡Claro que sí! El niño calladito. Qué bonito. Esta noche hablará más... o se quedará sin palabras."

(Of course—the quiet boy. How sweet. Tonight he'll either talk more... or be left speechless.)

I smiled, even if I only caught half of it. "Was that about Nate?"

Mariella grinned. "She says he'll either talk more because you look so pretty, or he'll be too stunned to speak."

"Oh," I replied not finding any reply to that compliment.

"Maddie, you're up, Mija," Mrs. Preston said, gesturing to the chair.

Maddie's phone buzzed just as she stood. She glanced at the screen and her expression shifted—worry flickering across her face.

"Everything okay?" I asked.

She read the message, then looked up at us. "It's Drew. His dad's MS flared up—bad. His mom had to take him to the hospital. Drew's home with his sisters."

The room went quiet for a beat.

"Oh no," Ivy said softly.

"Is he okay?" Aria asked. "Drew's dad, I mean."

"Drew didn't say much. Just that he can't make it tonight." Maddie's voice was steady but I could see the concern in her eyes. "He said to have fun."

Emilia moved closer. "Do you still want to go? We'd understand if—"

"No, I'm going." Maddie managed a small smile. "Drew would want us to. And Dayne's still picking me up. It's just... I wish there was something I could do."

Mrs. Preston touched Maddie's shoulder gently. "Sometimes being a good friend means going and having a good time when they can't. You can check on him tomorrow, yes?"

Maddie nodded. "Yeah. You're right."

"Now sit," Mrs. Preston said kindly. "Let's make you beautiful."

Maddie sat, and Mrs. Preston worked her magic—pinning Maddie's hair into a soft, elegant style that framed her face perfectly.

When she finished, Maddie looked in the mirror and smiled—smaller than before, but genuine. "Thank you, Mrs. Preston."

"De nada, Mija. You look lovely."

The boys arrived at seven, one after another, like a pick-up-your-date parade. Tyler's rumbling truck was heard before we saw it.

Emilia smiled. "Here comes the Beast." She glanced out the window with affection. "Question is, will the boy be louder?"

"I'd bet on the boy being quiet after he gets a look at you," Ivy teased.

"Shush, you," Emilia said, her cheeks turning rosier—but she was smiling too.

A knock came at the door, followed by Miggy's shout: "Let me open it!"

He pulled it open and announced, "You don't look like Farm Guy tonight."

"¡Miguelito!" Mrs. Preston said, half-scolding, half-laughing. "Tyler looks very handsome dressed up tonight." She moved Miggy aside and opened the door wider. "Come in, Tyler."

Tyler stepped in, bringing a gust of cold October air with him. He looked both proud and nervous.

"Hola, Mariella," he said, voice suddenly polite.

"Hi, Miggy." He crouched for a quick fist bump. "Farm Guy's taking the night off."

"Hi, Em." His eyes found her and seemed to do a mental head-clear. "Wow, uh, you whoa, um..."

Mrs. Preston turned the phone toward him so Luz could see.

Luz's laugh came through the speaker. "Ay, Tyler—¡por el amor de Dios! You tell her she looks pretty, ¿sí? Usually you can't stop talking, and now you forget all your words?"

Tyler groaned. "Hola, Mamá." Then he straightened, smiling at Emilia. "Sí, sí—she's more than pretty. She looks amazing."

"That's better, Mijo," Luz said warmly. "Enjoy tonight. And see, Emilia, I told you—speechless. Enjoy it, that won't last."

Tyler took Emilia's hand and gently led her toward the door. "Told you she loves you more than me now." Then he leaned down and murmured something that made Emilia soften completely.

They both said goodbye to Tyler's mom, and Emilia looked back at us with a grin. "See you there."

Marcus arrived next to pick up Aria. He stopped in the doorway when he saw her, clearly stunned. "Wow. You look—wow."

Aria smiled. "Thanks, Marcus. You clean up pretty well yourself."

They headed out together, comfortable and easy.

Dayne showed up a few minutes later, alone. He spotted Maddie and gave her a small, smile, "You look beautiful Maddie-Monster. Going to have keep all the country boys away from my cousin tonight."

Maddie laughed, "Don't be a dork. Anyway, you cleaned up good too so I'll be making be protecting you from the girl vultures tonight."

"Bummed for Drew, though. He texted you too, right?" Dayne asked.

"Yes, he did. I let everyone know about his dad," Maddie said. "If we don't hear more tonight, I'll check in with him tomorrow."

Maddie looked over her shoulder at us. "See you in a few, beautiful ladies."

Finally, Mrs. Preston opened the door again to find Aiden and Nate standing side by side—both in dress shirts and ties, letterman jackets because it was late October in North Dakota and the weather would do whatever it felt like.

All Aiden could say to Ivy was, "Wow, you look...wow. Like, really wow."

She ducked her head, smiling. "Thanks. You look really wow yourself."

Meanwhile, Nate's gaze found me—and stayed there. I walked toward him and slipped my hand into his.

He leaned closer, voice low. "I thought I had a better vocabulary than Aiden, but 'like really wow' seems to fit best here."

His eyes traced the dress, softening. "It reminds me of your ninth-birthday dress—but grown up."

"I shouldn't be surprised you'd remember my dress from then," I said. "That's why I picked it, though. I thought the same thing."

He smiled—small, quiet—and I was struck by how many versions of that smile there were.

All subtle. All meaningful.

This one felt like I see you.

We all said goodbye to Mrs. Preston, who stood in the doorway like a proud mama hen.

"Get pictures there too," she said, wagging a finger. "And drive carefully."

She laughed, shaking her head, and waved as we stepped into the cold October evening, the porch light spilling gold across the gravel.

The school gym had been transformed to look like every homecoming dance everywhere—and still uniquely ours.

Purple and gray streamers hung everywhere, string lights draped in zigzags across the ceiling, and a DJ booth was set up near the stage.

The air smelled faintly of punch, perfume, and hair spray. Teachers in semi-formal wear casually ringed the gym, pretending not to watch.

We found Dayne and Maddie already there—they'd snagged a big table for the group.

Tyler was already on the dance floor, pulling Emilia with him despite her protests. Aiden and Ivy found a spot near the wall, heads bent together, talking quietly. Aria and Marcus were at the edge of the crowd, laughing about something, looking relaxed and easy.

Nate stayed close to me, steady in the chaos.

"You want to dance?" I asked.

He looked at the floor, then at my boot. "Can you?"

"Probably not well."

"Then we match."

We found a spot near the edge of the dance floor where I could sway without putting too much weight on the boot. It wasn't graceful. It wasn't Instagram-worthy. But Nate's hand was warm in mine, and it felt like its own kind of perfect.

The DJ transitioned from pop to something slower—the kind of song that made people hesitate before deciding to stay or sit down. Nate didn't move.

"You good?" I asked.

He nodded. "Yeah."

We stood there, just moving enough to count as dancing, the rhythm slow, easy, real.

"I think we're officially terrible dancers," I said.

He smiled slightly. "That's what the data's saying."

The announcement came about halfway through the dance. The DJ faded the music, and Principal Andersen's voice filled the gym—cheerful and way too loud.

"Alright, Riverbend High Mustangs! It's time to announce your Junior Homecoming Court winners!"

The crowd erupted. Tyler immediately straightened, crown-ready, posture and all. Emilia looked resigned and a bit green, but steady. Nate looked like he'd been expecting to be hazed, not possibly crowned.

Principal Andersen continued, milking the suspense. "Your Junior Prince is..."

You could practically feel Tyler's confidence from across the room.

"...Tyler Alred!"

Tyler's arms shot up like he'd just hit a game-winning shot. "LET'S GO!" The gym cheered—partly because it was Tyler, and partly because Tyler made cheering feel mandatory.

Emilia covered her face with one hand but she was laughing, watching him with affection. He bounded up to the stage and accepted his crown with enthusiasm.

Principal Andersen raised his hand for quiet. "And your Junior Princess is..."

A pause. A beat. Then—

"...Aria Cooper!"

Aria looked genuinely surprised, then smiled and headed up to the stage. She accepted her crown, waved once, and took her place beside Tyler, who said something that made her roll her eyes but smile anyway.

The gym cheered louder—warm, happy, sincere.

Nate leaned toward me. "Dodged that one."

"Completely."

I watched Tyler and Aria under the lights—his grin unstoppable, her composure steady—and felt nothing but happiness for them. And relief that it wasn't me.

That felt like growth.

The DJ started the next song as Principal Andersen left the stage. Tyler did a manly version of a royal wave he'd been practicing while Aria walked off the stage. He followed, grinning, heading straight for Emilia.

Emilia protested weakly when he pulled her onto his lap, but she smiled anyway and straightened his crown.

We all gathered around them—congratulating, laughing, taking photos. Tyler was in his element, crown slightly crooked, arm around Emilia who looked simultaneously embarrassed and happy.

"We should send these to Drew," Ivy said, scrolling through the pictures on her phone. "He's missing all of this."

"Good idea," Maddie said, pulling out her phone too.

We took a few more—silly group shots, Tyler making ridiculous faces, Aria holding her crown like a trophy. Someone snapped one of all of us squeezed together, everyone laughing.

"Okay, sending," Ivy said, typing quickly. "Hope your dad's doing okay. Wish you were here."

"Perfect," Aria said.

The rest of the night blurred into laughter, photos, and too much sugar.

By the time we made it back to the Preston farmhouse, the October cold had settled in for real. Our breath hung white in the air as we hurried inside.

Mrs. Preston had left the porch light on, and the kitchen was warm and bright—a table already covered with empanadas and other delicious food. Mugs waiting by the stove.

"Your mom is a saint," Maddie said, heading straight for the food.

We filled the kitchen. Tyler's crown sat crookedly on the counter. Aria still held hers, twisting it absently in her hands. Dayne had claimed a chair and was already eating. Miggy appeared at the top of the stairs, clutching his stuffed dinosaur. "Is it over?" he whispered loudly.

"Miggy, you're supposed to be asleep," Emilia said.

"I couldn't. There are princesses downstairs."

Aria waved up at him. "Hi, Miggy."

He came down a few steps, eyes wide when he spotted the crown in her hands. "Were you the princess?"

"I was," she said, smiling. She lifted it carefully and set it on his head.

He stood with perfect posture. "Now I'm a crowned prince."

Sofía padded down after him, rubbing her eyes. When she spotted Nate, her face lit up. "Nay-nay!"

He stood immediately and scooped her up. She tucked her head against his shoulder, content.

"Up," she mumbled, already half-asleep.

"I've got you," he said softly.

Tyler leaned over. "Hey, Fía, you want my crown?"

Her sleepy eyes widened, and she nodded.

He kissed her forehead. "It's all yours," he said, placing it gently on her head.

We lingered, talking and eating until the kitchen was mostly crumbs and empty mugs. Maddie's phone buzzed and she glanced at it.

"Drew," she said, reading. "His dad's stable. They're keeping him overnight but he's okay." She smiled. "He says thanks for the photos."

"That's good," Emilia said.

Relief settled over the table—quiet but real.

Gradually people began to drift out—Maddie and Dayne first, then Aria and Marcus. Ivy helped with cleanup before heading out with Aiden.

Eventually it was just Tyler and Emilia in the living room and Nate and me in the quiet kitchen.

He set Sofía down on the couch beside Tyler, where she stayed asleep leaning against Tyler, still wearing the crown.

Miggy was asleep on the stairs, crown tilted off one ear, a fleece blanket laid over him, dinosaur tucked under his arm.

"I should get you home," Nate said quietly.

"Yeah."

We said soft goodbyes—Emilia walking us to the door, Tyler waving from the couch without moving enough to wake Sofía.

"Thanks for tonight," I said. "Tell your mom thanks, Emilia."

The night air was sharp when we stepped outside, our breath clouding in the porch light. Gravel crunched under our feet as we walked to his truck.

Nate opened the passenger door first, steadying me while I climbed in.

The heater hummed to life, filling the cab with warmth. We sat there for a moment, watching the windshield fog clear. The quiet felt easy.

"Tyler won," I said.

"As he predicted."

"You're relieved?"

"Deeply."

"Me too."

He glanced over, smiling faintly. "I thought it didn't matter much to you, but you really didn't want to win?"

"No, not like I might have before." I looked out the window at the dark fields sliding past. "It would've been part of what I expected. Tonight, though—winning wouldn't have compared to being with friends... and you."

He didn't speak right away, just kept driving, his hands steady on the wheel.

"I surprised myself by enjoying what I thought I'd hate," he said finally. "But yeah—people make it okay. Well... you make it more."

Something warm and certain settled inside me.

He pulled into my driveway, put the truck in park but left it running. The heater whirred between us.

"I feel like there's a lot I could do..." He reached over and brushed a loose curl from my face, careful, gentle. "Things I could be okay doing—with your help."

He kissed me goodnight in my driveway, the truck still running, the heater humming between us. Promises not ready to be spoken out loud swirled around us.

41

Sharing the Goods

Jenna

Monday lunch started out like normal. Then Nate showed up with a large cardboard box and set it in the middle of the table.

"What's that?" Tyler asked immediately.

"Lefse. Rosettes. Krumkake. Some other stuff." Nate opened the box. The smell of butter and cardamom drifted out.

"Where'd you get all this?" Ivy asked, leaning forward.

"Church bake sale," Nate said simply.

"Which church?" Emilia asked.

"Trinity Lutheran. About forty minutes west."

Tyler paused mid-bite. "You drove forty minutes to a church bake sale?"

"Saturday," Nate said. "After Thanksgiving."

"Why?" Drew asked, genuinely curious.

Nate glanced at me. I tried not to smile.

"Captain celebration," I said.

The table went silent for exactly three seconds.

Then Tyler exploded. "WAIT. Your big celebration for making captain was driving to a church basement to buy cookies from old Norwegian ladies?"

"Essentially," Nate said.

"That's—" Tyler gestured wildly. "That's the most YOU thing I've ever heard. Congratulations, Captain." Then, after a beat, "But also, DUDE."

"What's wrong with it?" I asked.

"Nothing's wrong with it," Tyler said. "It's just—most people would go to a movie. Or out to eat. Or literally anything that isn't a rural Lutheran church basement."

"The cookies are really good," I said defensively.

"I'm sure they are," Emilia said, clearly trying not to laugh. "But you have to admit it's extremely on-brand for you two."

Aria reached for a rosette. "I think it's perfect, actually. Very practical. You get to celebrate and discover good baking."

"Thank you," I said.

"Plus," Aria added, taking a bite, "these are incredible."

Ivy picked up a piece of lefse. "This is so sweet. You two driving out there together. Was it romantic?"

"It was a church basement," Nate said.

"With folding tables," I added.

"And four Norwegian grandmas," Nate continued.

"Who gave us extra for free," I finished.

Ivy smiled. "Sounds perfect to me."

Maddie grabbed a sandbakkel. "Okay, but did the church ladies adopt you? Because that's what always happens."

"One of them asked if we were dating," I said. "Then said we should bake together to test compatibility."

"Did you tell them you already do?" Maddie asked.

"Yes."

"And they loved it, didn't they?"

"They were very pleased."

Maddie grinned. "Called it."

"One of them gave us her number," Nate added. "Agnes. Said we should come bake with her before Christmas. Learn how to make proper krumkake."

"See?" Maddie said. "Adopted."

"One of them is Mr. Olson's aunt," Nate added. "Mildred. She was very proud when I said I have him for physics."

"Wait, Mr. Olson?" Drew said. "Our Mr. Olson?"

"Small world," I said.

"Small state," Emilia corrected. "Everyone's related to everyone here."

"I kind of want to go," I admitted.

"Of course you do," Tyler said. "You two are going to end up with like six Norwegian grandmas."

"Could be worse," Nate said.

Dayne picked up one of the thin, rolled cookies. "What's this one?"

"Krumkake," Nate said. "Norwegian. It's flavored with cardamom."

Dayne took a bite, eyebrows raising. "Okay, that's actually really good. We didn't have stuff like this growing up—my family's all over. African American, Puerto Rican, white. Military bases don't really do regional baking."

"What did your family make?" Maddie asked.

"My abuela makes these coconut cookies—besitos de coco. And flan. Always flan." He grinned. "Different vibe from this, but just as good."

"I'd try those," Ivy said.

"Next time she visits, I'll bring some," Dayne said.

"Wait, your grandma visits?" Tyler asked. "I thought you just moved here."

"We did. This past summer." Dayne reached for another cookie. "My dad's ex-Air Force. We moved around a lot—Germany, Virginia, California. Then he got out and took a job in the oil industry. Hence, North Dakota."

"That's why our moms were so excited when they moved here," Maddie added. "They're first cousins. Grew up together, but we've never actually lived in the same place until now."

"So you two are—what, second cousins?" Aria asked.

"Yep," Dayne said. "We spent summers and holidays together growing up, but this is the first time we've been in the same town."

"That's cool," Ivy said. "But also—this is probably the smallest place you've ever lived, right?"

Dayne laughed. "By far. Riverbend's the most...
homogenous place I've been. It's an adjustment."

"I bet," Emilia said. "Military bases are way more diverse."

"Yeah. Different cultures, different backgrounds, people
coming and going." He shrugged. "Here, everybody knows
everybody, and everybody's Norwegian or German."

"Or both," Tyler said.

"Exactly." Dayne smiled. "But I'm figuring it out. And
apparently, Norwegian church ladies make excellent cookies."

"See?" I said to Tyler. "Good celebration."

Tyler was quiet for a moment, which was unusual. Then his
eyes lit up.

"Wait," he said. "This is actually perfect."

"What is?" Emilia asked warily.

"Lutheran church basement bake sale as a rom-com
meet-cute." Tyler was already gesturing like he was framing
a scene. "Think about it. Small town. Elderly Norwegian
ladies with secret family recipes. Young couple bonding over
cardamom and lefse. Four church ladies who adopt them. It's
wholesome rom-com gold."

"You're going to write this, aren't you?" I said.

"Already writing it." Tyler pulled out his phone. "I'm calling it 'Baked with Love.' No—'The Krumkake Connection.'"

"Those are both terrible," Aria said.

"I'm workshopping," Tyler said, typing notes.

"This is my magnum opus." Tyler looked up, grinning. "You two are my muses. I'll dedicate it to you."

"We're honored," Nate said dryly.

"You should be."

"How long until you actually write this?" Emilia asked. "What am I saying. You'll have a first draft screenplay by next week."

"Probably," Tyler admitted.

"You're welcome for the inspiration," I said.

"At least they're being themselves," Drew said, reaching for more lefse. "Better than trying to do what everyone else does."

"Exactly," Aria agreed.

Tyler grabbed a rosette, still looking at his phone. "Okay but seriously, these are amazing. You two can cater my premiere."

"There's not going to be a premiere," Emilia said.

"Not with that attitude."

Tyler took a bite, then pointed at us with the cookie. "You two are weird. But like, good weird. Wholesome weird."

"I'll take that," I said.

The box made its way around the table. Everyone trying everything, comparing favorites, asking questions about which church lady made what.

"Now someone tell me what krumkake means," Tyler said, "because I need to know if I'm pronouncing it right for my screenplay."

"You're not," Emilia said.

"How do you know?"

"Because I can hear you."

The conversation shifted—arguing about pronunciation, debating which cookie was best, Tyler insisting we needed to find more church bake sales for "research purposes."

But I caught Nate's eye across the table. He gave me that small, quiet smile. The one that meant thank you. The one that meant this is good.

"So," Maddie said, leaning back in her chair. "Church basement bake sales are now a couple activity?"

"Apparently," I said.

"I support it." She raised her milk carton like a toast. "To the weirdest but somehow most perfect celebration ever."

And somehow, in that moment, with an empty cookie box and a table full of friends who got it—who got us—everything felt exactly right.

42

Captain in Action

Nate

The locker room felt different.

Not physically—same scuffed floors, same smell of sweat and old gym equipment, same white boards with Coach's scribbled plays. But something had shifted. The weight of the C on my jersey wasn't just fabric. It was responsibility.

I'd worn the uniform a hundred times. But this was the first time as captain.

Coach was at the board, diagramming Williston's defensive scheme. The team was scattered on benches—Tyler stretching, Drew re-taping his ankle, Marcus staring at his shoes with that pre-game nervousness he always got.

"Berglund," Coach said without looking up. "Come here."

I crossed to the board.

He handed me the marker. "Talk them through it."

Right. Captain responsibilities.

I studied the diagram, found the weak spots, explained them. The team listened. Nodded. It felt almost normal until Coach took the marker back and looked at me expectantly.

"Hands in," he said.

We circled up. Usually Coach said something here. But this time he just waited.

For me.

My throat went dry. Every eye in the locker room was on me.

"Just play our game," I managed. "Trust each other. We're ready."

Not eloquent. But it was true.

"Riverbend on three. One, two, three—"

"RIVERBEND!"

The sound echoed off the walls.

I hoped I was as ready as I'd just told them we were.

The gym was packed—Williston always brought their crowd. I spotted my mom and Tía Mariella in their usual seats. And there, three rows up, sitting with Aria and Emilia—

Jenna.

Still in the boot, but dressed in school colors, holding a poster that said CAPTAIN in neat block letters.

She caught my eye and smiled.

Something settled in my chest.

I could do this.

The game was everything I expected—loud, physical, competitive. Williston came to play.

We traded baskets through the first half. Aiden was smooth, making everything look effortless. Tyler was everywhere on defense. We were up four at halftime, but it felt fragile.

Then the third quarter hit.

Williston came out with full-court pressure—trapping, forcing turnovers, feeding off their crowd's energy. We turned it over three times in four minutes. Their lead grew.

Two points. Four points. Six.

The team was rattled. I could see it—Marcus's wide eyes, the frustration in Drew's posture, even Aiden looked uncertain.

Coach called timeout.

We huddled. Coach started to speak, then stopped. Looked at me.

This was mine.

My heart was pounding, but I made myself focus. Made myself remember what Jenna had written in that folder: *You're already the captain.*

"Hey." I waited until everyone was looking at me. "We knew they'd make a run. This is it. This is the run."

"We're down six," Dayne said quietly.

"So we come back." I looked around the huddle. "We're better than this. We know what to do. Stay patient. Move the ball. Get stops."

Silence.

Then Drew nodded. "Let's go."

We broke the huddle.

It took three minutes, but we found our rhythm again. Aiden broke their press with smart passes. Tyler got two steals. We chipped away at the lead.

By the end of the third, we were up three.

The fourth quarter was all focus and discipline. Every possession mattered.

With two minutes left, we were tied. Williston had the ball, but Tyler forced a miss. Drew grabbed the rebound and we pushed.

Aiden drove, drew defenders, found Tyler on the wing.

Tyler finished.

60-58, Riverbend.

Forty seconds left.

Coach drew up the defense. "Stay disciplined. No fouls."

Williston's point guard drove hard, but Tyler stayed in front. I stepped up to help, and the shot missed—contested, awkward.

Drew grabbed the rebound. Got fouled. Hit both free throws.

62-58.

Williston's final three-pointer missed at the buzzer.

Game.

The team mobbed Drew first, then me. Tyler was yelling. Marcus was grinning. Aiden pulled me into a quick hug—"Good leadership, Cap."

Coach shook his head, half-exhausted, half-proud. "Good job, Captain."

I looked for Jenna.

She was waiting by the bleachers, boot propped on the bottom bench, still holding the poster.

"Captain," she said when I reached her.

"Hey."

"That was incredible."

"We almost blew it in the third."

"But you didn't." She adjusted her weight, favoring her good leg. "You steadied them. I watched you during that timeout. You knew exactly what to say."

"I just told them what they already knew."

"That's leadership, Nate." She smiled. "Go shower. I'll wait."

"You don't have to—"

"I want to. Go."

The locker room was loud—music playing, everyone still riding the high. Tyler was singing off-key in the shower. Drew was on his phone, probably already checking stats.

I showered quickly, changed into street clothes. By the time I came out, most of the team was ready to go.

Coach caught my eye on the way out. "Good game, Captain."

"Thanks, Coach."

"See you Monday."

Jenna was still by the bleachers, talking to Emilia. Tyler appeared beside them, freshly showered, grinning.

"The Round Up," he announced. "First win tradition. Everyone's going."

"Let's go," Jenna said immediately, folding her poster.

The Round Up was packed—team filling booths, girlfriends, fans. The place buzzed with post-win energy: loud voices, fries being passed around, milkshakes at every table.

Jenna slid into a booth, and I sat beside her. Tyler and Emilia squeezed in across from us. Aiden and Ivy grabbed the booth behind us with Drew and Marcus. Dayne held court at a nearby table with some sophomores.

"Fancy," Jenna said when a waitress dropped menus.

"Only the best for captain celebrations."

Tyler was already re-enacting the third quarter with dramatic gestures. Drew leaned over from his booth. "Captain speech before the game was solid. Short. No BS."

"It's all that needed to be said," Jenna offered.

"Exactly." Drew pointed at her. "She gets it."

A massive plate of fries appeared at our table.

Tyler grabbed a handful. "That timeout in the third—you didn't panic. Just told us what we needed to hear."

"You guys did the work."

"Yeah, but you're the one leading it now," Aiden added from behind us. "That's what matters."

A milkshake appeared in front of Jenna. She looked up at the waitress, confused.

"Courtesy of the table," the waitress said, gesturing vaguely at the team.

"Team tradition," Tyler explained. "Captain's girlfriend gets a milkshake on first win."

Jenna raised the milkshake in acknowledgment. "Appreciated."

Several players raised their drinks back.

She took a sip. "Okay, this is actually really good."

Jenkins, one of the sophomores, approached hesitantly. "Hey, Captain? Coach said you might have film notes for me?"

"Yeah. I'll send them tomorrow."

"Thanks. And congrats."

Jenna nudged me gently as Jenkins left. "Captain responsibilities already starting."

"Apparently."

Dayne wandered over, stealing a fry. "Good timeout in the third. I was panicking a little. You settled everyone down."

Tyler's phone came out. "Team photo. First win. Everyone get in."

We rearranged—some standing, others leaning in. Tyler set up his phone with the timer. Jenna stayed beside me, my arm around her shoulders. Ivy and Emilia squeezed in. The team clustered around.

"Say 'undefeated!'" Tyler called.

"UNDEFEATED!"

The flash went off—chaotic, half the people mid-laugh, but genuine.

Tyler posted it immediately. "Season opener energy."

An hour later, things wound down. Parents texting. Early curfews. The celebration settling.

Jenna shifted beside me, adjusting the boot. "Ready to go?"

"Yeah."

We said our goodbyes. Tyler gave me a rough shoulder bump. Drew nodded approval. Aiden and Ivy waved. Dayne saluted with a fry.

Outside, the December air was sharp and cold.

I helped Jenna into the truck, the boot making it awkward but manageable.

"Good first game, Captain," she said as I started the engine.

"Good?"

"Great. But I didn't want to over-inflate your ego."

I almost smiled. "Appreciate the restraint."

She leaned her head against the window as I pulled out, watching The Round Up's lights fade. "You know what's nice?"

"What?"

"This. All of it. You being captain. The team. Us celebrating together." She looked over at me. "It feels right."

It did feel right. The game, the win, the celebration. Jenna beside me, comfortable and close.

First game as captain: complete.

And not just survived—actually good.

43

Boot Free

Jenna

The exam room smelled like antiseptic and old magazines. I sat on the paper-covered table, boot-clad foot dangling, regular foot tapping against the metal frame. Mom scrolled through her phone in the chair by the window, but I could tell she wasn't really reading anything. Just occupying her hands.

Ten weeks. Two and a half months. Seventy days of clunking around in this thing.

And maybe—hopefully—today it came off.

Dr. Patel knocked once and entered, pulling up my X-rays on the computer screen. "Let's see how we're doing."

She studied the images, clicking between views. I held my breath.

"Excellent," she said finally. "Bone's healed beautifully. No complications. Range of motion has been improving on schedule."

"So..." I couldn't quite finish the sentence.

She smiled. "So we're taking the boot off today."

Mom exhaled audibly from her chair.

"Really?" I asked.

"Really." Dr. Patel rolled her stool closer. "Let's get you out of that thing."

She unfastened the velcro straps one by one—the sound loud in the quiet room. Each release felt like something loosening in my chest.

The boot came off.

My ankle looked pale. Smaller than I remembered. Vulnerable.

"How does it feel?" Dr. Patel asked.

"Light," I said. "Weird. Like my leg forgot what normal feels like."

She manipulated my ankle gently—flexing, rotating, testing. "Any sharp pain?"

"No. Just... stiff."

"That's expected. We'll get you set up with physical therapy to work on strength and flexibility." She stood, stepped back. "Okay. Let's see you walk."

I stared at her.

"Just to the door and back," she said. "Take your time."

I slid off the table carefully. Both feet on the ground. No boot. No crutches. Just me.

The first step was tentative. My left ankle held, but it felt fragile. Like I was testing ice.

"You're favoring it," Dr. Patel observed. "That's normal. Your body's been compensating for ten weeks. It'll take time to trust it again."

I took another step. Then another.

By the time I reached the door, I was almost walking normally. By the time I got back to the table, I was smiling.

"Good," Dr. Patel said. "Very good. You'll have some stiffness, probably a slight limp for a few days. But you're cleared for normal weight-bearing activity. Just ease back into things."

"What about running? Jumping?"

"PT first. Build up strength and stability. We'll reassess in a few weeks." She pulled out a prescription pad. "I'm referring you to Cascade Physical Therapy. They're excellent. Plan on twice a week for the next month, then we'll evaluate."

She handed me the paper. "And Jenna? You did everything right. You rested when you needed to. Followed instructions. This healed as well as it possibly could have."

Something in my throat tightened. "Thanks."

Mom hugged me in the parking lot. Just pulled me in, careful of my ankle, and held on.

"I'm okay, Mom," I said into her shoulder.

"I know. I just—" Her voice caught. "You're okay."

We stood there for a moment, December air cold around us, her arms warm.

"Let's go home," she said finally. "I'll make lunch. Something celebratory."

"Grilled cheese?"

"Obviously grilled cheese."

I was on the couch—both feet on the floor, no boot, no pillows, no ice pack—when I texted the group.

ME: boot is OFF ME: i can WALK

The responses came immediately.

EMILIA: JENNA!!!

IVY: FINALLY

ARIA: OMG YES

MADDIE: this calls for celebration gifs

MADDIE: [GIF: Beyoncé strutting in heels]

ARIA: [GIF: Kid doing victory dance]

IVY: [GIF: Penguin waddling confidently]

ME: why is the penguin me

IVY: because you're walking boot free for the first time in 10 weeks

IVY: waddle energy is appropriate

EMILIA: what you can do now: [GIF: Person doing high kicks]

ARIA: [GIF: Someone running through a field in slow motion]

MADDIE: [GIF: Tap dancer going crazy]

ME: i don't think dr patel cleared me for any of that

IVY: fine what you can ACTUALLY do now
[GIF: Person putting on matching socks]

ARIA: [GIF: Someone walking up stairs normally]

EMILIA: [GIF: Person taking a regular shower]

MADDIE: [GIF: Someone spinning around in an office chair]

ME: the shower one is real though

ME: do you know how hard it is to shower with a garbage bag taped around your leg

ARIA: i can only imagine

EMILIA: so what now? PT?

ME: yeah twice a week starting next week

ME: dr says i did everything right and it healed perfectly

IVY: of course it did

IVY: you're weirdly good at following medical instructions

MADDIE: most responsible injured person ever

ME: i just wanted it to heal

ARIA: and it DID [GIF: Confetti cannon explosion]

EMILIA: we should celebrate properly

EMILIA: girls night this weekend?

ME: yes please

IVY: i'll bring snacks

MADDIE: i'll bring face masks

ARIA: i'll bring the ridiculous rom-coms

EMILIA: perfect

ME: you guys are the best

MADDIE: we know [GIF: Group hug]

I was making tea—standing at the counter, weight on both feet, no boot—when I texted Nate.

ME: boot came off today

Three dots appeared immediately.

> NATE: That's great. How does it feel?

> ME: weird but good

> ME: dr says i did everything right

> NATE: You did.

> ME: want to come over after practice?

> NATE: Yeah. I'll be there around 6.

> ME: perfect

He showed up at 6:03, still in his practice clothes, hair damp from a quick post-practice shower. I opened the door with both feet on the ground, no boot, no crutches.

He stopped. Just looked at me for a second, then smiled—real and warm.

"Hi," I said.

"Hi." He stepped inside, pulled me into a hug immediately. Careful of my ankle, but solid.

"You're walking your feet.

"Feet are walking boot free," I said into his shoulder.

He pulled back, eyes dropping to my feet. Both of them. Matching socks. No boot. We moved to the couch. I sat, and he settled beside me, turning slightly to face me.

"Can I—" He gestured to my left ankle.

"Yeah."

I shifted, bringing my left foot up onto the couch between us. He took it gently in his hands, studying it with that calculating look as he examined my ankle.

"It's thinner," he said. "From being immobilized. And paler."

"Very romantic observation, Nate."

"But it's healed." He looked up at me. "You're healed."

"Yeah." I smiled. "I am."

He pressed a kiss to my knee—quick, affectionate—then let my foot rest back down, his arm going around my shoulders. Then he reached into his jacket pocket and pulled out a familiar white bakery box.

I lit up. "You didn't."

"Celebration snickerdoodles," he said.

He pulled out something else from his jacket pocket. Two packages of toe socks. I stared at them. The first pair was compression toe socks—plain, medical-looking. The second pair had tiny emoji faces on each toe.

"Are those...compression toe socks?"

"They help with circulation and reduce swelling during recovery. Especially good after being immobilized." He held up the emoji pair. "But these ones are just for fun."

"You researched recovery socks."

"I researched a lot of things." He handed them both to me. "One pair for healing, one pair for personality. Both feet covered."

I untied the string on the cookie box, took one of the snickerdoodles, broke it in half. Offered him part.

"To ten weeks of healing," I said.

"To walking without a boot," he added.

"And to you getting your life back."

I smiled. "That too."

We ate in comfortable silence. His free hand found mine, fingers lacing together automatically.

"Thank you," I said quietly. "For coming right after practice. For the cookies. For the toe socks. For being here."

"Where else would I be?"

"How was practice?" I asked, settling against him.

"Fine. Tyler complained about defensive drills for forty minutes straight." He pressed a kiss to the top of my head. "What about PT?"

"Starting next week. Twice a week for a month, then we reassess."

He nodded, processing.

I shifted to face him better, both feet tucked under me on the couch—no boot in the way, no awkward positioning around the injury. Just...normal.

"This is the first time we've sat like this," I realized. "Without the boot between us."

He looked down at our intertwined hands, at the way I was curled into his side. "Yeah."

"It's nice."

"Very nice." He kissed my forehead, then my temple. "You want to watch baking shows?"

"Of course."

I pulled up the episode we'd been working through. He settled deeper into the couch, pulling me closer. My head rested on his chest, his arm secure around me.

On screen, someone's soufflé collapsed.

"That's a temperature regulation issue," Nate said.

"Nate Berglund, still math-analyzing the Bake Off"

"Still providing valuable structural feedback."

I laughed, tilting my head up to look at him. He was already looking down at me, that soft expression he got sometimes.

"What?" I asked.

"Nothing. Just—" He brushed a strand of hair behind my ear. "I'm glad you're okay. That it healed right."

"Me too."

He kissed me then—gentle, unhurried. Like we had all the time in the world and nowhere else. When we pulled apart, I settled back against his chest. His hand found mine again, our fingers lacing together.

My ankle didn't hurt. The boot was gone. Nate was here, warm and solid beside me. And for the first time in ten weeks, everything felt exactly right.

44

Practice Pies

Jenna

"Want to come over after practice?" I asked between classes. "I need to practice making pies before Thanksgiving."

Nate shifted his backpack. "Practice pies?"

"My mom noticed I've been baking again and asked me to bake the pies."

I closed my locker. "I've baked pies before. Filling's the easy part. Pie crust is a pain. I need support for this potential disaster."

"Math and science to the rescue."

My kitchen was quiet when Nate arrived. He knocked then came in. I was waiting for the day he came in without knocking. I wondered how many 'Doors open, come in' texts it would take.

Nate set his backpack by the door, then came to find me in the kitchen.

"What are we making?"

"And maybe pecan if we have time. I want to try lattice on the apple. And maybe leaf cutouts for the pumpkin."

"What makes pie crust so tricky?"

"It's the balance," I said, measuring out flour. "Too much water, and it's tough. Too little, and it falls apart. It's all about texture."

Nate nodded thoughtfully, cutting cold butter into cubes. "So—a baked chemistry experiment."

"Pretty much." I handed him the pastry blender and grabbed two dinner knives. "Cutting butter into the flour is the first step."

He eyed the knives skeptically. "Using those seems... inefficient."

"Hence the super-modern pastry blender." I nodded toward the one in his hand. "You can also use your fingers—or a food processor if you're soulless."

He looked at me. "Let's try them all and see which crust turns out better."

"Science-meets-Pie-Crust-Baking-Fair? Winner gets?"

"Let's just compete against the ingredients. Work as a team."

"You'll have an excuse if your science fails you."

"A contingency plan. Always."

We worked side by side, alternating tools and techniques. I tried to start a flour fight but failed and turned into a laughing truce—and a kiss that ended in both of us dusted with flour.

"That's like a chemistry experiment every time," Nate said when we pulled apart, resting his forehead against mine. "Combustible ingredients."

I laughed softly. "You don't think you are, but you get more adorable every time you say something like that."

"How was practice?" I asked.

"Fine. Coach asked again."

"About captain?"

"Yeah." He pressed the dough together, checking the texture. "Said he needs an answer by next week."

"What did you say?"

"That I'm thinking about it."

We started on fillings. Nate peeled apples with calm precision, almost every peel coming off in one long curl. I'd told him to let the peels fall to the floor, but that was too messy for him—he peeled over the sink instead. I peeked around him, pinched a long curl between my fingers, and tossed it over my left shoulder to land on the floor.

"That was kind of odd," he said, pausing mid-peel. "Family tradition?"

"It's a game," I said. "You throw the peel over your shoulder, and whatever letter it makes is the first initial of your true love's name."

He arched an eyebrow. "Played before TV was invented, I assume."

"Oh, definitely. Like my grandma's great-grandma's-grandma played it—way before science existed."

I peered down at the floor. The peel had landed in a way that actually sort of resembled an N.

"That could be an N," I said, smiling. "Or maybe a W. Or an M. Or—"

"Since we live now, in the age of science," Nate said, setting down the apple and peeler, "my official conclusion is that gravity twisted that peel into an N and only an N."

"I'm not fully convinced."

He pulled me toward him, backing me gently into the corner of the counter.

"Here's your data," he said before kissing me.

A minute later, he reached into the sink, plucked another peel, and tossed it over his shoulder without looking. "Definitely a J. No other possible conclusion."

"I've got data for that too."

We'd prepped four pie crusts, each now wrapped, labeled, and chilling in the fridge. The timer went off. Dough was ready. We pulled out two of the four chilled dough rounds to set the counter for rolling out. The dough was cool under my hands. The flour I pinched to sprinkle on the counter before rolling, soft between my fingertips.

Nate picked up the extra rolling pin. "Looks pretty straightforward."

"Pie crust can turn unscientifically finicky in a nanosecond," I warned.

"I'll proceed with extreme caution."

We rolled out two crusts, the squeaks and soft thuds of the rolling pins added rhythm to the kitchen. Bottom crusts went into the pans without issue, one to prebake, the other to fill with an apple mix and cover with a top crust.

We poured smooth pumpkin filling into the cooled, prebaked crust. This crust was simple just a bottom. But I wanted to try the leaf cutouts for the edge.

I rolled out extra dough and handed Nate a small leaf-shaped cutter. "Think you can make these look decent?"

"Probably not."

"Just try."

He pressed the cutter into the dough, lifted out a perfect leaf shape. Then another. Steady. Precise. Of course.

"Show-off," I muttered.

"You asked."

I arranged the leaves around the edge of the pumpkin pie, overlapping them slightly. It looked almost professional.

The pumpkin pie looked good enough to photograph before it went into the oven. I'd come too far from that curated version of myself to care. We slid it into the oven.

I pulled the remaining dough from the fridge.

"Okay. Technical challenge. Want to try a lattice top crust with me?"

"I've never done this."

"Me either. We'll figure it out."

I rolled out the top crust and cut it into strips. "Okay, so you weave them. Over, under, over, under."

"Like a basket."

"Exactly like a basket."

We worked side by side, his hands steady, mine less so. The first few strips went okay. Then I messed up the pattern and had to start over.

"Here." Nate gently lifted one of my strips. "Try this way."

We fixed it together, his hand guiding mine until the weave was right.

"There," he said.

It wasn't perfect—some strips were thicker than others, the edges uneven—but it looked like a lattice. Like something intentional.

"Not bad for practice," I said.

"It'll taste the same either way."

"Spoken like someone who's never cared about presentation."

"Guilty."

We crimped the edges, brushed egg wash over the top, and slid it into the oven. I'd already pulled out the pumpkin pie and it was cooling on a rack.

The kitchen stayed warm and quiet while the oven hummed. We didn't talk for a while—just cleaned up, waiting for the timer and for the pumpkin pie to cool to eating temperature.

Finally, I said, "I've got something for you."

He looked up. "Okay."

I went to my room and came back with a blue folder. My hands shook a little as I offered it.

"Here, sit down. I'm going to cut a couple pieces of pumpkin if it's ready."

I checked the pumpkin pie—still warm but cool enough to sample, though it really needed fresh whipped cream. I cut two pieces, put them on plates. I slid a plate and fork to where Nate sat on a stool. Then sat next to him and sampled my piece.

"Mmmm, pretty good," I said. "Pastry blender pie crust gave us a nice, good flaky crust."

I watched him open the folder slowly, my nerves kicking in. I knew the contents so I didn't lean over to read. He closed the folder carefully. Set it on the counter. Didn't look at me.

"Jenna, I don't—" He stopped. Started again. "I don't know what to say."

"You don't have to say anything."

He nodded once. "I just wanted you to have it. Before you give Coach your answer."

"Yeah. Okay."

He gave that small, quiet smile—the one that always meant more than words—then set the folder aside and reached for his fork.

He was still processing. I could see it in the way he sat there. Extra still, quiet. The way he got when he was calculating something too big to solve immediately.

"Tyler told me once that I see things differently," he said. "That I notice patterns other people miss."

"You do."

"But I never thought—" He gestured at the folder. "I didn't know other people saw it that way."

"They do." I leaned against the counter beside him. "The team voted for you, Nate. Not because they felt sorry for you or because there was no one else. Because they wanted you. You don't have to decide or tell me anything," I said gently. "Just... think about it all, okay?"

When he left, he slid the folder into his backpack.

An hour later, my phone buzzed.

NATE: I'm going to say yes.

ME: Good. You'll be great.

I set my phone down, still smiling, the scent of apples and cinnamon filling the kitchen.

Some data you didn't need to analyze.

You could just feel it was right.

45

Ways of Restoration

Jenna

Winter break passed faster than I expected. PT twice a week, Nate driving me to most appointments because Mom's schedule was packed.

My ankle got stronger. Not all the way back, but stronger. Dr. Patel was pleased at my last check-in.

"Right on schedule," she'd said. "Keep doing what you're doing."

What I was doing was exactly what Nate told me to do, which was exactly what the PT told me to do, which meant I was healing.

School started back up the second week of January. Cold, gray, everyone sluggish from break. I walked the halls without the boot, just a slight limp that was getting less noticeable every day.

I didn't expect to be called to Principal Hayes's office for a meeting after school. Mrs. Henderson, the front desk secretary, smiled when I walked in.

"Go on back, honey. They're waiting for you."

They?

I knocked on the half-open door.

"Jenna, come in." Principal Hayes stood, gesturing to a chair. Mrs. Wexler sat to one side, and beside her—

A woman I didn't recognize. Thirties maybe, athletic build, blonde hair pulled back in a neat ponytail. She wore Riverbend coaching gear but somehow made it look professional.

"Jenna, this is Coach Reeves," Principal Hayes said. "She's joining us as the new head cheer coach."

Coach Reeves stood, extended her hand. Her grip was firm, confident. "It's good to meet you, Jenna. I've heard a lot about you."

I glanced at Mrs. Wexler, uncertain.

Mrs. Wexler smiled. "Coach Reeves was one of my athletes. Back when I coached cheer."

"Best coach I ever had," Coach Reeves said simply. "When Mrs. Wexler told me what happened here and asked if I'd consider coming back to help rebuild the program, there was no question."

"You're from here?" I asked.

"My family farms near Belfield, so I went to high school here. I was on Mrs. Wexler's squad before she moved to counseling." She sat back down, and I took the remaining chair. "Then went to college, got my Master's in Sport Management. My focus was on creating positive team culture and preventing bullying in competitive athletics."

Oh.

"I've spent the last five years coaching at a high school in Minnesota," she continued. "But when Mrs. Wexler reached out... this felt like where I needed to be."

Principal Hayes cleared his throat. "The cheer program is still on hiatus for the remainder of this school year. But Coach Reeves will be working with interested students on the restorative justice taskforce we discussed before break."

Right. The anti-bullying initiative. Student council had presented it in December, got it approved. I'd been so focused on PT and Nate and getting through finals that I hadn't thought much about implementation.

"That's actually why we wanted to talk to you," Mrs. Wexler said gently.

Coach Reeves leaned forward. "I've read all the documentation from the investigation. I know what you went through. And I know you're still in PT, still recovering."

She paused. "But Mrs. Wexler tells me you're exactly the kind of leader this program needs."

My stomach flipped.

"We're forming a student taskforce to implement the restorative justice curriculum school-wide," Coach Reeves continued. "Student council will be involved, but we need a student lead. Someone who understands what happened, why it matters, and what real change looks like."

She looked directly at me.

"I'd like you to lead it. With my supervision, of course. But your voice, your perspective—that's what's going to make this work."

I stared at her. "I can't even cheer yet."

"This isn't about stunts or routines," she said. "This is about building something better. Creating a culture where what happened to you doesn't happen again. To anyone."

Mrs. Wexler's expression was gentle. "You don't have to decide right now."

"Actually—" I surprised myself. "I'll do it."

Coach Reeves smiled. "Good. Because there are some people who'd like to talk to you about it."

The former cheer squad—what was left of it—sat in a circle in the small gym. Maybe fifteen girls. Some I recognized from before. Jessie, who'd been dropped when the pyramid collapsed. A handful of younger ones who'd been on JV.

Coach Reeves stood at the edge of the circle. "Everyone, this is Jenna. She's agreed to lead our student taskforce on implementing restorative practices."

Jessie smiled at me. A real smile. Relieved.One of the younger girls—Emma, I thought her name was—raised her hand tentatively.

"Can I say something?"

Coach Reeves nodded. "That's what circles are for."

Emma looked at me. "I was on JV. I saw what happened to you. How you spoke up even though it was scary. How you told the truth when it would've been easier to stay quiet. You did what was right, even when it cost you everything."

"We don't want the old squad back," Jessie said quietly. "We want something different. Something better."

"And we want you to help build it," Emma said.

Then, like they'd planned it—maybe they had—the girls looked at each other and back at me.

"We want to nominate you for captain," Jessie said. "For when the program comes back. Not because you're the best tumbler or because you're popular. Because you're the kind of leader we need."

My throat went tight.

"You don't have to answer now," Coach Reeves said gently. "The program won't fully resume until next year anyway. But they wanted you to know."

I looked around the circle. At Jessie, who'd been hurt like me. At the younger girls, who'd watched everything happen and wanted something different. At Coach Reeves, who'd come back to rebuild this properly.

"I'm still in PT," I said. "I can't do everything yet."

"We know," Emma said. "But you can do this. And that's what matters."

Later at home I texted Nate.

> ME: they asked me to an anti-bullying taskforce

> ME: and nominated me for captain

> ME: i think i said yes to both

He texted back about the time practice usually finished.

> NATE: Of course you did. You're exactly who should lead it.

> NATE: How do you feel?

> ME: terrified

> ME: but also like maybe i can do this?

> NATE: You can.

NATE: Want to come over after PT tomorrow? We can talk about it.

ME: yes please

ME: also i need you to help me figure out what a restorative justice taskforce actually does

NATE: I'll research tonight and have a preliminary framework ready.

ME: of course you will

ME: this is why i love you

I stared at my phone.

I hadn't meant to type that. If felt it, but hadn't meant to say it yet. Three dots appeared. Disappeared. Appeared again.

NATE: I love you too.

My heart stopped.

Then started again, faster.

Oh.

Oh.

Jenna

I stared at my phone.

Oh god.

Oh god.

I'd just told Nate I loved him. Via text. Accidentally. And he'd said it back. My hands were shaking.

I sat on my bed, phone clutched like it might explode. This wasn't how this was supposed to happen. We were supposed to talk about it. Plan it. Say it at the right time in the right way.

Not like this. Not in a text about restorative justice frameworks. Although… maybe that was exactly like us.

I reread his message. *I love you too.*

He'd said it. He meant it. Right? My heart was doing something complicated in my chest. Part panic, part joy, part terror.

I should text him back. Say something. Anything. But what?

My fingers hovered over the keyboard.

Nothing. I had nothing.

I set the phone down. Picked it up again. Set it down.

This was ridiculous. We'd been dating for months. We'd talked about hard things. Been vulnerable. Been honest.

But this felt different. This felt like standing on the edge of something I couldn't take back. Not that I wanted to take it back.

I loved him. I did. I'd probably loved him for a while now, if I was being honest. The way he showed up. The way he listened. The way he researched ankle healing and bought me toe socks and made me feel seen.

But saying it—actually saying it—made it real in a way that scared me. What if—

No.

I stopped myself. We'd already done the "what if" spiral. We'd already almost lost each other because we were too scared to be honest.

Not again.

I picked up my phone.

> ME: I didn't mean to say it like that but I meant it

I hit send.

Stared at the screen.

No response.

One minute. Two minutes.

Maybe he was processing too. Maybe he—

I went downstairs, heart pounding. The front door opened. I stopped halfway down. Nate never just walked in. He always knocked.

But there he was, standing in the doorway, hair wet, clothes askew, slightly out of breath—like he'd texted me back from the locker room, taken the world's fastest shower, and driven here without thinking twice.

"Hi," I said.

"Hi." He stepped inside. Closed the door behind him. Didn't move farther into the house. Just stood there, looking at me.

"You drove here," I said stupidly.

"I couldn't wait."

"For what?"

He took a breath. "To say it. Out loud. Not just in a text."

My throat went tight.

"I love you," he said. Clear. Certain. "I've loved you for a while. I don't know exactly when it started, but I know it's true. The way you see people—really see them. The way you didn't let me hide. The way you're brave even when you're scared."

I couldn't speak.

"And I know you said it accidentally," he continued. "But I needed you to know I didn't. I meant it. Completely."

"Nate—"

"You don't have to say it back right now if you didn't—"

"I love you too." The words came out fast, certain. "I meant it. In the text. I meant it."

He went very still.

"I love you," I said again, stepping closer. "I didn't mean to say it like that, but I meant it. I've meant it for a while."

His hand came up to cup my face, thumb brushing my cheekbone. "Yeah?"

"Yeah."

He kissed me then—gentle at first, then deeper, like he was confirming something. Like he was making sure this was real. When we pulled apart, his forehead rested against mine.

"I was terrified," he admitted quietly. "That I'd said it wrong. That it was too soon. That you'd—"

"Me too," I said. "I panicked for twenty minutes."

"I panicked while I drove over here."

"You didn't look panicked."

"I'm good at hiding it."

I laughed, shaky and relieved. "We're ridiculous."

"We're honest," he corrected.

"We are," I agreed.

We stood there for a moment, close, his hand still on my face, my hands fisted in the front of his shirt.

"Come sit," I said finally.

We moved to the couch. He pulled me close, arm around my shoulders, and I settled against him like I always did now. Except this time it felt different. Lighter. More certain.

"So," I said after a moment. "When did you conclude that the data was telling you that Nate Berglund loved Jenna Lundquist?"

He thought about it. "There wasn't one moment. It was cumulative. Data points adding up over time. The way you laughed at my Bake Off analysis. The way you didn't let me deflect when I was scared about talking to my parents. The way you documented evidence for me like I'd done for you. The way you—"

He paused. "The way you saw me. Actually saw me. Not who I was supposed to be. Just... me."

My throat tightened. "That's when I knew too. When you saw me. The real me. Not the performing version. And you didn't want me to be different."

"Why would I want you to be different?"

"Exactly."

He pressed a kiss to my hair. "No more unsaid things."

"No more unsaid things," I agreed.

I tilted my head to look at him. "You know what's funny?"

"What?"

"We said it in a text about restorative justice frameworks."

He almost smiled. "Very on brand for us."

"Extremely on brand."

I shifted to face him better, both feet tucked under me—no boot, no awkward positioning, just comfortable.

"I love you," I said again, testing how it felt. Easier this time. More natural.

"I love you too," he said, like it was the simplest fact in the world.

And maybe it was.

Mom came home an hour later to find us on the couch, watching the Bake Off, my head on his chest, his arm around me, both of us exactly where we were supposed to be.

She smiled, didn't comment, just headed to the kitchen.

"Your mom knows," Nate said quietly.

"Moms always know."

On screen, someone's macaron tower collapsed. Nate made a small sound of disapproval about structural integrity. I smiled against his chest.

This. This was right. No more unsaid things. Just this. Us. Love.

46

Bonfire Light

Jenna

I climbed out of Nate's truck—no boot, no limp, just my regular shoes on solid ground. The string lights were already glowing between the oak trees, the bonfire crackling in the same spot.

"You good?" Nate asked, coming around the truck.

"Yeah." I smiled.

"Really good."

He took my hand. Natural now. Easy. No second-guessing what it meant or how it looked. We walked toward the fire together. The usual crowd had gathered—Ivy and Aiden on one log, Tyler helping Mrs. Preston arrange the food table, Emilia corralling Miggy away from the marshmallows.

Aria and Maddie were already laughing about something, heads bent together. And there, standing slightly apart, looking uncertain— "Dayne!" I called, waving. "Get over here!"

He grinned, relieved, and jogged over. "Wasn't sure I was supposed to just show up."

"Farm rules," Nate said. "Always just show up."

"Especially if you bring those," I added, eyeing the bag of cookies in Dayne's hand.

"My mom insisted." He held them up. "Apparently I can't go anywhere empty-handed."

"Your mom is wise," Tyler said, appearing to steal the bag. "These are going on the dessert table before Miggy discovers them."

Drew arrived then with his four sisters in tow—Mia with a notebook already out, Zoe carrying what looked like a rock collection, Lucy clutching her sketchbook, and Harper with Mr. Hops the secret agent rabbit.

"Hope it's okay," Drew said.

"Always okay," Emilia said immediately. "You know that."

Harper spotted Miggy and took off running. "MIGGY!"

"HARPER!" Miggy abandoned the marshmallows to meet her. "I got new chicken stories!"

The two of them disappeared toward the barn, Sofia toddling after them yelling "Wait! Wait me!"

Dayne settled onto a log, and I sat beside Nate across from him. The fire was warm, the evening air cool. Perfect.

"So," Maddie said, dropping onto the log beside me. "Junior year. We survived."

"Speak for yourself," Tyler said. "I didn't survive, I thrived."

Emilia threw a marshmallow at him. "You complained about calculus every single day."

"Thriving includes complaining. It's part of the process."

I laughed, leaning into Nate's side. He shifted to put his arm around me automatically. Across the fire, Aiden leaned over and kissed Ivy's cheek.

NOOOOO!" Miggy came running from the barn direction, Harper and Sofia trailing behind him. He skidded to a stop in front of Ivy and Aiden, hands on his hips. "You're breaking the RULES!"

He looked genuinely betrayed. "No kissing at the farm! You KNOW that, basketball dude!"

Aiden pulled back, trying not to laugh. "Sorry, buddy."

"You made RULES," Miggy continued, turning to address the whole group. "And nobody follows them! First rule: NO kissing at the farm. The cows could faint!"

"First Farm Guy kissed Meela—" He pointed accusingly at Tyler. "MY OWN SISTER. Then basketball dude kissed Ivy. And now Nate kissed Jenna!"

"Kissed!" Sofia echoed happily, not understanding but enjoying Miggy's energy. "Kissed, kissed!"

"It's NOT good, Sofía," Miggy told her seriously. "Kissing is the worst thing people do."

Harper nodded solemnly. "My cousin Brady kisses his girlfriend. It's very gross."

"See?" Miggy gestured to Harper. "Harper gets it. We're the only ones who understand."

Zoe wandered over, abandoning her rock collection. "I think kissing is okay when you're old. Like sixteen."

"Sixteen is FOREVER away," Miggy said. "And when I'm sixteen, I'm still not gonna do it."

Tyler leaned toward Nate and me. "Miggy's having a crisis."

"I can see that," Nate said, fighting a smile.

He wasn't done. He turned to face the whole group, incredibly serious. "When does it STOP? How many people get caught by kissing?"

"Probably all of them eventually," Emilia said gently. Miggy looked at her with the kind of betrayal usually reserved for major deception.

"Meela. You're supposed to be on MY side."

"I am on your side. But I also really like Tyler."

"But he's FARM GUY," Miggy said, as if this explained everything. "He's supposed to be about tractors and chickens and fixing The Beast. Not...that."

Tyler was trying very hard not to laugh. "I can do both."

"No you CAN'T," Miggy insisted. "Once you start kissing, everything changes. I've seen it. You get all weird and smiley." "

"Isn't smiley good?" Harper offered.

"Smiley's suspicious," Miggy corrected.

Sofia had lost the thread of the conversation but was now walking around the circle pointing at people.

"You kissed? You kissed?" She stopped in front of Dayne. "You kissed?"

"No," Dayne said quickly. "No kissing here."

Sofia patted his leg approvingly. Then looked at Miggy. "He no kissed."

Miggy studied Dayne with newfound respect. "You're safe. So far."

"Good to know," Dayne said, clearly trying not to laugh. Eventually the kissing crisis passed and Miggy returned to the barn with Harper and Sofia in tow, determined to show them the new baby chicks.

"That was something," Aria said.

"He's been like that for weeks," Emilia explained. "Ever since he realized Nate and Jenna were together. It was the final straw."

"The kissing apocalypse," Tyler said solemnly.

"Someone should warn him about middle school," Maddie added. Mr. Preston appeared with hotdogs for roasting, buns, and all the toppings.

"Who's hungry?" Everyone migrated toward the food table. I stayed on the log for a moment, watching. Drew helping his sisters make plates. Aria stealing a cookie before dinner. Tyler and Emilia moving around each other with easy familiarity.

Nate talking basketball with Dayne. All of it felt right. Real. Not performed.

"You coming?" Nate had circled back, holding a plate.

"Yeah." I stood, took his hand. "Just thinking." "

About?"

"How good this is."

He smiled. "It really is."

After dinner, someone started music. Maddie pulled me up to dance, and soon Aria and Zoe joined us.

Lucy sketched from her spot on the ground, capturing the chaos. Harper tried to teach Miggy a dance she'd learned at preschool.

"¡Mamá! ¡Mamá, mira!" Sofia came running from the direction of the house, making a beeline for Mariella, who was bringing out the makings for S'mores.

"¿Qué pasó, mija?" Mariella scooped her up. Sofia pointed across the fire at Dayne with great urgency.

"Pelo! His pelo muy bouncy!"

"Bouncy?" Mariella looked confused.

"His hair," Emilia translated, laughing. Sofia squirmed to get down, ran straight to Dayne. Stopped in front of him and stared up, way up, at his face.

"Hi Sofia," Dayne said, crouching down to her level. She reached out carefully, touched one of his curls. It sprang back. Her eyes went huge.

"Boing," she whispered reverently. She touched it again. "Boing, boing!" Then she whirled around to Emilia.

"¡Meela! Look! Goes BOING!" She demonstrated with her hands, making springing motions.

"I see," Emilia said, smiling.

Sofia ran to Tyler next. "Ty! Day's hair muy bouncy! Like this!" More hand springs.

Tyler nodded seriously. "That is very bouncy hair."

"Sí!" Sofia ran back to Dayne, looked up at him with total adoration. "You tall. Gots bouncy hair." She paused, thinking hard. Then turned to look at Nate across the fire.

"Sowwy, Nate!" she called. "Day's the up now!"

Nate raised his eyebrows. "What about me?"

Sofia toddled over to pat his knee sympathetically. "Nay-nay's nice, Day's hair boings." The entire group lost it.

"Displaced by superior curls," Tyler said solemnly. "That's rough, Berglund."

"Day gots boing hair," Sofia explained to Nate very seriously. "You got...."

"Regular hair," Nate said, deadpan.

"Si!." Sofia nodded. Then brightened. "Nay-nay nice, Day gots boing hair."

She ran back to Dayne and held up her arms. "Up?"

Dayne glanced at Emilia, who nodded encouragingly. He picked Sofia up carefully. She immediately grabbed a curl and pulled it gently, watching it spring back. Giggled. Did it again.

"This okay?" Dayne asked.

"You're stuck now," Emilia said. "That's the rule. She's claimed you."

"I have younger siblings," Dayne said. "This feels familiar."

Sofia patted his cheek. "You nice, Day. Muy nice."

Then she spotted Wobby, her stuffed rabbit, on the ground near Emilia.

"¡Wobby! Day, need Wobby!" Emilia retrieved the rabbit and handed it up. Sofia very solemnly placed Wobby on Dayne's shoulder.

"Wobby wikes Day's boing too," she informed him.

"Does he?" Dayne adjusted Wobby so the elephant wouldn't fall.

"Sí. He like boing."

Across the fire, Nate caught my eye and shook his head, smiling. Officially replaced by bouncy hair. Miggy emerged from the barn with Harper and the chicks-are-getting-big report, saw Sofia on Dayne's shoulders, and stopped short.

"Sofia, you can't pick NEW favorites every week," he said, exasperated.

"Can," Sofia said simply.

"But Nate's our tall person!"

"Now Day," Sofia pointed out with toddler logic. "Boing."

Miggy looked at Dayne, then at Nate, clearly torn. Finally he shrugged. "Okay, but Nate's still MY favorite. You can have Dayne."

"Si," Sofia agreed happily.

"Also," Miggy added, turning to Dayne, "have you done any kissing?"

"Uh...not recently?" Dayne looked alarmed.

"Good. Keep it that way. It's gross and it makes people weird."

Harper nodded agreement. "Very weird."

"We're the normal ones," Miggy told Dayne seriously. "Everyone else has the kissing plague. But we're safe."

"Good to know," Dayne said, carefully lowering Sofia back to the ground. She immediately grabbed his hand.

"Go see chickys! Dey funny!"

"Okay—" Dayne shot a helpless look back at the group as Sofia dragged him away, Miggy and Harper trailing behind to provide commentary.

"He's been fully adopted," I observed.

"Happens fast here," Emilia said. "One minute you're a visitor, next minute you're explaining moon chickens to a toddler."

As the fire burned lower, people started settling into quieter conversations. Drew's sisters had integrated completely—Mia deep in discussion with Mr. Preston about crop rotation, Zoe showing her new rock collection to anyone who'd listen, Lucy sketching everything. I found myself back on the log beside Nate, his arm around me, watching the flames.

"You're quiet," he observed.

"Just thinking."

"About?"

"Being okay, being healed," I leaned my head on his shoulder. I looked at him. "This. Being here without pretending. Having people who see me—actually see me—and stay anyway."

His thumb traced circles on the back of my hand.

"I see you."

"I know." I smiled. "That's the point."

The group by the barn returned, Sofia riding on Dayne's shoulders again, hands buried in his curls. Miggy was explaining something very seriously to Harper about secret agent rabbits.

"Day!" Sofia announced to the group. "No kiss!"

"That's the highest compliment she can give right now," Emilia explained to Dayne.

"The non-kissers are the good ones," Miggy added.

He shot a pointed look at Nate and me, then at Tyler and Emilia, then at Ivy and Aiden.

"We're surrounded," he told Harper mournfully. "But we're strong. We'll survive."

"Vive!" Sofia echoed, pumping her fist in the air from her perch on Dayne's shoulders.

As the evening wore on and the little kids started fading, Drew began gathering his sisters.

"Do we have to go?" Harper asked sleepily, clutching Mr. Hops.

"School tomorrow," Drew said. "Come on."

"Can we come back?" Lucy asked, carefully tucking her sketchbook away.

"Anytime," Emilia promised. "Farm's always open."

Mia hugged her notebook to her chest. "Mr. Preston said I could help with the garden next month."

"He meant it," Emilia assured her.

Sofia, still on Dayne's shoulders, looked devastated. "No! Day stay!"

"I'll come back," Dayne promised, carefully lowering her down. She threw her arms around his leg. "Si?"

"Si."

Satisfied, Sofia let go and toddled to Emilia. "I like Day."

"I know, mija."

"Day no kiss."

"That's very important to Miggy right now."

"Sí." Sofia nodded seriously. Then yawned hugely. After Drew and his sisters left and Dayne had followed, Maddie and Aria headed out. Then Ivy and Aiden.

Miggy had fallen asleep against Tyler's side, and Sofia was drowsing in Mariella's lap. Mr. Preston and Tyler worked together to bank the fire while Mariella carried Sofia inside, Emilia following with a half-asleep Miggy. Soon it was just Nate and me, sitting close by the dying embers.

"Hey," Nate said quietly.

"Hey."

"I love you." Simple. Easy. True.

"I love you too." He kissed me then—soft and unhurried, tasting like marshmallows and smoke and summer promises. From somewhere in the house, Miggy's sleepy voice drifted out.

"I HEARD THAT! Still gross!"

We pulled apart, laughing.

"He's got supersonic hearing," I said.

"And strong opinions," Nate added. The string lights glowed above us. The fire crackled in the distance. Inside Sofia was probably asleep, dreaming about bouncy hair and chickens that flew to the moon.

And I was here. No boot. No fake smile. Just me. Just us. Just real.

"Senior year next" I said against his chest.

"Senior year," he agreed.

"We've got this."

"Yeah. We do."

And standing there in the warm May night, after being surrounded by people who loved us the future felt wide open.

Epilogue

BADLANDS AND BAD TRADS
Horror Comedy Stories from Western North Dakota

An anthology by four mixed ethnicity authors who grew up near Theodore Roosevelt National Park.

Excert from *The Gnomes are Watchting* by Tyler Alred

If you didn't grow up in a Norwegian household in North Dakota, you might think garden gnomes are cute. Whimsical, even. Little bearded fellows in pointy red hats, fishing in your petunias.

You would be wrong.

Norwegian nisser are not garden gnomes. They are household spirits. Protectors of the farm. Ancient beings who have seen things—terrible things—and they remember every slight, every forgotten offering of porridge, every time you laughed at Grandma's lutefisk.

My girlfriend Emilia's grandma has forty-seven of them.

I counted.

They're everywhere. On shelves. On windowsills. Tucked into corners where you don't expect them. One is inexplicably IN THE BATHROOM, watching you with those painted eyes that follow you no matter where you stand.

"They're traditional," Emilia's grandma told me the first time I visited. "They bring good luck."

Good luck. Sure. If your definition of good luck includes never being alone, never having privacy, and developing a permanent sense that something small and bearded is judging your life choices.

The worst part? You can't move them.

"Why can't we move them?" I asked Emilia once, after I'd accidentally knocked over a particularly aggressive-looking nisse while reaching for a glass of water.

"Because they'll be angry," she said, completely serious.

"They're ceramic."

"Are they?"

Reader, I have no answer to that question.

Because here's the thing about growing up in western North Dakota: the line between tradition and horror is surprisingly thin. Your grandma serves you fish that's been soaked in lye and calls it a delicacy.

Your church basement hosts polka nights where the dancing never stops and Lawrence Welk plays on an endless loop. The walls are covered in rosemaling—those beautiful, intricate Norwegian painted flowers that definitely, absolutely, are not watching you.

Except they are. Everything is watching.

The nisser. The rosemaling. The cards during your great-uncle's weekly whist game, where the rules change every hand and nobody will explain them to you because "you should know this by now, Tyler."

I don't know it by now. I will never know it.

Last Christmas, Emilia's family invited me to their traditional Norwegian celebration. I was honored. Touched, even. I wore a nice sweater. I brought wine.

What I did not bring was an understanding of what I was walking into.

The lutefisk was served first. It jiggled. I smiled politely and took the smallest piece possible, which was still too much. Emilia squeezed my hand under the table—a gesture I interpreted as support but later learned was a warning.

"Try the lefse," her grandma said, passing me a plate.

Lefse, I can handle. It's basically a potato tortilla. I took two pieces, relieved.

"With butter and sugar," Grandma added.

Fine. Acceptable.

"And now the rakfisk."

I looked at Emilia. She looked at me. Neither of us spoke.

Rakfisk, for the uninitiated, is fermented trout. You take a perfectly good fish, bury it in salt for months, and then—when it has achieved the proper level of decay—you eat it. Raw.

"It's traditional," Grandma said.

There's that word again.

I ate the rakfisk. I smiled. I did not gag, which Emilia later told me earned me significant respect points with her grandfather.

After dinner, we played whist. I don't know how to play whist. I still don't know how to play whist.

But I played anyway, because when Emilia's eighty-year-old grandfather asks if you know how to play whist, you say yes. You say yes and you hope context clues will save you.

They will not save you.

At one point, I played a card that caused Grandma to gasp. Audibly gasp. Like I'd committed a war crime.

"That's not how we play," she said.

"How do you play?" I asked.

"You know how."

Reader, I did not know how.

But here's what I learned that night, and what I've learned growing up in this strange, beautiful, terrifying corner of North Dakota:

Tradition isn't about the thing itself. It's about the people.

Yes, the lutefisk is objectively terrible. Yes, the nisser are watching your every move. Yes, whist has rules that exist in a quantum state of being both fixed and constantly changing.

But these traditions—these weird, uncomfortable, occasionally horrifying traditions—they're how we show love. How we say "you belong here."

How we pass something down that matters, even if what matters is just the memory of your grandma laughing while you try not to cry over fermented fish.

So now I have my own nisse. Emilia's grandma gave it to me. It sits on my desk while I write, right next to the ceramic calavera my mom gave me—a Día de los Muertos skull painted in bright marigold and turquoise, grinning with that knowing smile that says "I see you, mijo."

The nisse and the calavera face each other across my desk. One Nordic, one Mexican. Both watching. Both judging. Both reminding me that my heritage is deeply committed to decorative items that never let you forget about death.

But they also remind me that I'm part of something. Something bigger than myself. Something that smells vaguely of lutefisk and sounds like accordion music and looks like forty-seven ceramic gnomes arranged on every available surface.

Is it horror?

Absolutely.

Is it also love?

Yeah.

It really is.

TYLER ALRED grew up in North Riverbend City, North Dakota, where he developed a healthy fear of fermented fish and ceramic gnomes. He currently lives with his girlfriend Emilia, a nisse, and a calavera who judge his writing in shifts. This story is dedicated to Drew, who died heroically in Tyler's first screenplay about haunted lutefisk. Very brave. Very Obi-Wan.

Fascinating Math Concepts: The Golden Ratio, Fibonacci Sequence, and More

The Golden Ratio, Fibonacci Sequence, and More

The Golden Ratio (φ)

The Golden Ratio is approximately 1.618 and is considered one of the most aesthetically pleasing proportions in mathematics.

Where It Appears in Nature

• Spiral patterns in nautilus shells, sunflower seed arrangements, and pinecones

• Proportions in flowers and plant growth patterns

• Hurricane and galaxy spiral shapes

In Human Design

• Architecture (the Parthenon and other classical buildings)

• Modern logo design (Apple, Twitter, Pepsi logos)

- Photography's 'rule of thirds' is a simplified version
- Book page proportions and typography spacing

The Golden Ratio creates proportions humans find naturally pleasing to look at - balanced but not boring, dynamic but not chaotic.

The Fibonacci Sequence

The Fibonacci sequence: 0, 1, 1, 2, 3, 5, 8, 13, 21, 34, 55, 89...

Each number is the sum of the two before it (0+1=1, 1+1=2, 1+2=3, 2+3=5, etc.).

Found Throughout Nature

- Flower petals (lilies have 3, buttercups have 5, daisies have 3,4 or 5)
- Pinecone spirals and pineapple scales
- Tree branching patterns

Connection to the Golden Ratio

As the Fibonacci sequence progresses, the ratio between consecutive numbers gets closer and closer to the Golden Ratio (1.618). For example: 89 ÷ 55 = 1.618...

The Fibonacci Spiral

When you create squares with sides that follow the Fibonacci sequence (1, 1, 2, 3, 5, 8, 13) and draw quarter-circle arcs inside each square, they connect to form the elegant Fibonacci spiral.

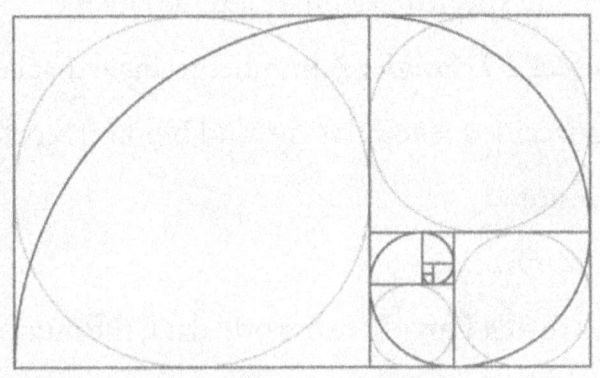

The golden ratio is approximately equal to 1.6181. It is considered aesthetically pleasing and is found in nature, art, and architecture.

Other Fascinating Math Concepts

Paradoxes & Brain-Benders

- **Monty Hall Problem:** A probability puzzle that feels completely wrong even when you know the right answer

- **Infinity Paradoxes:** Some infinities are literally bigger than other infinities (a hotel with infinite rooms that's full can still fit infinite new guests)

- **Möbius Strip:** A paper loop with only one side and one edge

Beautiful Patterns

- **Fractals:** Patterns that repeat at every scale (coastlines, snowflakes, broccoli)
- **Prime Number Spirals:** When you plot prime numbers on a grid, unexpected diagonal patterns emerge
- **Pascal's Triangle:** A number triangle that contains the Fibonacci sequence, fractals, and binomial coefficients all hidden inside

Practical Magic

- **Benford's Law:** In real-world data, the number 1 appears as the first digit way more often than 9 (used to catch fraud!)
- **Birthday Paradox:** In a room of just 23 people, there's a 50% chance two share a birthday

The Most Beautiful Equation

Euler's Identity: $e^{(i\pi)} + 1 = 0$

This equation is considered the most beautiful in mathematics because it connects the five most important numbers in math (e, i, π, 1, and 0) in one elegant statement.

Why These Matter

These mathematical concepts show up in unexpected places, connecting logic to beauty, pattern to chaos, and revealing the hidden structure of our world. They remind us that math isn't just about calculations - it's about discovering the elegant patterns that make the universe work.

The Sacred Sixth-Grade-Sleepover-Pact

THE SACRED-SIXTH-GRADE-SLEEPOVER-PACT

Established: September 14 of sixth grade year Among: Jenna Lundquist, Maddie Thompson, Ivy Preston, Emilia Preston & Aria Cooper

OFFICIAL RULES:

Article I: The Invocation Any party may invoke the Pact at any time by stating: "I'm invoking the Sacred-Sixth-Grade-Sleepover-Pact." Once invoked, the Pact is BINDING.

Article II: The Questioning Window

- The Invoker has exactly **15 SECONDS** to ask their question after invoking the Pact.

- If no question is asked within 15 seconds, the Pact is

VOID for that instance.

- The other party may count down out loud to apply pressure (this is allowed and encouraged).

Article III: The Sacred Answer

- The person being asked MUST give **ONE HONEST ANSWER.**

- No deflecting, no lying, no "I don't know" unless that's actually the truth.

- Whining is permitted but does not excuse you from answering.

Article IV: The Answering Window

- Once the honest answer is given, the Answering Window remains open for **ONE FOLLOW-UP QUESTION ONLY**.

- After the follow-up (or if the Invoker chooses not to ask one), the answering party may declare "Sacred Window is closing" and the subject is OFFICIALLY CLOSED.

- No one may bring up the subject again for at least 24 hours.

Article V: The Sacred Part

- This Pact is SACRED and will never expire.

- It doesn't matter if we're 16, 26, or 86—the Pact stands.

- Anyone who breaks the Pact has to buy the other person ice cream. Premium ice cream. With toppings.

Article VI: Amendments

- No amendments may be added without unanimous agreement and a sleepover to make it official.

Signed: *Jenna Lundquist* [with a heart dotting the 'i'] *Maddie Thompson* [in purple gel pen] *Ivy Preston* [in perfect cursive] *Emilia Preston* [with a little doodle of a cow next to her name] *Aria Cooper* [in all caps with stars]

Witness: Mr. Snuggles (Maddie's stuffed bear)

Afterword

I'm more interested in math now than I ever was in school. I don't blame math teachers. Maybe it's the system and how teachers are *supposed* to teach.

And I also think we have access to more information now. More ways to learn. It's a shame that so many kids graduate and still think they're no good at math. I've to keep learning about math and maybe actually take a math class or two.

If you think that you're no good at math. Think again. Everyone can learn math.

A book to read about how capable all minds are at math is Jo Boaler's *Limitless Mind.*

Almost Missed Our Shot

Cozy Endings in Riverbend Book 1

Finally Found the Words

Cozy Endings in Riverbend Book 2

Cozy Endings in Riverbend Book 4

Releasing Spring 2026

Riverbend High Happy Ending Book 5

Releasing Early Spring 2026

Guarding Molly: A Riverbend World Novella

Releasing Spring 2026

Five Sisters on the Prairie

A cozy coming of age YA Romance Series

Book 1 coming Summer 2026

Cozy Romances and Laughs

M.C. Danielsen writes heartfelt, cozy YA rom-coms with equal parts humor, emotional depth, and small-town charm. A lifelong North Dakotan at heart, she pays close attention to the smaller places that often get overlooked. Her current series delivers authentic rural vibes, slow-burn romance, and fiercely loyal friendships.

Her stories follow girls finding their voice, boys growing into heart, and the emotional chaos that comes with figuring out who you are—especially when feelings, playlists, and group chats get in the way.

When she's not writing, you can find M.C. playing merge-three games, rabidly cheering for the Minnesota Twins, the Minnesota Vikings, and the Buffalo Bills by marriage (she admits they're worth following).

By training, she's an expert in child development, trauma, and resilience. She believes every teen deserves a safe place to land

and to have people who light up when they walk into the room. She's certain that today's young people are capable of more than any generation before them.

Find Me

https://linktr.ee/mcd_ya_author

https://mcdanielsenyaauthor.com/

https://www.facebook.com/author.mcdanielsen#

https://www.instagram.com/mcdanielsenyaauthor/

https://www.tiktok.com/@mcdanielsenya_author

Join the crew and signup for my newsletter through my website. Goodies, bonus material, and all the cozy news your heart needs.